Maggie's Dilemma

Maggie's Dilemma

a novel by

Jennifer Wixson

Book 5 in The Sovereign Series

For Becky ...

who—I have no doubt—is already planning our

Girlfriend's Reunion Party in Heaven.

Acknowledgements

Nearly six years ago I began this little writing adventure that has come to be known as *The Sovereign Series*. Meant only to be one book, *Hens & Chickens*, the project somehow morphed into five novels (and maybe someday I'll get to that cookbook), thanks to the overwhelming response of fans. Thus I'd like to acknowledge first those early supporters who encouraged me to continue with these tales from Sovereign, Maine. Without you, Sovereign and her lovable and endearing inhabitants would long ago have disappeared into the sunset. Now, however, as we finally watch the sun go down over places like the Sovereign Union Church, Gilpin's General Store, Ma Jean's restaurant, the Millett Rock, Black Brook, Scotch Broom Acres, the Corn Shop Museum, and Maggie's little red schoolhouse, we experience a sense of nostalgic contentment knowing that our old friends will always be here for us to visit. We can escape to Sovereign whenever we want simply by opening one of the five novels.

In every book in the series the major characters attend a dinner at the old Russell homestead at which quite often the loquacious woodsman Leland Gorse tells one of his tall tales. In *Maggie's Dilemma* Leland gets to tell two stories (one at the regular dinner and one at a church breakfast), both of which originated from a woman I met at the Waldo County fall extension meeting in October of 2015. After listening to my presentation on *The Sovereign Series*, which included a reading of Leland's tipping over the outhouses story, Jeanette Jack shared with me two humorous tales her husband Ronald used to tell. I loved both stories and asked if I could include them in my next book. Jeanette agreed and graciously emailed me the particulars. Fortunately, before Ronnie passed she wrote down the tales in his own words and I'm grateful to both of them for providing me such great Maine color.

In addition, at church one Sunday (the First Universalist Church of Norway, Maine) Pat Shearman shared with me a story about attending Thursday evening prayer services as a child with her father, the Reverend Phil Shearman, a Baptist minister. Those services, she said, began with an enthusiastic hymn sing for 15-20 minutes and the way Pat told the story amused me so much I appropriated it for David and Duncan Faulkner's mother in *Maggie's Dilemma* (which should be a reminder to everyone to be careful what you tell me!) So thanks, Pat, for that!

I'd also like to thank my editorial team, which was the most thorough and experienced team I've ever worked with on a book. Helping keep me to the straight and narrow and negotiate all the Oxford commas this year were: Tracy Fritze, Laura Jones Farnsworth, Robin Follette, "Aunt" Wini Mott, and Jessica Wixson Shaw. My cousin Adeline Wixson was the first to read *Maggie's Dilemma* (in all of its various states and stages over a two-year period) and she continually provided me with encouragement and support, for which I'm eternally grateful as otherwise the book would never have gotten itself written.

Final thanks go to Peter Harris of Peter Harris Associates for his cover art, which says in one image what took me 80,000 words to convey. I hope you enjoy this final story in *The Sovereign Series*.

Jen Wixson
Troy, Maine
Sept. 14, 2017

Table of Contents

Two roads diverged in a wood, and I—

I took the one less traveled by,

And that has made all the difference.

-- Robert Frost

Chapter 1
The Ravens

From the comfort of her antique rocker, which was situated just the right distance from the toasty woodstove in her old-fashioned country kitchen, Maggie Walker Hodges gazed out upon the snowy February landscape. At sixty, she was still youthful-looking, despite having survived breast cancer and the unexpected death of her husband and childhood friend two-and-a-half years earlier. Her bright blue eyes still sparkled and the short white fuzz that had appeared after her chemotherapy was restored to its original color, only now the shoulder-length brown hair was interlaced with interesting strands of silver. Enchanted by the antics of her mating pair of ravens, Maggie leaned forward in her padded rocking chair.

The ravens looked like young lovers today, perched upon their accustomed branch two-thirds the way up the towering pine on the opposite side of the snow-covered gravel road. As Maggie watched the black birds a gust of wind toppled the light, dry snow from the branch above the pair, releasing a miniature squall upon their heads. The male hopped protectively closer to the female, squawking loudly. He ruffled the white dusting off his dark feathers and admonished his companion to do the same, which she did.

Perhaps there would be babies this spring? Maggie wondered, idly. She had witnessed—or thought she had witnessed—nascent signs of nest-building in a hard-to-see section of a nearby dead oak, a hollowed-out area in the craggy remains of the tree that was formerly used by a family of porcupines. Intrigued by the ravens, Maggie had been studying Corvids of late. She was amazed to learn that not only were ravens long-lived— ten to fifteen years in the wild and up to forty years in captivity—but also that they usually mated for life. For life! How many years of enjoyment might she not garner from this mating pair? Tears of joy filled Maggie's eyes as she realized with a rush of gratitude how blessed she was to live in a place where the inherent goodness of the world was constantly being revealed, if only one took the time and trouble to see it.

She had first noticed the ravens late last fall, when the days in the 45th parallel north were becoming depressingly short and when one of the nastiest Presidential elections in U.S. history nearly disrupted the bucolic life in Sovereign, Maine. Normally, politics had no place in Sovereign beyond the office of Road Commissioner, of course; however, the bitterness and divisiveness must have seeped into the well water, for friends and neighbors began to suspect one another of "not being quite right." So the passerine pair—naturally christened Romeo and Juliet—were a welcome distraction from the squabbles and bickering at Gilpin's General Store and the inanity on television, radio, and the

18

Internet, all of which Maggie had eventually abandoned for the simplicity of her daily life as minister of Sovereign's only church, the support of her daughter and son-in-law, the comfort of her close friends, and the entertaining antics of the ravens.

Like most Mainers growing up in an agricultural community, Maggie was raised to believe that all black birds—ravens, crows, grackles, starlings—were nothing more than scavengers, common thieves, and pests. Even an image of black birds on a book jacket caused the hair on the back of her neck to stand up, conjuring up as the picture did creepy presentiments of death and dying. But during these past few months her long-time prejudices had gradually been replaced by respect and admiration for Romeo and Juliet, which birds she had discovered through daily observation were certainly more intelligent and self-aware than most of the people on Facebook or Twitter.

The sound of a chair scraping against the battle-scarred pine floor, the succinct clearing of a masculine throat, and the scintillating aroma of perked coffee wafting from the six-cup percolator she left warming on the back of the woodstove reminded Maggie that she wasn't alone. The ravens had so completely hijacked her attention she had forgotten all about David, who had dropped in unannounced (but not unexpected, for she knew his lecture schedule at the college) for an afternoon chat and a piece of her homemade blackberry pie.

"You haven't heard a word I've said for the past five minutes," David Faulkner complained, shifting restlessly in his chair at the oak kitchen table. He pushed

19

his coffee mug to one side and laid his forearm on the cream-colored woven tablecloth, one of Maggie's winter favorites. "You're worse than my students. What's so important out there that you can't listen to what I have to say?"

Sixty-two-year-old David Faulkner was a handsome, athletic man, slightly below the average height, with dark curls and a neatly-clipped black beard reminiscent of Abraham Lincoln's. A well-known environmentalist hailing from Harvard, he was a guest lecturer at nearby Unity College for the current school year. He was also the uncle of Maggie's young friend 'Walden,' who had introduced them.

Maggie pivoted away from the window, somewhat reluctant to leave the peaceful world of Romeo and Juliet behind. "I'm sorry, my mind wandered. What did I miss?" She had discovered during the past few months in which they had known each other that David expected to be the center of attention, which was understandable given the national awards he had won for his environmental work and writings. Less fathomable, however, the erudite professor and lecturer appeared to have developed an interest in her, despite the fact that she was nothing more than the hard-working pastor of a small Union church in a community that numbered more bovines than two-legged residents.

"Forget it," David replied. He unconsciously picked up his teaspoon and tapped it against the table.

The muffled rapping sound reminded Maggie of the particular noise Romeo made when Juliet flew to another tree and he wanted her attention. Tap, tap, tap.

"It's not important," he continued. "At least not to you, obviously."

Aware that he was taking advantage of her well-known need to placate, Maggie nevertheless responded as he expected. "Oh, don't be disagreeable, David. Tell me again," she encouraged him, giving the pine baseboard a little push with her stockinged foot to turn the rocker so the chair was facing his direction. "I promise I'll pay attention this time. What did you say?"

Pacified, David laid down the teaspoon and leaned forward. He interlocked his hands on the table. The cuffs of his light blue oxford shirt hitched up to reveal a Rolex watch. "I said—we've been seeing each other now for five months. We met on the seventh of September, when Nick brought you to my first public lecture." Nick was David's nephew, who two or three years ago had shown up in town, introducing himself by the far more interesting sobriquet of 'Walden Pond'. Only months later had they learned his real name, but by then the die was cast and Nick Faulkner was known to all simply as Walden. David paused expectantly, apparently waiting for her to respond to his pronouncement.

"Five months? Really?" Feeling she had done her part, Maggie lapsed into silence. A Quaker, she was comfortable with extended silences and utilized this one to contemplate the possible implication of his remark, which obviously held some significance for them both that she was expected to acknowledge. Was David affirming that they were, in fact, a couple? Or did he mean that as they had already become an item, it was time to take their relationship to the next level? What was the next level? Did she want to go there? If so, did she want to go there with him? And where was she headed, during this next stage of her personal journey through life?

In truth, Maggie wasn't sure how she felt about David Faulkner or about their relationship in general. These were subjects she had been carefully avoiding since she had not yet answered the much more important question about the destination of her metaphysical voyage since Peter's death had changed everything. Several times lately she had brushed off a parishioner's subtle question about David and ignored pointed comments about how much time she and he had been spending together. Widowed now two-and-a-half years, Maggie had lost her husband, Peter Hodges, when he died of a massive heart attack while folding laundry at the kitchen table. One minute he had been rolling a pair of her pink ankle socks together and the next minute he was gone, taking her life's vision with him. Since then, she had been largely treading water, unable to chart a new course for her future.

Suddenly, a heightened focus descended upon her like a bright light from Heaven. In this altered state of mind she was painfully aware that David was sitting in the very same chair in which Peter had died. Was it a sign from across the Great Divide? Was it possible she could—and should—pick up from the very spot where her life had been altered, rendered so profusely?

No, that was not possible. A farmer's daughter, Maggie knew that rendered pork never became living flesh again; it was simply lard.

David rapped his teaspoon against the table again to remind her he was still waiting for her response to his pronouncement. Unwittingly, Edgar Allan Poe's poem, *The Raven*, popped into her head:

> *Once upon a midnight dreary,*
> *While I pondered, weak and weary,*
> *Over many a quaint and curious*
> *Volume of forgotten lore,*
> *While I nodded, nearly napping,*
> *Suddenly there came a tapping,*
> *As of someone gently rapping,*
> *Rapping at my chamber door.*
> *" 'Tis some visitor," I muttered,*
> *"Tapping at my chamber door;*
> *Only this, and nothing more."*

"I'm sure you must remember the day we met, Maggie," he rushed on, unable to bear the silence any longer. "That was my lecture on the effects of neonicotinoids on honeybees and grassland birds."

"Oh, yes. That was a good lecture," Maggie agreed. She remembered the lecture well because at it she had learned some new and shocking statistics. Thanks to David, she had learned that only five percent of the neonicotinoid seed coating was taken up by the corn, soybean, or canola plant; the remaining ninety-five percent of the poisonous chemical simply leached into the groundwater. In addition, she discovered at David's lecture that neonics were responsible for the dramatic decline in grassland bird populations. She stole a glance at Romeo and Juliet, momentarily worried that they, too, might be affected by the increased use of GMO corn in Maine.

Ah, distinctly I remember,
It was in the bleak December,
And each separate dying ember
Wrought its ghost upon the floor.
Eagerly I wished the morrow;
Vainly I had sought to borrow
From my books surcease of sorrow,
Sorrow for the lost Lenore,
For the rare and radiant maiden
Whom the angels name Lenore,
Nameless here forevermore.

Despite the fact that David was certainly one of the smartest and most interesting men Maggie had ever known, she wasn't quite prepared to accept that they were a couple. She wasn't even sure she wanted romance in her life anymore. At sixty, she found herself satisfied with herself and her age for the first time in her life. She wasn't too young—she wasn't too old—she was just right. She was relieved to be liberated not only from her menstrual cycle but also from menopause. For the first time in nearly half a century she was no longer under the influence of pesky hormones. She felt very comfortable, indeed. Was a romantic relationship worth the bother of introducing a permanent partner into her life? Wasn't it good that she paid attention to herself for a change, rather than to a man or a child?

"I remember the first time I came home with you," the professor continued. (Maggie winced at the term: "came home with you," which sounded to her ears as though she had picked him up in a bar and brought David back to her house in order to have sex.) "You cooked those biscuits I love."

"Bakewell Cream biscuits," she murmured. The biscuits were a Maine tradition and she had frequently served them with some of the many home-cooked meals that David, a lifelong bachelor, enjoyed. No wonder he spent so much time at her house!

"I ate them smothered in real butter from Ryan and Trudy's farm," he recollected fondly. "I had some of Wendell's unprocessed honey on top. Do you remember? That's when I became even more obsessed with the negative effects of neonics, I tell you." As though to emphasize his conviction, David rapped the teaspoon again.

Back into the chamber turning,
All my soul within me burning,
Soon again I heard a tapping,
Something louder than before,
"Surely," said I, "surely,
That is something at my window lattice.
Let me see, then, what thereat is,
And this mystery explore.
Let my heart be still a moment,
And this mystery explore.
" 'Tis the wind, and nothing more."

Open here I flung the shutter, when,
With many a flirt and flutter,
In there stepped a stately raven,
Of the saintly days of yore.
Not the least obeisance made he;
Not a minute stopped or stayed he;
But with mien of lord or lady,
Perched above my chamber door.
Perched upon a bust of Pallas,
Just above my chamber door,
Perched, and sat, and nothing more.

Maggie cast her mind back, recalling in greater detail when she and David had first met. It was not long after her sixtieth birthday last August. She had found herself with time on her hands that fall, none of her parishioners either desired to get married or felt the need to expire. In addition, Maggie's daughter Nellie had abandoned her mother (appropriately so, but still!) for her newly-married life to Doctor Bart and their non-profit medical clinic. Unused to so much free time Maggie considered broadening her horizons. That was when Walden had suggested attending one of his uncle's lectures. When David had taken an interest in her that evening it had seemed natural to return the compliment. At first they had gone to the movies and to concerts— Dutch treat, at her stipulation, even though he earned four times her modest salary. Later, however, at his expense she accompanied David on a few one-day field trips. Then she began inviting him to her house for a home-cooked meal, feeling it only proper to give some return for the obligation she felt. Like idle, untied riverboats she and he had drifted along since; she stopped issuing formal invitations to visit and he had begun to drop in when the spirit moved him, especially around meal time.

She glanced out the window at the pair of ravens, to discover Romeo was now grooming Juliet. She averted her eyes, overcome by the raven's display of tenderness. Perhaps the longing for unconditional love never died?

Then, methought, the air grew denser,
Perfumed from an unseen censer
Swung by seraphim whose footfalls
Tinkled on the tufted floor.
"Wretch," I cried, "thy God hath lent thee –
By these angels he hath
Sent thee respite---respite and nepenthe
From thy memories of Lenore!
Quaff, O quaff this kind nepenthe,

26

And forget this lost Lenore!"
Quoth the raven, "Nevermore!"

But then—love brought with it so much pain! Who knew better than she that one would eventually lose everybody and everything one had ever loved? What beloved friend, family member, or parishioner might not be snatched away from her tomorrow? Maggie shuddered inwardly thinking what her future losses would most certainly be. Did she want to add the potential for one more—a partner? Or even, God forbid! Another husband, who could drop dead at any moment with absolutely no warning at all?

And the raven, never flitting,
Still is sitting, still is sitting
On the pallid bust of Pallas
Just above my chamber door;
And his eyes have all the seeming
Of a demon's that is dreaming.
And the lamplight o'er him streaming
Throws his shadow on the floor;
And my soul from out that shadow
That lies floating on the floor
Shall be lifted---nevermore!

"Jesus, Maggie! You're not listening again."

Startled by the intensity of David's rebuke, Maggie jumped in her seat. Romeo and Juliet—who had in truth been eyeing her as much as she had been eyeing them—were startled in turn and flew off to a nearby maple tree, squawking so loudly she could hear them through the closed window.

"I'm sorry, David," she apologized again. "My mind is wandering. Perhaps we should continue this conversation another day?"

"What is it you're so damned focused on?"

There was nothing for it but to tell the truth. "A pair of ravens," she admitted, tucking her toes beneath the rocker. "I think I have a mating pair."

David leapt from his seat, his demeanor completely altered. Full of interest and enthusiasm, he strode to the window. "A mating pair of ravens! Well, why didn't you just say so in the first place?"

Chapter 2
Maple Syrup Season Comes to Sovereign

Maple syrup season arrived in Sovereign prematurely, but not as early as the prior year, which had broken all records in Maine. Wendell Russell, sixty-nine, one of the town's celebrated Old Farts—a nickname accorded themselves by the group of old timers who gathered regularly at Gilpin's General Store—at the urging of his venerable octogenarian buddy Leland Gorse, hunted up his spiles, a 7/16th drill-bit, and a couple of antiquated tin pails and covers, which had been part of his family's mapling supplies for nearly a hundred years. He tucked the cuffs of his coveralls into his boots and strapped on a pair of snowshoes in order to reach a pair of ancient sugar maples that guarded the entrance to the old Russell homestead. Sovereign had received fifty-five inches of snow over the course of the prior week, nearly thirty inches from 'The Blizzard' alone. "I'm jest doin' this so as I kin shut you up, Leland," Wendell informed his friend, slogging through the deep snow to the nearest tree. Leland carefully stepped along behind the old chicken farmer, taking the easy route by following in Wendell's snowshoe tracks.

Wendell ran his calloused paw around the tree trunk, fondling the rough bark. Finally, he selected a good spot to drill his first hole. He placed the tip of his hand-crank drill against the tree trunk, leaned in and began twisting the wooden knob, stopping every now and then to pluck the cold, damp shavings out of the hole with his forefinger. In a minute or two he was satisfied and fished in his coat pocket for a wooden spile that Bud, his grandmother's hired hand, had carved during the Depression. He carefully tapped the spile into the hole. Leland handed him an old tin pail and he hung the bucket. Wendell hadn't expected much and therefore was almost discomposed when he heard the sound of sap dripping into the tin pail. The sap plunked melodiously into the cold bucket in a sweet song of spring. "By Gawd, she's runnin'," Wendell exclaimed. He squared his shoulders and took in a deep breath. "Wintah cain't hurt us now!"

"Told ya," crowed Leland. He tossed his buffalo plaid hunting cap up into the air, exposing short white stubs of hair. He retrieved his hat and peered over Wendell's shoulder, curiously. "She runnin' good?"

"Ayuh." Wendell patted the maple tree fondly on the shoulder. "Good to see you still got it, old gal," he remarked. He turned back to his buddy. "'Tain't natural though. Last year warn't normal, neither." Like most traditional Maine farming families, the Russells had kept a nature and planting journal for two hundred years. Entries in the journal recorded everything that occurred on the homestead from when the ice went out of the pond to when the peas were planted to when children were born and old folks died. "I don't know nuthin' 'bout global warmin', but she sure ain't like the old days."

"Nope," agreed Leland. "But whatcha gonna do?"

"Put in my taps," Wendell replied, succinctly. He scouted a second spot to tap the mature maple—not too close to a previous tap and just the right height on the southwesterly side—and hung a second bucket. He snowshoed off to get more pails, covers, and spiles from the shed and spent the rest of the afternoon happily tapping trees around the homestead. He passed over the largest maple tree, however, which after more than a century of sharing her liquid gold, had earned a rest. He glanced up the old tree's barren crown, or what was left of the crown after a big windstorm the prior summer had clipped off two more branches, to calculate the maple's chances of surviving another year. One more big wind with her leaves on would pretty much bring her to her knees. But he already had a replacement maple for this one waiting in the wings, a jaunty young sapling that had sprouted in the middle of a mock orange bush about eight feet away. The upstart maple had tried to keep itself hidden amongst the woody stems of the shrubby bush, but three years ago Wendell had spotted the intruder. Although generally inclined to keep volunteers from overtaking his lawn and shrubbery, he nevertheless had allowed the pert young maple to grow. He himself would never be able to tap this new addition in his lifetime—maples needed to be at least forty-five years old and twelve inches in diameter before they were tapped—but Wendell was preparing everything on the homestead for his three-year-old son George, known in town as 'Tad,' short for tadpole due to the child's propensity for perpetual motion. The carroty-haired boy was a great favorite with the little old ladies of Sovereign most of which were in their eighth decade or beyond. Wendell had inherited the old Russell homestead with all the good things his ancestors had left for him to enjoy and he would pass the place on to his own son with at least as many if not more good things. He keenly appreciated the fact that Tad, an unexpected late sprout, was his own replacement. Still, like the maple tree he was by no means ready to be brought to his knees just yet.

31

All told, Wendell placed twenty-six taps in twelve trees. That would give him more than enough sap for the syrup he and his family used and gave away as gifts. He trudged back to the shed, removed his snowshoes and hung them up on the wall. A conscientious man, he cleaned and oiled his drill and bit and replaced his tools before returning to the cozy country kitchen where his fifty-three-year-old wife, Rebecca, was cutting up potatoes for supper. Wendell placed his cap on its hook, gave his wife a buss on the cheek, and dropped down into his usual spot at the kitchen table. He turned toward the stove and put his feet up on the radiant bricks of the hearth. "Where's he at?"

"Down for his nap. Finally! I thought he'd never go to sleep." Rebecca, who hailed from Boston, had become used to the fact that Mainers generally spoke about their loved ones utilizing pronouns rather than first names or even nicknames. For outsiders, this idiosyncrasy could make conversations downright difficult to follow and occasionally produced some embarrassing moments when one didn't know who was being referenced.

Wendell flashed his signature, gold-toothed grin. "'Druther have him up at night, Mother?"

"Heaven forbid! Would you like some tea, dear? You look cold."

"Ayuh. Thet'd be good."

Rebecca made her husband a mug of herbal tea using fresh herbs and boiling water from the large copper kettle on the back of the woodstove, which perpetually breathed steam into the hot room. She set the cup and a small plate of molasses cookies on the table in front of him. "I know you're hungry, but don't spoil your supper."

He swung his long legs back around under his chair and smiled up at her. "'Tain't likely."

Rebecca returned his smile, her hand alighting like a friendly chickadee on his shoulder. She dropped a kiss on top of Wendell's head, which was still thickly-covered with gray hair despite his advancing years. As she bent over him, her soft brown curls brushed up against his face and neck. Feeling the sap rising within him, he turned his wife around and pulled her down onto his lap. He kissed her affectionately.

Rebecca giggled and returned the salute. "I guess I don't need to ask you if the sap is running!" she added. She was a comely, plump brunette, dressed today in jeans and a feminine flannel shirt, looking every inch a country wife. A stranger stepping into the cozy, picturesque scene would never have guessed that she had spent most of her life in Boston, having removed to the small, rural town of Sovereign, Maine on the whim of a friend only five years earlier.

Five years! Had it only been five years ago when Lila had quit her job at the insurance company in protest of Rebecca's firing, and the two of them had motored up to Maine from Massachusetts at the invitation of Miss Hastings? Now, Miss Hastings, the late beloved music teacher, was lying under a little patch of sod and snow in the cemetery at the top of Russell Hill, and Lila and her husband and two children were residing happily up north in The County, as Aroostook County was commonly known. Most amazing of all—she and Wendell were blessed with a child of their own!

What, Rebecca wondered idly, would the next five years bring?

"Watch thet pot!"

Rebecca leaped up from Wendell's lap and sprang to the stove, where the potatoes had begun to boil over. She grabbed a pot holder, removed the lid, and slid the pan to the right side of the woodstove, which was cooler. The angry boil immediately subsided to a cheerful simmer and she replaced the cover, leaving it open a tiny crack. "Goodness! That one almost got away from me."

Rebecca poured herself a cup of tea and pulled out the matching pressed-back oak chair to sit at the table with her husband. "Do you know?" she said, her mind automatically reverting to the pleasant pondering, "I've been watching Maggie and David lately, and I think David's going to pop the question." Maggie the minister was one of their special set of friends and recently Rebecca thought she had seen nascent signs of a romantic relationship in that corner.

"'Tain't likely," Wendell opined. "Leland told me today thet she told him they was jest friends."

"And people say men don't gossip! Friends, indeed. Take my word for it—David's in love with her." Rebecca added a thick dollop of Wendell's honey to her tea. The teacup tinkled as she stirred, releasing the sweet scent of anise hyssop into the moist kitchen air. "I predict there will be wedding bells by August for those two."

"Wal, you know, jest 'cause he likes her, don't mean she likes him," Wendell pointed out.

Rebecca made a dismissive motion with her pretty hand. "Women don't generally spend all their free time with someone they don't like. Besides, you should see David at church. He's always underfoot. That is, when he goes to church," she amended honestly.

"Bet the old ladies like thet." Wendell took a gulp of tea and wiped his mouth on the cuff of his plaid flannel shirt.

"Of course they do! And for your information so do middle-aged ladies, like Maggie. David is a very charming man. I'm surprised he's never married."

Wendell harrumphed. "Too busy saving the planet probbly."

Rebecca was surprised by her husband's words and negative tone. Generally, Wendell was generous and open-hearted, always accepting newcomers at face value. He almost never offered the slightest bit of criticism. She regarded him closely. "Why, Wendell! Anyone would think you don't like David?"

He shrugged. "Course, 'tain't whether I likes him as matters."

"No-o-o," Rebecca agreed, slowly. She reached over and gently tilted her husband's face up, pushing back the graying hair from his damp forehead so she could search his childlike countenance for clues. "You think he won't make her happy?" she guessed.

"No, I don't. He'll be drugging her hither 'n thither, when what she likes best is to stay here to home."

"But ... she went to Spain not so very long ago," Rebecca countered. "Remember when Maggie hiked the Camino de Santiago?"

"Thet was only account of him dying." The "him" referred to in this case was Maggie's late husband, Peter. "She ain't even been out o' state since she come back from thet."

Wendell's wife pondered his words. "You could be right; it might not be a good match, in that regard. Walden says his uncle has lived in a lot of amazing places, Tibet, Australia, and even Antarctica, I think. But maybe David's ready to settle down? He's in his early sixties, after all. Maybe Maggie and the way we live here have made him see what he's been missing all these years? Maybe he's realized that fame and national awards can't compete with a loving wife and a community of caring friends...?"

"May-be. May-be not." There was a slight pause as husband and wife each fell to their own contemplations. "Wal, one way or t'other, Leland ain't going to like it," Wendell stated finally.

"Do you know something about Leland and Maggie I don't?"

Wendell grinned. "'Tain't likely." He quickly became serious again. "David jest don't seem like Maggie's type, is all."

"And Leland is?"

"Aw, Leland ain't sweet on her so much as he feels responsible for her." Wendell cupped his mug with his hands.

"That's understandable," Rebecca agreed. "Especially considering how close Maggie and Leland became during her cancer treatment."

"He shore ain't much like ole Peter, neither."

"Poor Peter! And poor David. It isn't fair to compare the two," Rebecca countered. She leaned over and straightened the collar of his flannel shirt, brushing off a few flakes of wood shavings from the tree. "Maybe it's a good thing David and Peter aren't alike? Maybe Maggie doesn't want someone who constantly reminds her of him? But maybe I'm reading their relationship all wrong? Maybe they are just friends?"

Wendell shrugged. "Wal, she kin make her own choice, I guess."

Realizing that Maggie's relationship with the noted environmentalist was one upon which they couldn't agree, Rebecca tactfully changed the subject. "Are you entering the maple syrup contest this year, dear?" Every March, in conjunction with Maple Sunday when all the sugar houses in Maine threw open their doors, the Sovereign Union Church held a fundraising pancake breakfast and maple syrup contest. Wendell, Leland, and Maynard Nutter (another octogenarian Sovereign farmer) typically vied for the top three spots in the contest. The first place winner was awarded a new piece of mapling gear. More important to the participants, however, the first place spot bestowed on the winner bragging rights as the town's best maple syrup producer.

Wendell's face brightened and his grip around the vintage mug relaxed. "Ayuh. Fust run for shore. She's awful sweet, might be twenty, twenty-five to one." The usual ratio of sap to maple syrup was forty gallons to one; however, the first sap run of the season often contained much higher sugar concentrations than later runs. "Jest as soon as he saw the sap was runnin' Leland scooted home to tap his own trees," Wendell added with a chuckle.

Rebecca laughed. "I bet he did! He came over here today to make you do his dirty work. He never has to lift a finger to see if the sap is running, not when you'll do it for him."

Suddenly, from a distance came the cheerful, bird-like chirps of a young child, followed by a steady thumping of a foot against a wall. Rebecca sighed and glanced at the clock. "Well, he was down almost an hour," she said. She eyed the simmering potatoes. "Could you go get him, dear?"

But Wendell needed no encouragement from his wife. He was already up out of his chair to liberate his own replacement, the young upstart who would one day take over the old Russell homestead.

Chapter 3
"'Tain't None O' My Bees-whacks!"

The ravens had netted Maggie a reprieve of sorts from a potentially perilous and certainly uncomfortable discussion with David about the nature of their relationship. She took full advantage of the reprieve knowing her primary duty was to herself. She must determine what direction she wanted to take in her life before any dialogue with David.

Maggie had always charted her own course—for better or worse—except once, when she had allowed Nellie's father to take the helm. That voyage had ended in disaster as far as the relationship went, although it did net Maggie her wonderful daughter. Peter, by contrast, had never wanted to take the helm. Instead, her late husband had stood beside her on deck, as he had stood beside her throughout their lifetime of friendship.

To give herself time to think, Maggie discreetly absented herself from David's company for a few days and avoided messaging him, although she did reply the few times that he texted her. She was surprised he didn't visit, but knew that this was a busy time of year for him, what with his over-capacity lectures, his classes, and his other commitments. If David was thinking relationship kinds of thoughts, however—and it appeared that he was—Maggie knew he would raise the subject again.

Her right foot pushed absently against the worn floorboard moving the rocker back and forth in a soothing fashion. She leaned back against the soft cushion and gazed out the window. Her hair lent fullness to her slightly elongated face and its few silvery threads highlighted her bright blue eyes.

Maggie had appropriated her rocker with her personal journal in hand—journal #18, the latest of the 8" by 5½" notebooks she had kept for nearly thirty years. Her journal was her tool for talking with herself. Sometimes the talking-to was of the cheerleader sort, but more often than not she utilized the journal for some honest soul-searching.

She was almost grateful to see that Romeo and Juliet were off foraging today, for the antics of the ravens would most certainly have distracted her. She pulled her eyes away from the glistening snow-covered scene outside and settled the journal onto her reading pillow. The tea kettle bubbled merrily on back of the woodstove filling the antiquated but charmingly old-fashioned eat-in country kitchen with its steady, moist exhale. The steam stimulated the dried herbs hanging in bunches from the hand-hewn pine beams—bunches of marjoram, oregano, rosemary, and thyme for cooking, and mint, anise hyssop, lemon and lime balm for tea—causing the herbs to exude their sweet and zesty bouquets in a delightful and uplifting symphony of aromas.

Maggie ran her hand over the smooth red cover of her journal. She remembered without looking when it was she had penned the last entry in the journal. She had last written when she returned from her pilgrimage along the Way of St. James—el Camino de Santiago, still grieving Peter. After his sudden death, she had challenged herself to walk the grueling eight-hundred mile trek from Le Puy in France to the city of Santiago de Compostela in Spain—one of the routes Christians of all ages had followed to seek penance for their sins and save their souls. Maggie's pilgrimage was commenced not only to find a physical means to escape the pain and loss of her beloved best friend and husband (and the aches and pains of her blistered feet and tortured knees during the ordeal did help offset the emotional pain), but also as a self-inflicted penance for not having accepting Peter's marriage proposal sooner. Years sooner!

She recalled some of the razor-sharp anguish of those first days and weeks of widowhood, when she'd walked nearly doubled over with grief. The pain was not as acute now, having dulled over the years to an ever-present throbbing, much like the constant ache of an old back injury. She even remembered without looking at them the last words she had written in her journal when she had returned from Spain: *Peter is dead. Life goes on. I will never love again!*

Of course she had known at the time that she would love again. She loved her daughter Nellie and she loved Doctor Bart, Nellie's husband, who was the son of her best friend, Jane, whom she also loved. And she loved her special set of Sovereign friends: Wendell and Rebecca; Ryan MacDonald and his wife Trudy; her particular friend Leland Gorse (Trudy's father); and former Sovereign residents Lila and Mike Hobart and their family up in The County. Finally, she loved her parishioners, each and every one of them, whether or not they attended church or even knew that they were her parishioners.

But ... had she really meant that she would never love a man—a life partner?—again? Never allow someone to get close to her? Never have someone to provide an arm she could lean upon when the going got tough, as the going was most certainly going to get in the years to come?

Maggie opened her journal, flipped to the next blank page without rereading the last entry, and began to scribble stream of consciously:

41

When Peter died I thought Love was over for me. I thought I'd never again be able to experience the kind of love we shared and cherished, the deep and abiding love that flourishes between people who have been together many, many years. That's what I believed then and I still believe it. There's simply not enough time left in my life for that kind of love to develop. Peter and I built our love slowly over nearly six decades; our love was solid, like a stone wall created over a lifetime by a master stonemason.

Yes, that kind of love is definitely off the table. But does that mean all love is off the table? Is it possible that David and I can build a mutually-satisfying relationship based upon a different type of love?

I'm happy living alone, but I remember when Peter moved in how wonderful it was to have him to lean on, to share my daily cares with, my silly little worries and rewards. Would I feel comfortable sharing those small but sacred things with David? Likewise, do I want to be the recipient of David's cares and concerns?

What about sex? Why hasn't David even tried to kiss me? Doesn't he find me attractive?

As soon as the last paragraph spilled out upon the white-lined page in bright blue ink, David's bearded countenance popped into her head. Maggie closed her journal and rested her head back against the chair. She certainly found David attractive. He was often mocking and sardonic, which lent his countenance the air of a romantic desperado. Still, there was little sexual tension between them. Maggie wasn't sure whether the lack of passion could be laid at his door or hers, or both of theirs. It took two to tango, and maybe they just weren't a matched pair? Or maybe they were too old to dance?

I hope not, she thought. I want to enjoy sex again!

She knew that Peter—if he could somehow reach her beyond the grave—would be the first to congratulate her if David turned out to be someone whom she could love and make love with, someone with whom she could celebrate life and being alive. "Those who have the remainder of their earthly days to live out need physical love," he'd say. "Don't let me hold you back." (She could hear him now.) "You know I've only ever wanted you to be happy!" (She did know it.)

Still ... would she listen to Peter? She had rarely taken his advice during their years of friendship and look what it had cost her to ignore him! So many years without him by her side. Of course, he had always been home on the farm in Winslow when she needed him, but it wasn't the same as having him physically with her, as she did when they finally were married.

And what would people in Sovereign think if she took up with a new man so soon after Peter's death? Did it matter?

Of course it mattered what Nellie thought, and Wendell and Rebecca thought, and what all the rest of their close group of friends thought. But it mattered more to her what she thought, and right now Maggie thought she couldn't do it.

If someone had come to her for pastoral counselling about the same issue, Maggie knew she would be the first to encourage her parishioner to grasp love with both hands and hang on tight, no matter what. The only problem with her pastoral advice, as Peter liked to point out, is that she never took it herself.

A roundly-given rapping on the old schoolhouse door woke Maggie from her reverie. She hadn't seen or heard anyone pull into the dooryard and quickly peered out the window, surprised to see the slanted, late-afternoon sunlight reflecting from the tail-end of a familiar dark Chrysler parked in her driveway. Shirley!

She quickly placed the journal and pen on her little book stand and covered the journal with a gardening magazine. Before she could rise up out of her rocker, Shirley Palmer, the indefatigable, seventy-something retired postmistress of Sovereign and local busybody, popped into the kitchen without knocking on the inner door.

"Hello, dearie! Don't git up," Shirley instructed her. "I ain't a-going to stay long. I was jest drivin' by 'n seen you settin' in the winder, so I thought I'd step in. There's somethin' particular I been wantin' to speak to you about." The spry old lady shifted out of her ankle-length wool coat and draped the coat and her hand-knit scarf over the back of a kitchen chair, making herself quite at home. She was dressed neatly in one of her usual plaid wool skirts and white blouses, with a red button-up cotton cardigan, sturdy winter boots, and black wool leggings.

"Oh?" Maggie sank back into her chair with an uneasy feeling. She suspected Shirley had stopped in to question her about David. It would be just the thing Shirley would do. The retired postmistress was the unofficial social maven of Sovereign, the sort of woman who would say what she felt needed to be said—if she thought it was the right thing to do—no matter how unpleasant or how much pain her directness caused everyone involved, even herself. She meant well and while Maggie respected and often appreciated the older woman's frankness, she would much rather not be on the receiving end of it.

"I hope I ain't interruptin?" Shirley set her clutch purse and knit gloves down on the kitchen table. She carefully removed her black felt cloche hat.

"Oh, no," Maggie lied.

Shirley targeted a free chair and drew it away from the table so she was facing the minister. Despite her age, her back was straight as an arrow when she sat down; however, her hands, curled and twisted, betrayed nearly sixty years of mail-handling and letter-sorting. She placed her arthritic hands in her lap, keeping her knees together modestly, her wool skirt falling several inches below her kneecaps.

Maggie said nothing, waiting for her friend and parishioner to begin the conversation. Shirley opened the volley with a feint to the left. "Glad you ain't busy. You got yer sermon all writ, then?"

Shirley's words hit their mark. Maggie had been so busy worrying about her relationship with David that she had forgotten all about her pastoral message for this coming Sunday. "Um, almost," she lied again, promising to seek penance later. In fact, she hadn't even begun to write her sermon. "Was there something in particular you wanted me to include in the service?"

"Nope, 'twas jest a reminder, dearie. You only got two days. Sunday will be here afore you know it." Shirley's gaze flitted about the room, immediately landing on the colorful new wallpaper with a chicken and egg motif. David had helped Maggie hang the new paper on New Year's Day. "My, I ain't nevah seen sech a variety o' poultry afore! Not on wallpaper, leastways."

"The kitchen was always dark, you know."

"Wal, 'tain't dark no more!"

Maggie decided that rather than beat around the bush, she might as well determine the purpose of Shirley's visit. She did need to prepare her church service, after all. "What was it you wanted to see me about?" she asked boldly.

Shirley's eyebrows knit together. "Wal, now, I cain't rightly remember." She glanced up at Maggie, as though seeking the information from that corner.

Maggie, however, felt under no obligation to offer any more aid to her friend, especially if Shirley intended to dissect her love life. "Was it something about the pancake breakfast, maybe?"

"Wal, no, don't think so. Warn't even on my way to see you a-tall. 'Twas jest on my way to Hannah's house 'n took the short cut ovah the Cross Road. I'm surprised I got as far as I did. Yer road ain't fit fer a donkey!"

Maggie smiled to herself, knowing that if Shirley Palmer wanted to go someplace and a donkey was the only means of transportation Shirley would surely ride the beast. "The snow will melt soon enough and then we'll be complaining about the mud," replied Maggie, sagely, she thought.

"Wal, I'm a-going to call John Woods when I git home and give him a piece o' my mind!" In Sovereign, there was a perpetual tug-of-war between the town's First Selectman, John Woods, who held the purse strings, and Asa Palmer, Shirley's husband, who was the annually-elected Road Commissioner and therefore responsible for maintaining the town's roads.

"I suppose a few truckloads of sand wouldn't hurt," said Maggie, always careful not to take sides. "We did get a lot of snow in that last storm."

Shirley scoffed. "'Twould take more 'n a few loads to make yer road safe! I ain't sure how I'm a-going to git up the hill to Hannah's house without gettin' stuck. Thank the Good Lord I can still walk!"

The older woman fell silent, as if picturing herself marching up the snow-covered road, offering Maggie an opportunity to shift the course of the conversation. "Is Hannah making you a new hat for Easter?" One of her close neighbors, Hannah Shorey Trow (Doctor Bart's

46

aunt) was the town's seamstress and often did millenary work for Shirley.

"Lord-y, yes!" Having taken the bait, Shirley settled back into her chair assuming a comfortable, conversational attitude. If there was one thing Shirley Palmer liked more than being a busybody, it was being a busybody with a new hat. She patted her tight gray curls. "That's what I'm a-going to see her about. When we was young, we gals all-ways hed new bonnets for Easter," Shirley reminisced gaily. "Dinn't they make hats back then! Nowadays, a body cain't even locate a department store let alone find one that carries Easter bonnets. Do you know Macy's in Bangor is closing? 'Twas all over the news. Ain't things changed," she added sadly.

Things had changed, Maggie agreed soberly—and silently.

Both women paused for quiet contemplation. In the silence, Maggie heard the snow dripping off the eaves. Added to that was the slow, methodical ticking of her Regulator wall clock. Maggie suddenly had the awful sensation that Time was running out.

How much time did she have left before she crossed the Great Divide and joined Peter? How many years were left to her to do the things she wanted to do? Say the things she wanted to say? Hug the people she wanted to hug? Pick all the blackberries she wanted to pick and bake all the pies she wanted to bake!

Maggie glanced over at Shirley and caught the older woman gazing unseeing into space. It occurred to Maggie that Shirley—fifteen years her senior—might be asking herself the very same question: 'How much time do I have left?' She recollected how Shirley had stood by her and comforted her not only during her death-defying bout with breast cancer, but also during those dark days after Peter's unexpected heart attack. A wave of gratitude and affection washed over her for her friend and parishioner. Yes, things certainly had changed—for both of them. Shirley had lost two of her sisters since Peter's death and was constantly plagued by financial anxieties relating to her motherless nephews and nieces and their offspring.

"Tell me about the hat," Maggie prompted, cheerfully.

Shirley perked up. She shook a knobby finger at the minister. "Oh, no—I know yer tricks," she replied, teasingly. "I'm not telling you a thing, Miss Margaret! Hannah 'n I is a-going to surprise all you gals. Them men 'n their contest won't hold a candle to us!"

Maggie smiled. "I know plenty of women who tap trees, but none of them ever enter the maple syrup contest. I wonder why? Why should we let the men have all the fun? Maybe this year we should give them a run for their money?"

"I ain't a-following you, dearie."

Maggie leaned forward in her rocker. "Why don't we hold a hat contest on Maple Sunday? That would give the women something fun to do, too."

Shirley clasped her hands to her breast. "Lord-y! A hat contest! 'Twould be jest the thing."

"We don't need to run out and buy new hats either. Why, I bet every woman in town has hats in her attic. I know I have half a dozen upstairs."

"'Twould be terrible fun!"

"As long as we give the men their moment in the sun, I don't think they'll mind if we add a second contest."

"But who's a-going to jedge us?" Shirley worried. "Every gal in town will want to participate."

Maggie hardly thought that assertion was true, but didn't contradict Shirley, especially as there was an easy way to allay her concern. "Pooh! Who says we need women judges? We'll just use the same judges we already have."

"You mean—men?" Shirley asked, swallowing hard. Historically, the maple syrup judging had always been left to the male sex, although a motion to change that had been introduced several times over the years. The motion was always voted down, however,—by the women themselves—who were much more interested in eating and socializing than in taking the contest seriously.

"Anyone with a refined taste in maple syrup surely has a refined taste in hats, too."

"Wal, I don't rightly know 'bout that. But I suppose it don't make much difference. Some gals have about as much fashion sense as a snowshoe hare—one set o' clothes fer winter and 'nother fer summer. Wouldn't Hannah Trow have a leg up, though! Her Henry's one o' the jedges."

"So is David—my friend David Faulkner," Maggie added. Too late, she realized her mistake. If Shirley had stopped in to chastise her about her relationship with David, Maggie had just let slip the perfect opening.

"Tut, tut! Friend, indeed," Shirley scoffed. Suddenly, her thin frame jerked upright. "Say! Now I recollect why 'twas I stopped in to see you in the fust place."

Maggie felt her shoulders droop. "You do?"

"Yep." Shirley eyed the minister critically. "I surely do, but …" she broke off.

"But what?"

"'T'ain't none o' my bees-whacks," she declared. Shirley popped up from the chair and retrieved her coat from the back with an air of conviction. "No—no more nor nobody else's business, neither. You got a right to make yerself happy, dearie. And don't let nobody tell you otherwise, neither." The retired postmistress shrugged into her wool coat and wrapped the scarf around her neck. "Besides, I ain't got time to lecture you 'bout yer love life—my word! I got to get Hannah workin' on that new bonnet."

Maggie laughed. She had been worried about a lecture from this notorious busybody and yet Shirley had given her the same advice she would have given herself— only not heeded!

Becoming aware that the matron was waiting to say goodbye, Maggie rose and offered her adieus. "Thanks for stopping in," she said, sincerely. She opened the shed door and walked her guest out into the unheated entryway. "Give Hannah my love."

"Ayuh. And remember what I told ya—ain't nobody but you can say what's right fer you, dearie."

"I'll certainly remember that. It's the kind of advice everyone wants to hear!"

"That's my gal." Shirley patted Maggie fondly on the shoulder. Almost as an afterthought, she leaned over and gave the minister a dry peck on the cheek. She tucked her purse under her arm and readjusted her cloche felt black hat. "Although, I do think it's high time you took yerself a lover, Maggie Hodges," she added with a wink.

A lover? This from straight-laced Shirley Palmer! Maggie was so taken aback she allowed Shirley to escape with the last word.

The spry matron stepped firmly down the stone path leading to her four-door Chrysler sedan. Maggie heard Shirley chuckling to herself as she went, sounding much like a satisfied mother hen clucking over a nest full of chicks. When the older woman reached her car she turned and waved. Maggie smiled and waved back. She remained on the threshold, hugging herself against the chilly March dampness, and watched as the retired postmistress maneuvered her vehicle out of the driveway and gunned the car up the over the snow-covered road.

The third-quarter moon rose in the east over the bare treetops. When she could no longer see or hear Shirley's vehicle, Maggie knew the retired postmistress had made it safely up the hill. She returned to the kitchen and immediately poked the fire, adding two more sticks of wood.

She retrieved her chair and recovered her journal from the side table. Maggie made one final entry before closing the book: *Shirley here this afternoon. Gave me permission to take a lover. Maybe I will!*

Chapter 4
Rabbit Hunting

On Saturday, Maggie was supposed to take David rabbit hunting—hunting, that is, with a camera rather than a gun. In January, David had developed an interest in the snowshoe hare after one of his friends at the Maine Department of Inland Fisheries and Wildlife informed him that the state's other rabbit species, the New England cottontail, was recently state-listed as an endangered species. The cottontail is rarely found north of Portland; however, the snowshoe hare is still numerous enough in the Pine Tree State to be hunted and has long held a popular spot in the heart of inveterate Maine hunters. After some cajoling on David's part, Maggie, who had hunted the snowshoe hare as a child with her uncle, her mother's brother, reluctantly agreed to act as his guide.

David told her he was intrigued by the snowshoe hare's seasonal fur change, which facilitated the hare's ability to blend in with the ever-changing New England groundcover. When the Maine woods were leaf-covered and brown, the hare was brown; when the natural world was blanketed with soft, white snow, the hare was white; and when the ground was covered with snow one day and washed by rain the next, the hare's fur was a mottled, white-spotted brown. By contrast, the cottontail stays brown all year-round. Hoping to eventually publish an article on Maine's snowshoe hare, David was eager to photograph and document the hare during the interesting transitional time of year. He calculated the only way for him to approach the creatures near enough to photograph them was to enlist Maggie's aid.

"I was never so damn cold in my life as I was rabbit hunting," she told him with an involuntary shiver when they had made the date. "I always hated it as a kid."

"Why did you go, then?" He bestowed upon her one of his mocking smiles, which Maggie was pretty sure she found sexy.

"I suppose I wasn't smart enough to say 'no'," she replied, much to his amusement. David's hearty laugh was filled with genuine admiration for her frankness. The admiration was both pleasant and flattering.

"Did you actually carry a gun?" he inquired, obviously impressed by the fact that Maggie had hunted rabbits as a child.

"I did. A 20-gauge shotgun with bird shot. The dear creatures were safe from me, though," she added.

"Why? Did you never have a good shot?"

"Oh, I had plenty of shots. My uncle always posted us kids—my cousin Ralph and I—outside the stretch of wood he and his buddies intended to hunt. They turned the hounds loose and drove the rabbits right at us, dogs braying and bellowing all the way. Those dogs were an awful racket!"

"Is that why you missed the rabbits?"

"I missed them because I intended to miss. I shot over their heads. If I never hear another rabbit scream it'll be too soon."

"I'm surprised nobody noticed your defalcation?"

"Ralph did, but he didn't mind. He got to shoot all the rabbits."

"Well, no furry lives will be lost on our date, I promise. I'm only hunting with my cameras."

David was supposed to arrive at nine-thirty on Saturday; however, he showed up nearly an hour early to grab a bite to eat first, as she had expected. She spied his white Land Rover as it pulled into the driveway and automatically set the coffee pot back onto the woodstove for a quick warm-up. She slipped into the cool, dry pantry, once a closet where the neighborhood schoolchildren had stored their coats, hats, and boots, and retrieved the raspberry pie she had baked the prior day. The pie, one of Maggie's favorites, was more for herself than for him. She had come to the realization that she didn't want to claim her Great Reward without eating a lot more of her favorite pies!

David let himself into the shed without knocking. Maggie heard him pause to hang his parka on the Shaker-style coat rack. He doffed his boots and entered the kitchen cheerfully, rubbing his cold hands together. She allowed him to give her a light kiss on the cheek before she stepped quickly away. Although she was considering adding a permanent partner to her life, she was on the fence as to whether or not David was right man for the job. She was determined to keep their relationship treading water a bit longer. In the meantime, she gave herself free reign to utilize the wide variety of stalling techniques known to both sexes.

Unabashed by her aloofness, David dropped his keys into a carnival glass candy dish atop the antique oak chiffonier and leaned back against the heavy serving piece. He launched immediately into the project at hand, with little preliminary chit-chat. "I'm taking three cameras," he informed her. "*National Wildlife* will give me a feature article, if I get some good shots today."

"Wonderful! Well, then, I hope we aren't skunked."

David's face fell. "Seriously, Maggie? I thought you knew the best places to go!"

"I did when I was a kid. We lived in Winslow then, remember?"

"So let's go to Winslow."

"We can't. There are two new McMansions where we used to rabbit hunt."

David folded his arms across his chest. "Well, you must have a Plan B?"

Maggie hesitated for the briefest of moments. "I was thinking of asking my friend Leland to show us where to go. He knows where all the local hare hang out. You remember my friend Leland, don't you?"

"Who could forget that old duffer?" David scoffed. "He tells such crazy stories. Worse, he actually seems to expect people to believe them."

David had previously expressed disgust with Leland so this response came as no surprise. Still, Maggie couldn't help attempting to amend his negative perception of her old friend. "I think some of Leland's stories are true," she countered. "Or, at least, are based on some facts, anyway."

"Please, Maggie! I swear I hear the song *Dueling Banjos* whenever I see that guy."

This pronouncement was hard on Maggie as Leland Gorse was one of her closest friends in Sovereign. She remembered well one afternoon during her chemotherapy when Leland had stayed with her while Peter went to Winslow to help his nephew Bruce with the haying. Leland had kindly and matter-of-factly cleaned her up after she'd tossed her cookies. Then he proceeded to tell her some of his favorite stories, just to help take her mind off her troubles. "He's a good man," she stated firmly. "You just don't know him yet."

"I don't intend to get to know him. If you can't figure out where we should go today, I'll wait until my friend at IFW can take me rabbit hunting."

Maggie was irritated by David's sulkiness, but nevertheless she was wise enough to abandon her plan to show him the true value of Leland's character. Trying to fix things only seemed to make matters worse. "I guess we could hunt around here. I've seen some sign lately."

"Good. Let's just keep today for you and me, OK?" David stepped in Maggie's direction, as though inclined to give her a make-up hug.

Maggie didn't need a degree in feminine intuition to pick up on David's sign. Quickly, she pulled out a chair at the kitchen table so that the chair was between the two of them, thus thwarting his forward movement. "Ready for some coffee and raspberry pie?"

He stopped in his tracks. "Sure. I only had two eggs for breakfast because I knew you'd feed me." He sat down and hiked the chair up to the table. "By the way, what did your family do with all the rabbits they shot? Did you eat them?"

"Don't ask," she said, slicing into the flaky pie crust. Thick red raspberry juice oozed out.

"It might be an important cultural distinction and an interesting slant to my article."

"I doubt that."

"How can you say that when you don't even know what angle I'm taking with my story?" he replied, annoyed.

"Because my uncle tossed the dead rabbits to the dogs. Is that cultural enough for you?" Feeling annoyed herself, she carelessly plated up the two pieces of pie.

"That was rather a waste."

"I'm sure the dogs didn't think so." Maggie slapped the pie onto the table. "Coffee?"

"Sure."

She poured out two cups of coffee and fixed David's just as he liked it. She fixed her own and took her seat at the table without saying anything. Sometimes he could be a bit of a prig!

The tension between them eased, however, as soon as David took his first bite of raspberry pie. "Ah! This is excellent! You're a great cook, Maggie."

Maggie felt her ruffled feathers smooth back down. "Thanks. Raspberry is one of my favorites. I have a patch of raspberries out back that gives me fifteen or twenty quarts a year."

They proceeded to eat their pie in silence. Maggie had added some dry birch to the woodstove and the bark crackled and popped as it caught fire. The kitchen was toasty and comfortable and she felt her mood continue to mellow.

"It's almost as good as your blackberry pie. In fact, I think I'll have a second piece before we go, just to help keep me warm while we hunt. Some rabbit guide I know told me rabbit hunting is damn cold work." He grinned and winked.

Completely appeased, Maggie giggled. "It's good to know you actually do listen to me sometimes." She rose to retrieve the pie, cut a second piece, and slid the pie onto his plate. Then she returned to her chair. "I hope you haven't forgotten you're going to be one of the judges for our maple syrup contest? Maple Sunday is only three weeks away."

David picked up his fork. "Don't worry. I have it in my calendar."

"Good. Because you'll also be judging a ladies' hat contest, although, I suppose it isn't politically correct to say it's a ladies' contest. Both contests are open to everyone."

He was slightly taken aback. "A hat contest? What do I know about ladies' hats?"

But Maggie could tell by the amusement sparkling from his hazel eyes that despite his protest he was not disinclined to act as one of the judges. She suspected that David, who regularly spoke to large audiences around the globe on environmental issues, appreciated the attention of a crowd, no matter its size, composition, or raison d'être. "What does anyone know about hats? Millinery knowledge isn't a prerequisite for judging, I'd say. I don't believe there's any such thing as fashion anymore."

"Surely you must be able to find somebody else in this one-horse town to judge the hats?"

David, when he first arrived at the college, had been surprised to discover a community of Amish in Unity. Since then, there had been a lot of 'one-horse' jokes from him, all of which irritated Maggie. She heard the message behind his jokes as a disparagement of the rural agricultural lifestyle, which was the lifeblood of the area. Was he deliberately trying to annoy her today? Or was he just completely unaware of—and unconcerned about—her thoughts and feelings?

"Really, it's no big deal, David. We just thought we'd use the same judges for both contests. Besides, how hard can it be? Just pick the hat you like the best."

David fondled his beard, as though giving careful consideration to the hat contest. But in the months Maggie had known him she had already discerned this habit meant that he had moved beyond the present topic. He was now mentally engaged in their next topic of conversation. Unfortunately, most of the time she had no clue what that conversation was likely to be about.

"Are you going to participate?" he said, finally. He laid his forearm deliberately on the table. His hand landed near hers.

Maggie instinctively pulled back. She averted her eyes, lest like a deer in the headlights she become mesmerized by the intensity of his gaze and get swept away. "Probably not," she replied, taking a bite of her pie. "It wouldn't be appropriate. I'm the minister, after all."

"Because if so I might be a bit biased," he continued, suggestively.

"You and every other man on the panel," she said, lifting her coffee cup to her mouth.

Once again, David appeared taken aback. "How many judges are there?"

"Six others besides you," she added, sweetly. "Six other men with six wives and the balance of their lives hanging over their heads."

David burst out laughing. "This town cracks me up. Why, every man in town must be one of the judges?"

"Almost, except for the three regular contestants, of course." Maggie was relieved to note that the sexual tension between them had been diffused.

"Who are our three regulars?"

"Wendell, Maynard Nutter—you don't know him—and Leland."

"Him again! I should have guessed. Promise me you won't do anything foolish like sit with that guy at the pancake breakfast, OK? I don't want to be trapped at the same table with him."

Stubbornly, Maggie refused to promise. Angry and frustrated, she almost wanted to cry. Merging their very different set of friends would be just one of many challenges if she and he got together as a couple. She had met several of David's male colleagues and had even gone on field trips with some of them. While all of them seemed nice, they had little in common with her and her quiet life in this small farming community.

David, oblivious to her distress, devoured his second piece of pie. He glanced at his Rolex. "Time to go." He took a final swig of coffee and carefully daubed his beard with his napkin.

Maggie shook off her apprehension and gathered her things. Despite what she had said about being cold rabbit hunting, they wouldn't need their down parkas this morning. The weather had cooperated by providing them with a gorgeous March day. The sun was bright and the temperature was nearly fifty degrees. Maine weather in March can be dicey—one day five below zero and snowing with forty miles per hour winds and the next day fifty degrees above and raining. But there was no snow or rain forecast and in fact there had been no new snow since February twentieth. The snow was densely packed—perfect for easy snowshoeing.

She decided to start the hunt in the ample fields and woods in back of her house. Once outside, Maggie expertly strapped on her snowshoes, a pair of Tubbs bear paws she had purchased with her own money when she was thirteen. David clamped into a light-weight set of aluminum snowshoes on loan from the college. One digital and two SRL cameras crisscrossed his chest. They both wore wool sweaters and turtlenecks under their fleeces, affording them the opportunity to doff layers if they got hot.

The sun already felt warm against Maggie's face. She pulled on her mittens, deeply inhaling the dry, fresh March air. She could almost smell the fertile, musky scent of the earth lying in wait beneath the snow. Soon, the delightful cheeping of the spring peepers and garbled croaking of the wood frogs would fill the evening air with their mating songs as the cycle of life kicked into high gear once more.

"Which way are we headed first?" David queried.

His question brought Maggie back to the moment. She pointed to a stand of balsams intermingled with second-growth poplar and paper birch situated at the back edge of the nearby field. The stand was immature and had filled back in naturally after the mature wood was cut and removed about a decade earlier. As a result, thorny blackberry and raspberry canes, hawthorn bushes, tree stumps, and dead branches helped fill in the spaces between the young trees. "We'll head over there and hunt that grove of balsam first."

"Seriously? We'll never get through that mess without getting torn to shreds."

"What are you—a wimp? If you want to find rabbits, you need to go where the bunnies hang out. According to my uncle, snowshoe hare like nothing better than puckerbrush, that is, when they're not feasting in my garden," Maggie amended. "But the deer have already beaten them to what was left of my Brussel sprouts."

David still seemed disinclined to tackle the stand of balsam with its thick undergrowth. "I thought snowshoe hare laid low in depressions? Forms, I believe they're called."

"They do. But not usually right out in the open, David. Were you expecting to just snowshoe along and get lucky enough to push a rabbit out of hiding?"

"My friend told me it was pretty easy to jump one."

"It is. If you go where you're likely to find them."

Maggie adjusted her wool cap and launched off, moving easily along on her snowshoes over the compressed snow. David hung back. She suspected she might have offended him by impugning his knowledge and calling him a "wimp." She hadn't meant to be harsh, but sometimes he was just too annoying!

Until that moment, Maggie hadn't realized how important good humor in a partner meant to her. If she couldn't laugh at—and laugh with—her partner, what was the point? Wouldn't she always be walking on eggshells around him, afraid she'd offend him without knowing it? She certainly hadn't expected David's ego to be so touchy. He probably wasn't used to women knowing more than he did, or at least having more practical experience, for Maggie was sure that David had more scientific knowledge about the snowshoe hare than she did. Imagine her rabbit hunting misadventures as a child offering her the opportunity to discover what type of man she wanted to spend her final years with!

Lost in thought, she hadn't noticed that he had snowshoed up beside her. "Hey," he said, as they trudged along in unison. "Sorry I acted like a jerk back there. I'm not used to being second in command. Just tell me where to go and I'll follow your lead." He grinned good-naturedly.

Maggie's reservations caved-in immediately. "Follow me, but not too closely. You don't want a branch in the face."

He saluted her. "Aye, aye, Captain!"

Maggie laughed, feeling rejuvenated. He had apologized and even poked fun at himself! What more could she ask for? If he was a big enough man to recognize own his shortcomings, he was a big enough man for her. "I'm the one who should apologize," she said, feeling contrite. "I'm sorry I called you a 'wimp.' I guess I've gotten a little too comfortable over the years speaking out."

"That's what I like about you, Maggie—you don't play games. You say what you think, even if the truth hurts."

"You mean, I blurt things out without thinking first."

"Don't worry—I can handle the truth." He hooked her arm, slowing them both to a standstill. He gazed around at the vista before them. The brilliant sun tossed sparkles across the snowy expanse, scattering twinkling stars upon the blue-white snow to light their path. "Do you know, on such a beautiful day as this, there's no place I'd rather be than right here in Sovereign, Maine? And there's no one I'd rather be with than with you, Maggie."

She snuck a peek at him to see if he was jesting. No, he was serious. "Really?"

"Really! Now, let's go tackle that—what did you call it?"

"Puckerbrush?"

"That puckerbrush, and find ourselves a snowshoe hare to photograph!"

Before the afternoon sun had set, David had taken more than a hundred photos of not one, but three snowshoe hare, each having distinctly different fur. One hare was nearly white, with only a few brown spots, and the other two were equally spotted half brown and half white.

David was excited about the photographs, certain they would earn him a feature article in *National Wildlife*. Despite the pains they had gone through to get the pictures, battling their way through the dense puckerbrush, it had been worth it. One of the hare had remained hunched in its form and so David was able to get several excellent still photographs of that. The other two hare leaped up just as Maggie was about to step on them with her snowshoes, presenting him with more challenging fleeing shots. However, on review the photographs came out perfectly.

They took the road home, carrying their snowshoes. Maggie good-naturedly listened as David detailed the nature and scope of his article. She was relieved they had jumped the three hare, knowing as she did that David would have been deeply disappointed if the outing had turned out to be a bust. For herself, Maggie was content with the afternoon. The day had been a success from the moment David had apologized to her. How could she not appreciate someone as self-aware and humble as he was?

The more time she spent with David Faulkner, the more Maggie realized she enjoyed spending time with him. Perhaps she *was* ready to open the door to her heart and let another lover in? And why shouldn't David be the one? Certainly, there was no other man looming large on her horizon!

Chapter 5
Maple Sunday

On the last Sunday in March, Maple Sunday, Maggie's alarm went off at 5:30 a.m. Forty-five minutes later she entered the banquet hall attached to the Sovereign Union Church, a traditional little white country church, where a group of ladies and a few men had gathered before dawn to prepare the fixings for one of their annual fundraisers, the pancake breakfast. Served up with bacon, scrambled eggs, toast and a variety of homemade jams and jellies, the main attraction, the pancakes, included whole-wheat, blueberry, strawberry, raspberry, and even cranberry pancakes.

The woodsy smell of bacon frying and the delicious aroma of fresh-perked coffee greeted Maggie when she entered the commodious banquet room. Through the server's window she could see Shirley Palmer hard at work mixing pancake batter in the commercial kitchen. The matron was wearing her new hat, a wide-brimmed straw affair decorated with a variety of colorful fabric birds setting in what appeared to be real bird's nests. Shirley had donned a ticking-striped cobbler's apron over her usual Sunday dress and, spying the minister, smiled and gave Maggie a cheerful thumbs-up.

The church ladies had outdone themselves decorating the banquet hall and tables. Sixteen, eight-foot banquet tables were covered in colorful linens, all of the same floral figured pattern, with complementary pastel cloth napkins. They were set with the church's hotel silver plate and six clear-glass maple syrup pitchers, each pitcher having a number from one to six hanging like a dog tag off its neck. The contestants—only the three regulars this year—were allowed to enter two syrups apiece in the contest. Small bouquets of spritely-looking yellow daffodils were intermingled with the syrup pitchers.

When Maggie arrived, the hall was scattered with volunteers putting out iced water pitchers and chilled butters. The fresh butter was plated on the church's green Depression ware and was a donation from Scotch Broom Acres, Leland's family farm now managed by his daughter Trudy and her husband Ryan MacDonald. The molded butter in the pretty green dishes featured the farm's well-known monogram, an "*S*" intertwined with a strand of the vetch-like flowering scotch-broom plant that was the farm's hallmark. Scotch Broom Acres had received many statewide awards and was now recognized for its many fine products. The marriage of the big city lawyer to the small-town farmer had been a big success not only romantically but also for the home-based business, melding as it did Ryan's expertise with finance and marketing with Trudy's farming knowledge and her creative design.

Seeing the butter reminded Maggie of David's dislike of and disdain for Leland. Anxious to prevent any possible hard feelings, she determined to take the matter into her own hands today lest David do or say something hurtful to her good friend. She calculated that if she spent some time with Leland before David arrived at the breakfast, hopefully he wouldn't notice that they appeared to be avoiding him later on. David had tried to make Maggie promise that they wouldn't sit at the same table with Leland; however, Maggie hadn't yielded to this request, knowing as she did that they would most likely end up with her particular group of friends, of which Leland was one. The best she could do was to be sure and seat her and David as far away from Leland as possible, and hope for the best.

Knowing that Leland most likely would have been the one to run the fresh butter down from the farm, Maggie went looking for him. She was disappointed, however, when in the kitchen she discovered that Trudy had dropped the butter off the day before. "I ain't seen hide nor hair o' Leland," said Shirley. "Want me to send him over to yer table when he comes?"

"No, no need," Maggie replied, hurriedly. "I'll run him down, eventually." She glanced at the sink, already piled high with dirty pots and pans. "Want some help with the dishes?"

Her assistance was accepted and Maggie cheerfully set to work washing up. As she worked, she kept an ear out for her loquacious friend. But by seven o'clock, the official start of the pancake breakfast, Leland still hadn't made an appearance.

At Shirley's insistence, Maggie abandoned the kitchen and took up her regular post at the main door, where she acted as the unofficial hostess of the annual event. She greeted members of her little flock as they and their families entered, and graciously pretended not to see the guilty looks on the faces of her 'Submarine Christians,' those who surfaced for Christmas and Easter services, and the occasional church breakfast or supper. By seven forty-five most of the tables were filled and still there was no sign of Leland or the Scotch Broom Acres crew.

The influx had slowed and Maggie was chatting at the back of the room with two or three parishioners when David entered. She saw him scan the banquet room looking for her and held up her hand so he could locate her. He smiled and began weaving his way through the bustling crowd to join Maggie. Shirley, however, had also seen David arrive and cut him off at the pass. "Jest a minute young fella," Maggie heard her say to him gaily. She knew that Shirley was working hard to gain votes for the hat contest and she watched the two of them together anxiously, unsure whether David would consent to remain in Shirley's clutches. But when she heard his brisk, energetic laugh in response to something the retired postmistress said Maggie realized he was being a good sport about the whole thing. Thank goodness David wasn't turned off by Shirley's downhome character like he was by Leland's!

While David was thus employed, Maggie attempted to locate a place for them to sit. Too late, she realized her mistake—she had been so busy working and keeping an eye out for Leland she hadn't reserved a seat in advance for David and herself. Now there were no two seats together to be found.

At that moment the Scotch Broom Acres gang arrived with Rebecca, Wendell, and Nick Faulkner in tow. Relief washed over her when she realized Leland wasn't among them. An extra table was quickly set up for the newcomers and Ryan MacDonald beckoned for Maggie to join them as the table was being prepared. She realized there was nothing for it but to sit with them. For herself, she was only too glad to join her special set of friends. She just hoped that if Leland did put in an appearance he would sit as far away from David as possible.

Maggie was greeted with enthusiasm. "Thank goodness you're here," said Trudy, attempting to unzip three-year-old Alice Rose's coat. "Now maybe the kids will behave themselves!"

"'Tain't likely," said Wendell, flashing a grin.

Maggie laughed and winked at Alice Rose, who giggled in response. "You're right. I'll probably incite them to further mischief-making."

Rebecca, who had already liberated her son Tad from his winter jacket, was now trying to catch him. Wendell grabbed the boy by the waist as he ran around the back side of the table. He scooped the child up and plunked him down in the wooden highchair. He plopped the high chair's tray down, effectively barring the child in place. "Thet should hold you fer a while," he said, satisfied.

"Mama, I'm *too old* for a high chair," announced three-year-old Alice Rose, beginning to hop from one foot to the other. "I'm much older than Tad." Trudy sighed and shot her husband a helpless look.

"Welcome to bedlam," said Ryan, cheerfully, pulling out a chair for Maggie. "Sit next to me. I'm only in charge of Hope. She's pretty safe." Hope was Ryan and Trudy's fifteen-month-old daughter, a thoughtful, silent child, quite the opposite of her lively older sister.

"Give me that child and go help your wife," Maggie directed him. Ryan agreeably handed Hope off to Maggie, who smothered the little girl's face with kisses and asked, "Whose girl are you?"

"Moo-Mooo," cried the cherub. She grabbed a loose strand of Maggie's hair and tugged hard.

Maggie gently released the child's hand. "Did you hear that?" she said proudly. "Hope knows my name!"

"Charming. She thinks you're a cow," Ryan replied, drily. "Where's David? Wait, I see him—Shirley has him in her clutches. I'll go and dislodge the old boy."

"Do that and he'll be grateful to you forever."

"Only problem is, I might not be able to get away from Shirley myself. I'm one of the judges, too."

But Ryan was successful at his task and in three minutes David slid into the open chair at Maggie's left.

The environmentalist smoothly greeted the others at the table and then leaned closer to Maggie. "Sorry, I got waylaid," he said sotto voce.

"I saw that. I hope Shirley wasn't too hard on you? I know she wants you to vote for her hat."

"Was that what she was up to? I thought she was just being a busybody. Thank God Ryan came to rescue me. He asked her who was minding the kitchen and she took off faster than that snowshoe hare we almost stepped on in the puckerbrush."

Maggie felt discomfort at David's use of the word "busybody" to describe Shirley, but not because he utilized the derogatory term to describe the retired postmistress. Her conscience pinged because she, too, had been guilty not-so-long-ago of the same thing. She certainly wouldn't attempt to chastise him, however. Instead, she unfolded her cloth napkin and spread it over her lap. "Did Shirley at least convince you to vote for her hat? Yes, please," she added to Sherry, the young waitress, who appeared at her elbow proffering a fresh pot of coffee. In the old days, Maggie's daughter Nellie was always one of the servers at the pancake breakfast. Lately, however, Nellie was too busy working at the couple's medical clinic to help out much at the church.

"Certainly not. Your friend Shirley would have done better to stay away from me. I might have voted for her then. Me too, thanks," he added, flashing the waitress a charming smile. Flattered—and a bit flustered—the teenager giggled.

Suddenly—to Maggie's dismay—Leland appeared out of nowhere. He must have entered the hall through the side door to the kitchen, where he would have been warmly greeted by the women in the kitchen and given plenty of hot samples to eat. Her old friend spotted their table and hoofed it across the room. The fact that all the chairs were taken didn't stop Leland; he never missed a beat. He grabbed an empty folding metal chair from another table, turned the chair around and parked it between Alice Rose's highchair and his son-in-law. "Mind if I butt in?" he asked the table as a whole. Without waiting for a reply, he squeezed in.

Ryan moved his long legs to make room for Leland. "As long as you don't try to influence my vote," he cautioned.

"Would I do thet?" the woodsman asked innocently.

"Yes!" replied Ryan, Trudy, Wendell, Rebecca, and even Walden, in unison.

Alice Rose banged her spoon upon the wooden bib of the highchair. "Grampa, Grampa!" Her carroty-haired playmate Tad, sitting across from Maggie, picked up on Alice Rose's cue and likewise pounded his fat fist against his tray.

"I hope the pancakes arrive soon," Rebecca said, sighing. She leaned down and rummaged through her bag looking for a toy to distract her son.

Leland gave his granddaughter a playful pinch. Alice Rose squealed.

Ryan bent his dark head over his daughter. "Hey, let's not get too excited until after we get something to eat, OK?" His words were directed to Alice Rose, but Maggie knew they were intended also for Leland.

"Spoil sport," Leland replied. He stuck his tongue out at Tad, who was watching intently. The boy giggled and mimicked the old man. Pleased with his work, Leland made himself at home. A waitress set some extra silverware on the table for him and he undid the napkin, dumped out the silverware, and tucked a corner of the light-blue cloth into the neck of the navy tee shirt he wore under his flannel shirt. Leland reached for his bread knife, most likely to bang the butt end against the tabletop in imitation of the impatient children, however,

73

Trudy's hand was quicker than her father's and she carefully moved the silverware out of his reach. "Please, Father," she said in a low tone. "You're setting a bad example."

Leland immediately became contrite. "Won't happen agin," he promised his daughter. "Whar are them durn tootin' pancakes, anyway?" He craned his neck for a better look at the server's window.

Maggie surreptitiously eyed David. He was frowning, the nostrils of his aquiline nose flared slightly in disdain. "I'm sorry," she whispered, painfully aware of Leland's foibles. "I didn't know he was going to sit with us."

"Forget it," he said. Still she knew he was greatly annoyed.

Fortunately, Sherry reappeared at that moment with a heaping platter of fragrant pancakes. She handed the plate and a pair of tongs to Ryan, who politely held the platter out first to Rebecca, who helped herself and then passed the plate on. The pancakes moved around the table accompanied by good-natured joking and jostling. David held the warm platter for Maggie, who selected two large pancakes, one raspberry and the other cranberry-chocolate.

Leland thrummed his fingers on the table as he waited his turn. When the platter finally arrived down to his end, he lifted two or three pancakes with his fingers, checking the moist, fluffy griddlecakes over looking for blueberries before making his selection. "Good grief," muttered David, under his breath. Maggie felt herself blushing for her old friend's manners, or lack thereof. Trudy rose wordlessly, took the platter from her father after he had made his selection, and retired to the kitchen to fetch a fresh batch of pancakes.

In order to distract David's attention from Leland, Maggie pointed out his choices for maple syrup.

Jennifer Wixson

Her distraction worked, much to her relief. Interested as he was in the variety among syrups gathered at the same time and basically from the same area, David eagerly sampled two or three pitchers, making thoughtful comments about each of the sweet amber liquids. As a judge, David, as well as Ryan, had been provided with a score card and he went to work assiduously making notes on each of the syrups he sampled. Maggie saw Ryan jotting a few things down as well. The contest was highly subjective and the non-judges at the table naturally felt compelled to offer their unsolicited analysis and appraisal.

"I like syrup #5," said Rebecca, who suspected by the syrup's dark molasses color and rich viscosity that it was Wendell's last-run of the season. "What do you think of #5, Walden?" she asked Nick Faulkner, who was sitting directly across the table from her.

"Don't know—haven't tried that one yet," replied Walden. "Pass the pitcher over, please." He was a rugged thirty-something, a larger but much more emotionally and spiritually sensitive version of his uncle. A few years ago he had relocated from Massachusetts to Maine with a heavy chip on his shoulder. Seeking a new life in the Maine woods, basically a life of self-pity and solitude, Nick Faulkner presented himself in town by the satirical pseudonym 'Walden Pond.' He shortly became known as the Mushroom Man, however, because he harvested and sold wild mushrooms for a living. Walden, instead of becoming an outcast as he might have become in so many communities, was accepted and welcomed by the locals for his many talents, which ranged from knowledge about wild mushrooms to familiarity with the work of eighteenth and nineteenth century poets, such as William Cowper and Emily Dickinson. Now, he was popular with most everyone in Sovereign and was one of Maggie's particular pets.

75

Rebecca handed the maple syrup marked #5 to Walden. She turned her smile upon David next. "You might like to try #5, too."

David motioned to his score card. "It's on my list."

To smooth over David's discourtesy, Maggie jumped into the conversation. "I like first-run syrups best," she offered up. "Trudy, would you mind sending #1 down our way?"

"That one gets my vote," Trudy replied, handing the #1 syrup to Walden, who leaned across his uncle to pass the glass container to Maggie.

Ryan raised an eyebrow. "You haven't even eaten a pancake yet," he chided his wife, who had in fact been busy trying to get some food into Alice Rose.

"What's your point, Sir?"

"My point is that a good judge would at least sample the syrup before she pronounces judgment upon it."

Trudy shrugged off her husband's criticism. "I like its color."

Leland poured a generous amount of syrup #4, which was also light-colored, over his pancakes. He took a bite and smacked his lips. "'Tain't bad—'tain't bad at-tall, if I do say so myself."

"Is that yours, Leland?" Walden asked, falling for the older woodsman's bait.

Leland puffed up like a mother partridge. "Wal, 'tain't like me to spill the beans, but ..."

Trudy stopped him. "Then don't, Father."

"Why, ain't hardly said 'boo' to a goose, yet!"

Ryan gave his father-in-law a consolatory pat on the arm. "Sometimes the goose knows it's cooked without having to be told."

Walden glanced around the table at large, a perplexed expression on his face. "I thought this contest was supposed to be anonymous?"

"It is," Ryan replied. "Leland just thinks he knows which two syrups are his. I wouldn't take his word to the bank, though," the lawyer cautioned. He paused to jot something down on his scorecard and looked back up. "He's been known to be wrong once or twice."

Leland shrugged off the jibe from his son-in-law and leaned forward to address Wendell down the table. "Didja evah hear 'bout the time me 'n Clyde Crosby tussled with a monster buck in the back o' Sam Lovejoy's '46 Hudson? Dem near kilt us," he said, stuffing a rasher of bacon into his mouth and masticating loudly. "We was jest kids, then."

"Father, please," Trudy admonished quietly. Leland snapped his mouth shut and swallowed hard. The wad of bacon stuck in his long turkey neck like an extra wattle.

"Don't think I have," Wendell obliged his friend, with a knowing wink.

Rebecca's eyes widened. "Whatever were you doing with a live deer in your car, Leland?"

"'Twarn't quite kilt."

"I think that's the moral to his story," Ryan said. "At least I hope it is. One shouldn't drive around with a live deer in one's vehicle."

The old farmer and woodchopper thumped his fist against the table so hard the butter plate jumped. "No-suh, by gawd! Ain't no moral to my story at-tall. 'Tis an honest-to-goodness real life tall tale."

"Glad you cleared that up," Ryan added. He reached across his father-in-law's plate to secure the butter before it bounced off the table.

"Go ahead—tell us the story, Leland," Walden encouraged the older man, whose woodsman skills he admired greatly.

Maggie, painfully aware that David didn't share Walden's sentiment, felt her date stiffen in his chair. She knew she was being codependent to keep worrying about David's animus toward her old friend. Still, she couldn't seem to help herself. If she and David got together—and the jury was still very much out on that, from her point of view, anyway—he would necessarily have to learn to accept Leland as one of her many friends. But how hard could it be to listen politely to one of Leland's tall tales without taking personal offense? Maggie decided to stop worrying about David and his relationship with Leland. What would be—would be. She settled back into her chair determined to enjoy her friend's story.

Leland leaned his elbows against the table and launched into his tale. "One evenin' when I was 'bout eight 'n Clyde was twelve o' thirteen, Sam stopped by our house to git Pa to go night huntin' with him. 'Twas back when folks warn't so particular 'bout huntin' …"

"By 'folks' he means game wardens," Ryan elucidated to the table at large.

"… as they is nowadays," Leland continued, barely missing a beat. "We kids 'n Pa piled into Sam's new vehick-kel, a '46 Hudson with fancy chrome trim 'n real purty upholstery like you ain't never seen since. She was a real beauty, alright! We drove ovah to the Bog Road so as we could scout them fields near Hannah's old place— 'twas a nice pocket o' deer theah back then. Pa lit up the first field 'n we seed a good half-dozen deer. Pa held the torch steady 'n Sam used his .45-70 to shoot out the open winder. When Sam squeezed the trigger, a two-foot flame come shootin' out the end o' thet gun. I couldn't see nuthin' at-tall at fust, but when the smoke cleared, I seed a ten-point buck down in the grass, dead as a doornail."

"You counted ten points in the dark with smoke in your eyes?" Ryan asked, innocently.

Leland scowled at his son-in-law. "Pa was still holdin' the torch."

"Never mind him," Rebecca interjected. "Keep going!"

Gratified, the old woodsman continued, sensing that he had most of the audience in his grip. "We kids 'n Pa jumped out to go git the deer while Sam run the gun back to Hannah's folk's place, jest in case the wardens was out 'n about, you know, as 'twas evidence thet could be used against us. We was gonna field-dress the deer, but Sam said, 'No, 'twould take too much time 'n we'd do thet at home,' so we drug him up to the edge o' the road waitin' fer Sam to come back. When he pulled up, Pa opened the door to the Hudson 'n we three pushed 'n shoved thet two hundred pound buck into the back seat as quick's we could. None of us was feelin' no pain—pr'haps the old man had let Clyde 'n me take a swig o' two o' his whiskey," Leland allowed, "'n when we got thet deer in Clyde 'n I clumb in 'n perched atop thet buck jests as proud's though we'd shot him ourselves."

"I thought you said the deer was alive inside the car?" Rebecca queried, curious.

"Ain't got to thet part yet. Wal, Sam drove along 'n we kids hooted 'n hollered out the winder—'n possibly hed a few swigs more o' whiskey—celebratin' our trophy buck, you know, but when we got ovah to Troy Corner Road thet deer come-To quicker 'n a Ju-ly thunderstorm. He started wheezin' 'n thrashin' 'n snortin'. Scairt the bejesus outta us! They was hoofs 'n antlers goin' every which way to Sunday. Sam hed shot the buck alright, but he'd only stunned him. Thet deer sure warn't dead!"

"Holy heck! What did you do?" Walden demanded eyes agog.

"We bailed, thet's what we did. We kids hopped ovah into the front seat quicker 'n a whiskah, right atop Sam 'n Pa. Dinn't Sam swear at us! 'You boys git back in thet seat 'n hold thet dem deer down,' he screamed. Neither Clyde nor I thought thet was a particularly good idea so we made for cover. We curled up on the floor by Pa's feet 's far away from thet buck's hoofs 's we could git. My Pa warn't the excitable type, but he didn't like the idea of any deer gettin' the better o' him. 'Jaysus, pull over, Sam,' he bellered, 'n I'll kill thet son of a ...' "

Trudy coughed politely.

"...thet son of a biscuit," Leland continued. "But Sam was of a stubborn disposition—them Lovejoys was all-ways stiff-necked—'n he wouldn't stop the car 'til we got home. By thet time, the deer hed shredded thet fancy upholstery in back and de-stroyed most o' the interior chrome."

"Did you learn anything from that experience?" Ryan asked.

Leland sat back in his chair. He folded his arms across his chest and regarded his son-in-law with a smug look. "Shore 'nuff did. Larned nevah to take a new vehick-kel out night huntin'," he concluded.

Everyone around the table laughed and Ryan good-naturedly joined in. Maggie stole a glance at David. He alone wasn't smiling, although the expression on his face was inscrutable. Well, at least he didn't appear completely turned off by Leland and his tall tale. That was a step in the right direction!

Out of the corner of her eye, Maggie saw Leland puff himself up for a second story and recognizing the sign that her old friend was about to launch into another tall tale, for David's sake, she decided to cut Leland off. One story at a sitting was enough. "May I try some of that syrup #4, please?" she asked Rebecca, in a loud voice. "Looks like it might be a winner," she added.

Rebecca quickly picked up on Maggie's diversion attempt. "Goodness, you've entertained us so much we've almost forgotten why we're here, Leland," she remarked in a flattering fashion. Pleased, the old woodchopper watched while the glass pitcher containing what he thought was his own syrup made its way down the table.

"Bettah watch out or you'll git fat, Maggie," Wendell said, tucking a forkful of strawberry pancake into his mouth.

"If I was worried about getting fat I probably wouldn't have had two pieces of blackberry pie for dinner last night!"

Wendell took a swig of coffee. "What's fore suppah?"

"Blackberry pie—I seem to be baking them a lot lately." The table laughed again.

Rebecca smiled at Ryan, holding up to his view pitcher #5, which she believed to be Wendell's maple syrup. "Have you tried this one yet? It's really very good."

"Not yet," Ryan replied. "But I can see which way the wind blows around here. No matter how I vote, I'm going to step on a lot of toes."

Walden made a quick calculation in his head. "Only thirty," he joked. "Unless one of you guys is missing some toes …?" he added with a grin, revealing a set of even white teeth through his bushy beard. Over the winter he'd allowed his hair and beard to grow longer, making him look a bit like one of Maine's notoriously elusive black bears.

"I don't know about you," David said to Ryan, "but this maple syrup contest is starting to make the hat contest look a lot more appealing."

Everyone laughed again. Maggie was relieved to see David enjoying himself. Apparently, Leland's tall tale was forgotten.

Breakfast continued in the same light-hearted vein. Thanks to Trudy's careful oversight, Leland behaved himself for the balance of the meal. Much to Maggie's relief, her old friend disappeared into the kitchen as soon as the table was cleared. When Ryan arose to supervise the two older children, who had been freed from their high chairs, she therefore felt comfortable excusing herself and going to spend some time with the kids. David would be safe under the kind care of Rebecca and the watchful eye of Trudy she knew.

The two children ran ahead of Ryan to get to the church's large toy chest. The lawyer and Maggie followed at a leisurely pace. "This works out well," he said. "There's an issue I want to speak with you about. It's personal and I didn't want to bring it up at the table." Gone was the good-natured dairy farmer and in his place was the former big city attorney.

Maggie was instantly concerned. "What's wrong?" she asked anxiously.

"Nothing's wrong … I hope." Ryan steered the two of them to a quiet nook where they could keep an eye on the kids and the toy box and yet speak freely. "I just wanted to give you a heads-up," he continued. "Some young guy stopped at the farm the other day and introduced himself as your financial advisor. Because of that I listened to his spiel for several minutes, but seriously Maggie, he gave me impression that he was not to be trusted. If this guy is your financial advisor I think you might be making a mistake letting him handle your money."

Maggie was taken aback. "But I don't have a financial advisor."

"You don't know anyone named Bill Gagnon?"

"Bill Gagnon?" Maggie thought a moment. "Oh, yes—he's the one who delivered Peter's life insurance check."

"Did he invest the proceeds for you?"

"What proceeds?" she replied sadly. "By the time I got done paying the bills and Peter's funeral expenses, there wasn't anything left to invest."

"I'm sorry for that. But now I'm confused. Was it Peter's financial affairs Mr. Gagnon handled, then?"

Maggie wrinkled her brow. "I don't think so, but you'd have to ask Bruce that." Bruce Gilpin, her nephew by marriage, had taken over his family's dairy farm in Winslow from his uncle before Peter had died. "He signed most everything over to Bruce—thank goodness for that! Otherwise, it might have been messy with the farm and all. I suppose there could have been some old family stocks and bonds that Mr. Gagnon managed."

"Hmm. This whole thing smells fishy to me. I'm glad to hear you didn't give Mr. Gagnon any money to invest. Still, it sounds as though he's using your name on the thinnest of pretexts to gain access to potential prospects. It would make perfect sense. Everyone in town trusts you, Maggie."

"But I didn't give him permission to use my name! I wasn't even his client—Peter was. Can he do that?"

A large rubber ball rolled their way and Ryan instinctively picked the ball up and gently bounced it back in the direction of his daughter. "What Mr. Gagnon is doing is unethical, but not illegal, strictly speaking, since you did have some financial dealings with him and his company. Frankly, I can't remember the exact words he used to introduce himself, either. I was doing the evening milking at the time and the guy cornered me in the milk room where the compressor makes a lot of noise. He might not have said anything that wasn't strictly true. I could have inferred that Mr. Gagnon was your advisor by the way he framed his introduction."

"Isn't there anything I can do to stop him?"

"You could give Mr. Gagnon a call and ask him not to use your name. Or you could let me make some inquires first and then suggest the best way for you to proceed. If he's a crook, we don't want him to know we're on his trail." Alice Rose came rushing up to her father and threw her arms around his legs. Ryan instinctively patted his daughter's dark head. "Game over?" he asked.

"We need you! Come play with us, Daddy," the dark-hair girl begged, grasping her father's hand and tugging him in the direction of several other children.

"OK, sweetie." Ryan allowed himself to be pulled back into the melee of the banquet hall and Maggie drifted with him. "In the meantime," he continued, over his shoulder, "if anyone says anything to you about Mr. Gagnon, be sure and let them know that he's not your advisor and that you have no recommendation about him one way or the other, OK? Don't say anything bad about the guy, please. You don't want to open yourself up to charges of libel."

"Advice heard and taken. How much do I owe you for the legal fee?"

Ryan picked up his daughter and tossed her into the air. Alice Rose squealed with delight. "No charge," he replied, setting the child down. "Maybe just a couple of hours of babysitting some night?"

"Love to—anytime. Well, anytime I'm available, that is," Maggie amended hastily, remembering how busy her calendar was getting these days.

"I knew there'd be a catch!" Ryan and Maggie both laughed.

At nine o'clock, the winner of the hat contest was announced. Much to her gratification—and not really to anyone's surprise—Shirley Palmer won. She excitedly accepted the large quilted handbag, which Hannah Trow had sewn specially for the prize. "'Tis jest what I was wantin' for my knittin'," Shirley crowed with delight. "Now, how do you suppose a body knew that?"

Wendell attempted a nonchalant attitude when the judges prepared to announce the winner of the maple syrup contest. But when Leland's name was called as winner, however, his charade fell apart. "Dang it! Thet's 'nuther year down the drain."

"Hush! How can you say that?" his wife chastised him in a low voice. "We put up fifteen gallons of lovely maple syrup."

"Ayuh, 'n all thet means is we got fourteen more gallons 'n we need," Wendell replied with his good-natured grin.

Leland ambled up to the podium to accept the prize, which this year was a new hydrometer. Assured of the crowd's attention, he hammed it up. Several of the church ladies flocked around taking photographs. Finally, the old woodsman waved the women away. "Let me say what 'twas I was a-going to say afore I fergit," he chastised them.

The ladies reclaimed their seats and Leland continued. "'Twarn't the best year we've had by a long shot, but warn't the worst, neithah." He turned the glass hydrometer over in hands, examining the measuring device. "Probably none o' you recollect the season—'twas 'bout thutty years ago now—when the sap didn't even staaht to run 'til summer. Juu-ly, I think 'twas."

Maggie, who had reseated herself next to David when the contest winners were being announced, caught her date rolling his eyes at what was obviously a taradiddle on Leland's part. Anxious to turn David's attention away from the woodsman, who looked as though he was about to launch into another tall tale, she put her hand on David's sleeve. "Let's go into my office," she said, quietly. "I've got to get ready for church."

She slipped from her seat and unobtrusively headed for the side door, which led directly into the two-hundred-year-old church. Maggie stepped inside the quiet, peaceful house of worship. As usual, she felt a calm, quiet strength seep into her when she entered the nave. To her relief David quickly abandoned his seat and followed her.

Why did she worry so much about what David thought and felt? Was it possible she was already in love with him?

Chapter 6
One of a Couple?

I thought your work was done after this breakfast?" David said, when Maggie closed the door behind them, shutting out the noise of the banquet room. "You don't mean you're not going on the sugar house tour with me?" He appeared hurt and disappointed.

Surprised, Maggie stared at him. "How can I go with you? You know I have a church service to lead." So much for love! Abruptly, she turned on her heel and headed toward her office.

David followed, grumbling. "I'd think this whole breakfast thing would be enough work for one day. You greeted people and said the prayer and everything."

Maggie stopped short at the door. Sometimes his ignorance and insensitivity astounded her. "Honestly, David! You know I lead services every Sunday at ten o'clock. If I don't do it, who do you think would?"

He reached across her, turned the doorknob, and swung the door open for her—further irritating her. A rush of cold air escaped. She had forgotten to turn up the propane heater in her office. "Don't you ever get a Sunday off, then?" he asked.

"I do, when the church is closed."

"When is that?"

"In summer," she replied, tartly. "July and August." She pushed past his outstretched arm. Although Maggie's office was small, having been cobbled onto the back of the little white church around the turn of the twentieth century, she was intensely fond of it. Her study was lined floor-to-ceiling with shelves of books, some of them eighteenth century texts bound in tan calf's leather, which had been left at the church by her predecessors. She also had brought into her office her theology and pastoral college texts and to those had added her favorite classical novels and poetry, including works by William Makepeace Thackeray, Anne Ritchie Thackeray, Robbie Burns, Sir Walter Scott, Jane Austen, and Walden's favorite, Emily Dickinson. The small room boasted a heavy oak desk and two filigreed mahogany chairs, each sporting a plush burgundy seat cushion. An elongated leaded window allowed the mysterious winter daylight (and some cold air) to fill the room. Suddenly, for some inexplicable reason, Maggie felt ashamed of her tiny office. "I work at home in winter to save money," she said awkwardly, feeling the need to explain away the cramped, chilly space.

"No worries," David replied, glancing around curiously. To Maggie's relief, he appeared impressed by the numerous volumes of leather-bound books. "I'm the one who should apologize," he continued. "I'm just not up to speed on church stuff, like Duncan is."

Duncan? Maggie was unable to place the name among David's colleagues. Probably he was one of David's old friends from Massachusetts. "Who's Duncan?" she asked, lifting a white robe from a handful of ankle-length garments in her tiny closet. She slipped her right arm into the vestment. "Someone you went to school with?"

"No, my brother. You know—Nick's father." He moved forward and helped Maggie into her robe.

Maggie had forgotten Walden's father an Episcopal minister. "Oh, right." She shrugged the garment into place on her shoulders and peered back inside the closet to select a stole. She chose a rainbow-colored cloth strip and draped it over her shoulders.

David watched her dress, hands in his pockets. "You look like Duncan wearing that thing. I keep forgetting you're clergy."

"David!" she cried, deeply offended. How could he forget her vocation? Her calling! Her job was every bit as important as his. True, she wasn't world-renowned like he was—she probably wasn't known much further than Thorndike—but they were both working to help make the earth a better place to live, albeit in different ways. She began to suspect that David rated her vocation on a par with a menial job like that of a housekeeper or a factory worker. Miffed, she gave the braided gold cord around her waist a little tug.

"Have I offended you? I have offended you," he said, reaching out to her.

Maggie sidestepped his clasp. She opened the top right-hand desk drawer and located her personal Bible. "Are you religious at all?" she asked, ignoring David's question.

"Of course I am. We were raised Episcopalian. Both my parents were active in the church. You know that."

"Yes, you've told me about your parents and their commitment to the church. But what about you? What do you think? What do you believe?"

David shrugged. "OK, so maybe I'm not a regular church-going guy. But I do believe in a Higher Power."

"You do?"

"Sure. I just don't like all the hoopla-ha and paraphernalia that goes along with churches and ceremony and stuff, although your services are always meaningful. I find your sermons very thought-provoking."

The obvious sincerity of this remark melted Maggie's anger. Mollified, she rewarded him with a smile. "Thank you."

"Your scarf's on crooked, though."

"It's not a scarf, it's …" Maggie broke off, seeing him grin. David had known all along it was a stole, not a scarf; he was teasing her.

"Sorry, couldn't resist."

She squared her shoulders. "I'll have you know this was a gift from a very dear friend," she enlightened him. "We went to Bangor Theological Seminary together." She suddenly felt the need to impress upon David the importance of her calling. "Cathy has a church in Alaska now."

"Well, since your friend's not here and I am let me fix your stole."

Maggie was about to protest that she didn't need any help "fixing" her stole, when the confident touch of masculine hands on her shoulders sent shock waves through her central nervous system. She realized how bereft of touch she had been since Peter died. She, a minister, who hugged people almost every day of the week! But the touch of her parishioners and friends wasn't the same as the touch of a loving partner, and Maggie knew it. "You really like my weekly service?" she asked meekly, suddenly anxious for masculine reassurance.

"I do," he replied. He adjusted her stole so that both sides hung evenly, stepped back, and regarded Maggie in full religious apparel. She could tell by the look on his face that, despite the clerical garb, he liked what he saw. He moved forward and brushed a stray lock of her hair back from her face.

Half afraid, Maggie glanced up at him. Amused hazel eyes revealed admiration and a sense of mutual camaraderie. "What do you say, Maggie?" he said cajolingly. "We've been beating around the bush with our relationship for weeks, now. Why don't we just agree we like each other and want to be together? It's not as though we're teenagers, after all."

Maggie felt an aching emptiness in her solar plexus and yearned to throw caution to the wind. It had been so long! Two-and-a-half years since she had leaned upon a man. One step, a half-step really, and she would be in his arms. Was it really so simple, then? No need to hash it all over first? Discuss their individual hopes and dreams and goals? No, they certainly weren't teenagers! When one was a teenager—and made a mistake—one had a very long lifetime in which to rectify one's mistakes. But when one was sixty-years-old, one didn't have the luxury of Time to make mistakes.

David's arm snaked possessively around her waist and he drew her close to his chest. She felt hot tears on her cheek before she even realized she was crying. She didn't surrender—but she didn't resist, either. She stood still, allowing the future to close in around her like the waters of an incoming tide.

He stroked her hair. "You've had a rough go of it the past few years, haven't you, babe? But it's going to be OK, now. I'm here for you."

Maggie leaned against his shoulder. She wept. It was so good to yield! Such a relief to let go and let someone else take the lead for a change.

"Go ahead, baby; let it out," he urged.

But the waterworks stopped as quickly as they had begun. Shakily, Maggie pulled away and fumbled for a tissue from her desktop. She wiped her eyes and blew her nose. "Sorry, I'm not usually such a crybaby," she said, tossing the used tissue into the trash.

"Hey, don't apologize. There's no need for that." He clasped her gently by the chin and tilted Maggie's head so he was gazing directly into her eyes. "We're a couple now—right?"

"I guess so."

David burst out laughing and released her. "I love the way you sugarcoat everything!"

Maggie giggled. "Sorry, I guess that wasn't very encouraging."

"You do want to be a couple, don't you?"

"I think so. I know I'm happier with a partner."

"That's my girl!" He dropped a kiss on her forehead. "You're one special lady, Maggie," he assured her, glancing at his watch. "But if you don't get going, your parishioners might not agree with me. It's almost ten o'clock."

"They probably won't start the service without me," Maggie replied with a smile. Already, she felt the warmth of romantic bliss enveloping her like a fine cashmere sweater.

"Well, anyway, I've got to run myself," he said, moving closer to the door. "I told my students I'd meet them around ten for the sugar house tour. I'll call you tonight, before I head off for St. Louis tomorrow."

"You're going to St. Louis tomorrow?" she exclaimed, startled by this unexpected announcement.

"Didn't I tell you?"

"No." Maggie felt the air being let out of her balloon. She had always hated the uncertainty and insecurity that came with being part of a couple, especially in a new relationship. She had experienced so much insecurity and angst with Nellie's father she had purposely steered clear of lovers after him, that is, until Peter had finally persuaded her to marry him.

"I'm sure I told you. I'm leading a workshop for the Society for Conservation Biology. They're hosting a big conference on deer ticks."

"No, I think I'd remember that."

David shrugged his shoulders. "They invited me to participate in the conference last fall. You probably forgot. It's a big deal. Biologists are coming to St. Louis from all across the country."

"I'm sorry, David, but I don't remember," she responded, and immediately kicked herself. Why was she apologizing? She was sure he had never mentioned he was leading a workshop for a national conference. It wasn't likely she would forget such an honor shared with her so early in their relationship.

"My workshop is on white-tail deer population biology. The deer population has exploded over the past century, thanks to forest fragmentation. We need to get a handle on the deer population in order to control the tick population and thus Lyme disease." David instinctively fell into professor mode. "What's good for *Ixodes scapularis* and *Ixodes pacificus,* the deer tick and the Western black-legged tick, carriers of Lyme disease, is bad for us Homo sapiens, I'm afraid. Did you know *Borrelia burgdorferi*—that's the Lyme disease bacterium—has been in the forests of North America for over sixty thousand years?"

"Really? I thought Lyme disease originated in Lyme, Connecticut?"

"That's what we all thought until the genomes of *Borrelia burgdorferi* were sequenced recently and a doctoral candidate at Yale reconstructed the bacterium's history on this continent. It's fascinating!"

"I'm sure it is," Maggie said. She was more interested in the fact that he was leaving, however. "Who's taking your classes and lectures while you're gone?"

"We're on break. Now, I'm sure I mentioned the workshop when we spoke about spring break a few weeks ago," he lectured her.

David was so confident—maybe she had forgotten? Maggie dutifully cast her mind back over their conversations, emails, and messages, but couldn't recall any that related either to the work shop or the tick conference. She hated herself for being picayune. What did it matter whether he'd told her or not? He was going away! How could he be so complacent about being apart from her when they had just gotten together?

"How long will you be gone?" she asked anxiously, immediately hating herself for appearing clingy.

"All week. Don't worry, I'll keep in touch, babe."

A frown spread over Maggie's face. David, likely realizing that the gate was about to close before his prize was secured, crossed the room in three strides. He clasped Maggie by the shoulders, forcing her to look up at him. "Promise me you won't worry about our relationship while I'm gone, OK? I'll call you every night. Believe me I don't want to lose you just when I've found you, Sweetheart."

Sweetheart!

Well, for better or worse, their relationship had moved up to the next level. The ship had shoved off. For what destination, God only knew!

Chapter 7
Kate, and a Word to the Wise

David was as good as his word. He messaged Maggie regularly and called her each night to check in from St. Louis, sharing the highlights of his day at the tick conference. Gradually, their conversations took on a more personal nature—it was easier to say things on the phone than to say them in person, after all—and Maggie found herself confiding things to him that she had kept to herself since Peter died, things she hadn't yet given voice to, not even to her daughter Nellie.

She was grateful for the opportunity presented by David's conference to ease into this new relationship with him. She certainly wasn't ready to hop into bed with David, despite Shirley Palmer's permission to take a lover. She wasn't sure when—or even if—she would be ready to be intimate with a man again. Maggie could only trust to time and pray that David wouldn't take advantage of her vulnerability.

One day, during the first week of April, the temperature stretched to nearly seventy degrees. Snow from the woods melted, and gay, glistening rivulets ran down the hill with abandon. The sun felt like a blessing on the earth. A little flock of robins scoured Maggie's front lawn searching for worms and chickadees switched to their spring mating call, which sounded almost like that of the phoebes—"phee-be." Altogether it was a glorious afternoon and Maggie threw open the windows to air out her home, which had become close and musty over the long winter. The fecund scent of spring permeated the little old schoolhouse. She inhaled the fresh air deeply and greedily.

While washing up her dishes, she heard the unmistakable garbled croaking of her Corvidae pair. She grabbed a dish towel and stepped to the window, wiping her hands. Romeo and Juliet were loudly conversing—one might almost have said arguing—from opposing trees on each side of the mud-puddled road. Too funny! Just like an old married couple.

With a jolt, Maggie realized that she, too, was now one of a couple. She felt both gratified and satisfied to be in a relationship again. "Go ahead and argue it out," she instructed the ravens. "Don't hold back—it's not healthy. Trust me, I've found that out the hard way!"

David's first few days back from St. Louis were naturally awkward; however, the two of them soon fell into an agreeable pattern of seeing each other almost every day. But their physical intimacy lagged several steps behind their emotional intimacy, which was perfectly fine with Maggie. There were hugs and a few kisses. As before, however, no sparks arose from their physical connection and much to Maggie's relief any discussion of sex seemed off the table for the time being. Probably David realized she just wasn't ready to become intimate with another man yet, and she was grateful to him for his understanding.

"I'm taking a small group of students to do a field assessment in Troy Saturday," David announced over lunch the first week in May.

"Oh?" Maggie said, taking a sip of hot coffee, which was organically-grown and quite good. She awaited the elaboration she knew would follow. Usually, she disliked eating at Unity College's Wyman Commons because their meal was continually interrupted by David's students. Today, however, he was short on time and because their lunch was late most of the students were in already back in class. It was nice to see the professor on his own turf, too, Maggie decided.

"Hey!" said David, responding with a wave to a fellow teacher. He returned his attention to his salad, punching his fork into tender pieces of red and green lettuces grown at a local greenhouse. The college prided itself on serving as much local food as possible and was one of the first in the nation to go green. "Want to join us on this field trip?"

Upon hearing the invitation, Maggie felt both excited and trepidatious. This was the first time David had asked her to accompany him on a trip with his students, so it was serious business. "Am I going to be able to help you?" she probed. "Or am I just going to be there as local color?"

"Both," he replied, laughing. "There's a potential housing development that could spell the end of a Significant Vernal Pool in Troy. You've had some experience with amphibians—and with local politics— and you might be able to help us stop the development. But it does mean getting your feet wet and maybe even your feelings hurt."

"Count me in," Maggie replied, happily. "You know I'm not afraid of either." She was reassured to find she wasn't going to be just a useless tag-along—the Girlfriend. She and Peter had always loved frogs and this sounded like an interesting project. "What do I need to bring?"

"A warm jacket, hip waders if you have them, polarized sunglasses, and your best local-color hat."

"I've got the first three, but I'll have to see Shirley Palmer about the hat," she demurred.

He laughed again. "God forbid! OK, you can skip the hat."

This time, Maggie made sure she had her sermon for Sunday written well in advance. When David phoned her Friday evening, she was able to assure him she was ready for the field trip.

"Good girl! Looks like the rain will end overnight, but it will still be cloudy. That's perfect for assessing vernal pools; we won't have to keep putting our sunglasses off and on. Makes the counting a whole lot easier. The frogs will be active, too."

"What are we counting?"

"Amphibian eggs."

"Isn't it a bit late for frogs' eggs?" Maggie suggested bravely. The garbled chuckles of the wood frogs and the sleigh bell sound of myriad spring peepers had been serenading her at night since mid-April. When she and Peter were kids, they had gathered plenty of the tapioca-like egg masses deposited by the frogs in several vernal pools in the woods near their homes. Sometimes they hatched the eggs out, but usually they simply flung the gelatinous globs at one another. She winced, thinking of what David might say to that, wasting what might now be a protected species at child's play!

"Hopefully not. And we're not just counting peepers and wood frog eggs we're also looking for fairy shrimp—I doubt we'll see any of those, though—spotted salamanders, and blue spotted salamanders. Basically we're assessing this particular vernal pool to see if it meets the criteria for a Significant Vernal Pool established by the Maine legislature's Natural Resource Protection Act, Chapter 335, under Significant Wildlife Habitat Rules. If we can establish that the pool meets these criteria, we can force the developer to abandon his project. That's where you come in with the local politicians. We certainly don't need another donut shop in the area—not a chain one, anyway."

"What are the criteria that vernal pools have to meet to be considered significant?" Maggie asked, curious to know how the powers-that-be in Augusta determined which of her favorite vernal pools might be worthy of protection and which not worth the effort. If she had her way every single vernal pool in Maine would be protected!

"There must be either an abundance of certain species present—and the Rules are very specific as to the numbers—or the presence of a rare, protected, or endangered species, such as the spotted turtle, the ringed boghaunter dragonfly, and the Blandings turtle. We won't see any of those species, however, because they don't use vernal pools to complete the critical portion of their life-cycles until June. But we can't wait that long because the developer in this case wants to start building later this month. We need you to get the Troy Planning Board to halt the project until they hear the results of our assessment. Think you can do that?"

"No problem! The Planning Board in Troy is very conservation-friendly, but just in case I'll have a chat with Brian Piper—he's chair of Board of Selectman in Troy—and see if he can put in a good word to the Board in advance of their next meeting."

"Excellent! I knew I could count on you, Maggie."

She was glad they were conversing over the telephone so that David couldn't see her blush, almost like a silly schoolgirl. Nevertheless, she was pleased by his compliment. If this was how a future with David was going to be, bring it on!

"We're going to concentrate on wood frogs and spotted salamander eggs hoping to get our numbers one way or another," he continued. "The fairy shrimp are more of a southern New England species, only found in about five percent of Maine vernal pools, but if we find them, we've struck gold."

In its way, intellectual stimulation can be as seductive as erotica and Maggie now felt herself becoming aroused by the subject under discussion and by the extent of David's knowledge. "How many?" she asked breathlessly, feeling an irresistible urge to know more. "How many wood frog eggs do we need to save the vernal pool?"

David laughed, obviously pleased by her interest. "The eggs are counted in masses. Wood frogs are the most common, so we'd need to find at least forty masses."

"Forty masses! That sounds like a lot," she worried, concerned not only about protecting the vernal pool but also about the impact the proposed chain donut shop would have on Gilpin's General Store and the local restaurant, Ma Jean's.

"It really isn't. Once you start counting, you'll be surprised how many masses we can find. Those wood frogs like to stick together—pun intended. Of course, much depends upon the size of the vernal pool, but I've already scoped this one out—it's about an acre—and thanks to the spring rains the pond has filled up from last year's drought. Spotted salamander eggs give us twice as much bang for the buck as wood frogs, too, and blue spotted salamander, four times. I have five students going with us—that's all I could round up because of finals—and having you along gives me three sets of assessors. I'll be verifying the egg masses you all discover and tallying the results. The whole assessment shouldn't take more than three or four hours."

"I'll wear my barn boots and bring my hip waders," Maggie told him. "That way I'll be ready for anything!"

"Looks like I've struck gold already—a woman who wants to spend a date counting frogs' eggs!"

"You know how much I like donuts, David, but believe it or not, I like frogs more."

"I do believe you," he said. His voice over the phone suddenly sounded low, husky, and seductive. "You're one-in-a-million, Maggie."

As she said her goodbyes and signed off, Maggie realized that her heart was palpitating and her palms were moist. Was she excited because she would be seeing David again soon? Or was the excitement because she was going frogging!

The next morning Maggie drank her coffee and ate her oatmeal in her pajamas. Once finished, she returned to the bedroom to select her outfit for the field trip. She couldn't remember the last time she had dressed with as much care as she took preparing for this date to count frogs' eggs! Feeling giddy and lighthearted, she laid out several pair of jeans in order to determine the most comfortable and yet most flattering pair. After the jean selection she rummaged through the plastic bin under the bed that contained her turtlenecks and pullover sweaters, searching for a combination that would be both warm and complement her hair and skin tone. She selected a lavender turtleneck and a purple-colored, tightly-knit V-neck sweater, mindful not only of the snagging hands of the puckerbrush but also of the way the sweater accented her mature curves. She donned her best bra, too—an underwire. She hoped she could last the afternoon without tearing the bra off, though. Her tolerance for bra discomfort these days was perilously low.

After a light lunch, Maggie found herself ready to go, an hour early, naturally. She took the opportunity to hunt down her full-length mirror, which she finally found upstairs in the back of her closet behind some old overcoats. She tugged the mirror out, stood it up against the bedroom door, and checked herself in the mirror. She was surprised to discover a mature woman staring back at her rather than the young girl who loved to hunt amphibians with Peter. Frogs, toads, salamanders, newts, turtles, garter snakes—all were fair game back then and had ended up in many a glass canning jar or terrarium. "Who are you?" she demanded of the woman in the mirror, arms akimbo. "And what have you done with Maggie Walker?"

Receiving no answer but an unsatisfactory grimace, she quickly stuffed the mirror back into its hiding place behind the coats. She stepped to the vanity mirror to examine her face closely. The eyes were the same bright blue they had been back in childhood; however, the wrinkles and dark wedges around her eyes attested to the hardships and losses she had experienced since then. In addition, her eyelids looked puffy and over-inflated and there was a small pouch of skin hanging beneath her chin that certainly hadn't been there years ago. How aggravating! Still, she thought she looked damn good for sixty.

Maggie squared her shoulders and sucked in her stomach. "Shoulders back. Chest out," she instructed the unfamiliar woman in the mirror. She ran a brush through her shoulder-length hair and expertly twisted it up into a bun. She pulled a few silver strands of hair out to soften her face. Maggie considered adding make-up, but elected not to paint herself. Witnessing too many poor face painting jobs attempted by heavy-handed undertakers had turned her off make-up in general.

She glanced at her delicate gold wristwatch, which had once belonged to her grandmother, her mother's mother. There was still half an hour before David arrived with the college van. She hesitated, staring at the timepiece, suddenly concerned. What if she dropped her grandmother's watch in the woods or in the water? What if she lost the precious family heirloom altogether?

After a brief deliberation, Maggie stretched the band and removed the watch. She was about to take the timepiece down and place the valuable in her jewelry box in the downstairs bedroom, when a faint knock at the front door turned her mind from her task. The knock sounded again and she instinctively slipped the watch into her back pocket and hurried down the stairs to answer the door.

"Henry!" she said, surprised to discover not David but her neighbor, Henry Trow, standing on the stone stoop. He was a short man in his mid-seventies, with rounded shoulders, hooded eyelids, and bushy gray eyebrows that stretched across the bridge of his nose. He moved with a perpetual shuffle, thanks to a hip condition. Henry's manner was characteristically curt; however, Maggie had learned over the years he'd been in town that his bark was much worse than his bite. He really was a very sweet man. Henry had become sort of an adopted grandfather to her daughter, Nellie, too.

"You busy?" he asked, abruptly.

"I have an appointment at one o'clock," she replied, opening the door wider and moving a step back. "But I'm free until then."

Accepting her reply as good enough for his purposes, Henry handed her his cane and hoisted himself up the step into the shed. He removed his brown wool fedora, holding it in his gnarled hands like a supplicant. "I'm sorry to bother you, but there's something weighing on my mind. I didn't know where else to turn."

Maggie, used to these sorts of confessions, quickly assumed a ministerial pose. "I'm glad you came to me. Would you like to talk about it?" She handed him back his cane.

"Yes, but can't we go inside? It's damn damp standing here." Henry thumped the head of his cane against the unvarnished shed floor. Several loose splinters in the floorboards jumped.

"Sorry, yes." Henry made a move to slip out of his rubber overshoes, but Maggie stopped him. "Never mind taking those off. My kitchen floor needs washing, anyway."

He ignored her direction and carefully kicked off the muddy rubbers. "Hannah would kill me if she found out. We didn't need last night's rain, did we?" He hung his fedora up on the coat rack.

"Not really, but probably the farmers appreciated it, after last year's drought." Maggie led her neighbor into the comfy country kitchen, which was toasty from the heat of the woodstove.

"Ah!" Henry exclaimed, moving next to the stove and rubbing his hands together. "This is more like it." After a few seconds he shrugged out of his plaid hunting coat and laid the jacket over the back of a chair. He seated himself at the head of the table.

Taking that as her cue, Maggie slid into the chair across from her neighbor. She glanced at the Regulator clock. Assuming David was on time or early as usual, she had about twenty minutes at best to give to Henry, which wasn't much. In her experience, people who sought her advice or counselling typically held onto the nut of the problem until the very last moment. Then, they tossed their nut out onto the table almost gleefully, knowing full well how hard a nut it was to crack and how long it would take to crack it!

Maggie should have known, however, that dissimulating wouldn't be an issue for her neighbor. Six words were all it took. "It's about Kate," he blurted out. "She's stealing again." Kate was Henry's granddaughter, his only natural grandchild, who ten years ago—when

Kate was about fourteen—had been caught shoplifting on more than one occasion.

Maggie knew that Kate was currently in a Master's program at the University of New Hampshire. She was shocked to discover the young woman had reverted to her old ways. Kate, now in her mid-twenties, was her daughter Nellie's age. "What a shame! How did that happen?"

Henry wrung his hands. "Evelyn—that's her mother—doesn't know. The only reason she found out about it in the first place is because Kate called her mother for bail money. Apparently, Kate lifted some kid's LL Bean boots at the university."

"Well, she's not the first," Maggie remarked, recalling a recent news article about that very same thing. "Funny how Bean boots are all the rage again! They were in style when I was young and then tanked for thirty years. Now, apparently, all the kids have to have them and there aren't enough Bean boots to go around—not that that gives anyone a right to steal them," she amended hastily, aware she was transgressing. "I'm sorry. I know how fond you are of Kate," she added, sincerely. "It must have been very hard to hear."

"Damned difficult." Henry wrung his hands.

Maggie realized her friend was close to tears. Kate, despite her failings, was the apple of her grandfather's eye. More than once Maggie had heard Henry say that Kate reminded him of his beloved first wife, Gerry, who passed away shortly before he came to Maine. His second marriage, to Hannah, Doctor Bart's aunt, was very recent, and was welcomed by his friends and family. Maggie laid a hand on her neighbor's arm. "What can I do?"

"You can tell me I'm doing the right thing by asking Kate to come live with us, at least until she gets her act together."

105

Maggie, trained at seminary to hide her emotions, nevertheless was taken aback. She averted her eyes so Henry couldn't read feelings, taking a few precious moments for further reflection before replying.

Could coming to live with someone who would undoubtedly spoil her be the best thing for Kate? Hadn't being spoiled and pampered her entire life created the girl's character defects in the first place? What about Henry? What would happen if his granddaughter used the opportunity to take financial advantage of him? Would he be able to recognize—and admit to—hogwash from Kate when he heard it?

And what of Hannah? Married to Henry just two years, Hannah was no relation to Kate. How would she handle the extra burden of having a spoiled and probably hardened young woman on her hands and in her house? There were so many negatives to the proposed situation that Maggie found it difficult to give Henry the stamp of approval for which she knew he was looking. "Well, it's a very generous offer," she said, finally. "But getting her act together could take Kate some time. What does Hannah say?"

"She says she has too many mouths to feed, which means she wants the girl to come. You know Hannah can't stand to see anything suffer—bird, dog, spoilt brat. She'll stuff Kate full of her chocolate Needhams and hope that makes everything better."

Maggie smiled to herself at the notion of Henry's grown granddaughter being 'fixed' by candy, even Maine's notoriously popular chocolate, coconut, and potato candy. "I think it might take a bit more than Needhams, although Miss Crump does swear by them," she added, referring to Hannah's good friend, for whom she often cooked.

Henry's watery blue eyes bore into hers. "You don't think we should do it, do you?"

"No, I don't," she admitted. "Kate's an adult—she's not a child any longer. I think you should let her sort out her own life and her own problems. But ... I don't think you're going to take my advice, because that's not who you are."

"I knew I could count on you to be honest, Maggie."

"Still," Maggie continued, as though he hadn't interrupted, "if anyone could help someone turn from the wrong path and find her true place in this world it's you and Hannah."

"Bless you," he cried, gripping Maggie's hand and giving it a heartfelt squeeze.

"We all have choices in this world, but a little push down the right path—given with disinterested love—won't hurt Kate. Robert Frost's words to the wise are worth remembering in this situation: *Two roads diverged in a yellow wood ... I took the one less traveled by, and that has made all the difference.* Just make sure you shove her down the right road."

Henry chuckled and released her. "Pretty top shelf, borrowing from Robert Frost. Makes me think of his 'good fences make good neighbors' poem." Having received the validation for which he was seeking—and reinvigorated—he was anxious to depart. He pushed himself up from the table and reached for his jacket. "Remember, the fence gate swings both ways—neighbor."

"Don't worry, I'll remember," Maggie assured him. "I'm sure there will come a time when I'll need more than a cup of flour." She ushered her neighbor into the shed and waited patiently as he seated himself on the bench and pulled on his rubber overshoes. A horn tooted out front. David had arrived!

Henry arose, retrieved his fedora, and peered out the shed window. "Hot date, huh? I suppose it's the Professor. Where's he taking you today?"

Maggie smiled and swung open the door. "If you must know, he's taking me to Troy—to count frogs' eggs."

Henry shuffled forward, pausing on the wooden stoop. "Frog eggs, eh? Well, you look damn good, woman. Too bad I'm taken or I'd give that upstart Paladin a run for his money." He thumped his cane for emphasis and the splinter in the floor jumped again. Unexpectedly, he leaned closer and dropped his voice. "A word to the wise, before I go, Maggie. You might want to consider dumping that financial advisor of yours."

Maggie was taken off-guard. "My financial advisor?"

"That young whippersnapper stopped in the other day and had the nerve to suggest I might be too old to handle my own money. Too old, indeed! I've been handling my own money and investments for sixty-five years, before he was even a twinkle in his mother's eye."

Maggie's stomach suddenly felt queasy. "Was his name Bill Gagnon?"

"One and the same! He was too greasy by half, and I'm not talking about hair cream, either. After I kicked him out Hannah told me I was rude to him. I just wanted you to know because no doubt he'll have some hard words about your crusty old neighbor when you see him next. Take care he doesn't pick your pocket!"

David tooted again and Maggie realized she didn't have time to explain to Henry that Bill Gagnon wasn't her financial advisor and was, in fact, using her name without her permission. She was relieved, however, to learn that Henry, who would be considered wealthy by Sovereign standards, hadn't given the man any of his money or investments to handle. Mentally she made a note to see Henry at a later date and fully explain the situation.

Satisfied that he had done his duty to his neighbor—and having received from her the validation for which he had been looking—Henry departed.

Chapter 8
The Significance of Blue Spotted Salamander Eggs

Maggie quickly collected her shoulder pack and hip waders. She slipped into her barn boots and stepped out into the freshly-washed spring air to meet the college van. One of the students popped out of the passenger seat and Maggie, taking that as her cue, waded through a mud puddle and climbed into the vacated seat. David grinned as he greeted her, but didn't proffer his usual peck on the cheek. Feeling self-conscious, she was careful to take her cue from him. As a result, when he introduced her to the students in back she failed miserably in hearing and remembering their names.

Soon the five young people were chatting amongst themselves, their happy banter acting as a screen of sorts between the front seat and the rest of the van. "Buckle up, Sweetheart," David directed in a low voice. "This road is a nightmare." He put the ten-seater into reverse and backed around, shifting again and headed back the way he had come. Maggie obeyed wordlessly. She made herself comfortable in the warm seat vacated by the student, content to be with him, part of the mission to save the vernal pool.

They drove several minutes in silence, as David concentrated on his driving so that the van wouldn't get stuck in the treacherous ruts in the muddy road. The rain overnight had brought the frost out of the ground, making navigation on the dirt road much worse. Mud splattered against the windshield and wet, loose gravel churned against the underside of the van. David whipped the steering wheel first to the right and then to the left, cursing under his breath.

"Does the landowner know we're coming?" Maggie asked, gripping the roof handle as the van jounced over a bump.

"Not now, Maggie."

Obediently, Maggie fell silent. She had forgotten this was David's first exposure to mud season in rural Maine.

Five minutes later he brought the van safely to a halt at the stop sign at the junction with the main road. Having reached pavement again, he visibly relaxed. "Whew! I think I'll go around the long way when I bring you home. Looked like your neighbor had a lot easier time of it going up the hill."

"That would probably be best. Don't worry, mud season only last a few weeks."

"A few weeks? One day is enough for me! Now, to answer your question—the farmer knows we're coming because he's the one who contacted me in the first place."

Maggie was surprised. "He did? Wasn't that rather against his interest? Doesn't the farmer hope to sell his land for the donut shop?"

After ascertaining that the way was clear, David pulled out onto the Ridge Road, which led out to Route 9/202. "Yes and yes. Yes, it's against his interest—sort of. And, yes, he wants to sell."

"Then, why …?"

"Because this farmer is nobody's fool. He's figured out how to take advantage of a tough situation. Either his vernal pool doesn't qualify as a Significant Vernal Pool—in which case he sells the property to the donut shop developer—or the pool does qualify, in which case he keeps the land but sells the development rights to the Maine Farmland Trust, becoming a Forever Farm."

"That's pretty clever! Did the farmer figure this all out by himself? Sounds complicated to me."

David preened himself in the rear-view mirror, primping his beard. "Let's just say, he might have had some inside information."

"You helped him!"

David lowered his voice again. "I did. But that's just between you, me, and the wood frogs, OK, Sweetheart?"

Maggie was thrilled. David had been in Maine less than a year and already he was effecting positive environmental change. Even more impressive in her book—he was working with landowners rather than against them, creating what looked to be a win-win situation.

Her gratification was short-lived, however. To her consternation, ten minutes later David slowed before a familiar farm in Troy. The dairy farm belonged to Sheldon Nutter, Maynard Nutter's nephew. She hadn't heard anything lately from Maynard about his nephew, but she hoped Sheldon wasn't being forced to sell some of his land because he was having financial difficulties. She knew how precarious the dairy industry was in Maine and would rather lose a vernal pool than another dairy farmer. She and Peter had both been raised on dairy farms in Winslow.

Sheldon must have heard them drive in because, before the van's engine had stopped sputtering, the fifty-something farmer ambled out of the tractor shed to greet them, wiping black grease off his hands with a shop rag. Dash, his tri-color Border collie, trotted at his heels. David rolled down his window to greet the farmer and the familiar scent of fermented corn, cow manure, and soured milk wafted into the van. Maggie, to whom the smell brought back sentimental memories of her early days on the farm in Winslow, inhaled deeply. She heard the lowing of Sheldon's cows and the indistinct music coming from the ubiquitous radio that most Maine farmers keep playing in their tie-ups and felt right at home. The old familiar longing for her family's farm returned. Why, despite her wonderful life in Sovereign, was she aching for her birthplace in Winslow? Did everyone else feel the same emotional pull to return 'home' when they reached a certain age?

"OK with you if I leave the van here?" David asked.

"As good as anywhere, Professor."

David pulled the keys out of the ignition and opened his door. Taking their cue from him, the little group of students piled out of the back of the van. Maggie waited with the five students while the two men greeted each other. David and Sheldon shook hands warmly, leading her to suspect that they must have had more than one or two meetings together. David was a decade or so older than the farmer and they could have very little in common, she knew. Sheldon had never been to college nor had he ever traveled; his biggest excursions were forays to Bangor or Waterville to pick up tractor parts.

"Ready to get your feet wet, Doc?" Sheldon asked, giving the environmentalist a good-natured slap on the back.

"Ready as you are, Boss. Why don't you go first and I'll follow your lead?"

"Ha, ha! Not on your life. I'm going back to my tractor. I'd druther work on Izzie any day than go chasing after frogs in a dang pond."

Dash, recognizing Maggie, trotted over to greet her. She bent down to fondly pet the Border collie.

114

Sheldon took a step forward to call his dog and his eyes fell on her face. "Maggie! What are you doing here? Are you with this guy?"

Maggie smiled and nodded. "I'm afraid so." She stood up.

"You must be slumming!" Sheldon snapped his fingers and whistled, and Dash leapt back to the farmer's side. "Although you could do a lot worse."

"I'm just along for the ride," explained Maggie. "How's Elizabeth?"

David had started to unload his equipment from the van, but paused when he heard their friendly exchange. "You two know each other?" he asked, surprised.

Sheldon gave an unconscious tug to his baseball cap, his demeanor suddenly serious. "Maggie did the funeral for both my parents. Mom died last year and Dad about nine years ago."

"I'm sorry. I should have realized ... small town," David replied, fumbling for words.

"Liz sometimes takes the grandkids to Maggie's church, too, so they don't become heathens—not that they aren't little heathens already. I don't put in many appearances, I'm sorry to say. I'd blame it on the cows, except Maggie knows what time we milk. She said your last service was crackerjack, by the way," Sheldon added, turning back to Maggie.

"Thanks! Is there a prize in that for me?" Maggie joked. She noticed, however, that David wasn't laughing.

He checked his Rolex. "Mind if we head out for the vernal pool? Some of the students need to be back for a class at five."

"Go for it, Professor. You know where 'tis. I'll be in the tractor shed if you need me." Sheldon watched as David corralled the students and herded them toward their task. When Maggie made a move to go with the others, the farmer gently held her back. "Not so fast. Are you really interested in this environmental stuff?"

Maggie knew that what Sheldon really wanted to learn was whether she and David was a couple. Rather than prevaricate, she felt as though she should acknowledge their relationship. "I am interested, but I'm also dating David. You probably think we don't have much in common, but ..."

Sheldon held up his hand, signaling for her to stop. "Hey, I'm not here to judge you. Just making sure you're OK."

"I'm OK—more than OK, actually." Maggie smiled as she realized how happy she felt despite the cloudy day. She was happy to be here with David and content to be in the moment. The sun's ultraviolet rays felt warm against her face, rejuvenation was in the air, and she suddenly discerned from amongst the many cheerful noises of spring one of her favorite sounds, the industrious tapping of mink frogs.

"Good to know. The Professor's not a bad guy— a little over-educated for my taste, but I wouldn't mind sitting down to supper with him. In fact, we already have. At the house, of course. Don't think I'd go down to Darby's with him."

By Maine standards, Darby's in Belfast was a highbrow eatery. Maggie pictured Sheldon in his dirty work coveralls at a fancy candlelit dinner with David and laughed aloud. "You might enjoy a night out, you know," she teased.

"Yeah, and I might be able to stay awake past seven-thirty, too—in your dreams! But I give you the green light to go anywhere you like with the guy. Even down to Darby's."

"Thanks for your permission," she said, amused to discover that Sheldon, like Shirley, felt the need to bless her relationship with David. Goodness! Was she going to receive consent from all her friends and parishioners?

"And if there's one thing I know about ole Peter," the farmer continued, in a serious tone, "it's that he'd want you to be happy. He was a good man, Maggie. One of the best I've ever known."

Maggie felt her throat tighten with emotion. Hot tears filled her eyes. She nodded, unable to speak.

Sheldon turned aside to cough and spit, giving her time to collect herself. She glanced toward David, watching, through blurred vision, as he strode over the greening meadow toward the pond, his students trailing behind him like baby ducklings. The damp spring breeze ruffled his dark hair and fluttered the tails of his LL Bean hurricane shirt. He looked every inch the environmental crusader. "You're right about that. Peter would want me to be happy," she said, brushing away her tears.

"Well, then—what are you waiting for?" Sheldon gave her a slight push and hip waders in hand she hurried to catch up with the rest of the group.

The vernal pool was situated near the tree line on an irregular piece of open ground that contained shallow ledge and some rock outcroppings. Hummocks of bleached, dead grass were threaded with bright green new shoots and tall stalks of exploded cattails screened the low-lying pond from the main road. She herself had driven by this particular vernal pool for years and had never known it was there. The location—less than a half mile from the junction of Routes 9 and 220—would be the perfect place for a donut shop, she admitted; however, now that she knew the pond existed, she was determined to protect it. To Maggie, who was used to the small vernal pools in which she and Peter had played as children, this pond appeared huge by comparison to them. How would they ever finish counting the frogs' eggs in two or three hours?

A pair of mallards announcing their territory squawked as the team converged at the edge of the pond. The ducks took flight, the beating of their wings sounding like sheets whipping on a clothesline on a windy day. A blue jay called out a warning from a nearby pine tree and several curious chickadees flitted from bush to bush gradually drawing nearer to them. Boots squished over soggy, dead vegetation from the prior season, cushioned by the spongy new undergrowth. The pond exhaled a pleasingly dank, fertile scent, reminding Maggie of the smell of rotting wood and regenerating plant life. Thin, milky clouds obscured the sun, but she still felt the warmth of UV rays on her face and hands. After six months of winter, Maggie's eyes were unused to even the brightness of clouded daylight and she was glad David had reminded her to bring polarized sunglasses.

David herded them together at the pool's southern edge. "We'll split into three groups of two," he said, opening his budget of instructions. "One person will count and the other will take notes. Before we do that, however, we'll divide the pool up into three sections and I'll assign one to each team. Stay in your own section, please! We don't want to double count. Remember, we're here today to count frogs' eggs; however, I want you to record any amphibians you see. There's a separate place on your clipboard for that. Also, if you're quick enough to snap a pic of a frog or toad, we'll upload your pic and the information to Herpmapper.com. Ashley, why don't you take Maggie? The rest of you, split up into teams as you please." He handed three clipboards to one of the students to distribute, and jotted a few notes on his own clipboard.

The students, partnering up, immediately began chatting amongst themselves. Maggie was unsure what she should do and elected to wait for David's nod before climbing into her hip waders.

Done with his note taking, David held up his hand for everyone's attention. "Now, I know you're all experts at identifying amphibian eggs—hopefully you brought your copy of my PowerPoint presentation with you—but if you have any doubts at all, please call me over to take a look. It's important we get our assessment correct, not only to save the pool from the donut shop, but also because as biologists we have a duty to correctly add to the database of scientific knowledge. Who knows what other important project our data gathered today might be used for?"

An excited murmuring rippled through the little group of students. Maggie felt her own pulse quicken at the significance of his words. David had a way of energizing people and spurring them to environmental action and she was thrilled to be a part of the day's assessment.

"All right—go to it!" he commanded.

The students immediately broke into pairs, leaving a tall, thin girl with stringy blonde hair and pale skin by herself. She moved over to Maggie's side. "Hey," the girl said. "I guess we're partners."

Maggie had been wondering which one of the girls was Ashley; however, she'd been too embarrassed to ask David, thereby revealing she hadn't been paying attention when he introduced them. "Maggie," she replied, holding out her hand, forgetting that they had been previously introduced."

The girl ignored the outstretched hand. "Yeah, I know. Mind if I count and you keep notes?" Without waiting for an answer, Ashley handed Maggie the clipboard and pen. She eyed the minister's hip waders. "Hey, can I wear those?"

"Please do," said Maggie. She was anxious to make a good impression so that David would know how well she got along with young people.

119

"You won't need 'em anyway—you've got barn boots on," the girl pointed out.

Maggie glanced at the student's feet. Ashley was wearing traditional LL Bean boots, the style that Henry's niece Kate was said to have stolen. The duck boots were good for hunting, but not so good for frogging since the uppers were leather and only the bottoms were waterproof. "Right," she replied.

Ashley carefully spread her jacket on the damp ground and sat down to untie her Bean boots. "David told us in class Thursday he was bringing his girlfriend today."

Maggie knew that most students and professors were on a first name basis at Unity College. Still, she was bothered by Ashley's familiar use of his name.

"David's pretty cool, isn't he?"

Maggie realized by the reverential tone of the girl's voice that Ashley had a crush on him. "Yes, very cool."

The student slipped her feet out of her boots and stood up. "Are you a biologist, too?"

Maggie held the hip waders out to Ashley. She hesitated before replying. She suspected David wouldn't be thrilled if she revealed her vocation, since it might become fodder for some college gossip about the minister and the environmentalist. "Technically not. But I've loved frogs ever since I was a kid. I guess you'd say I'm an amateur herpetologist."

There was a little plop to their left. "Hey! What was that?" Ashley asked, startled.

Maggie handed the girl the waders and moved closer to the water to inspect the area. She didn't see anything but widening circles in the pond water. "Most likely a wood frog."

"Cool!" The girl pulled on the hip waders and slipped the suspenders over her thin shoulders. "We've had several classes on amphibians, but this is my first field trip. I shouldn't have any trouble, though. David did an amazing PowerPoint presentation showing us what the different egg masses look like." She retrieved some white folded pages from her jacket pocket and held them out to her partner.

Maggie unfolded the pages and quickly skimmed through the PowerPoint presentation. "Have you ever gathered frogs' eggs before?" she asked, curiously.

Ashley frowned. "I'm from Tucson. We don't have frogs."

By this time, the three sections to be assessed had been laid out by the other students using colored flags and surveyor's tape. David held up his hand to get everyone's attention again and proceeded to give the green light. "OK, teams—begin counting! Maggie, you and Ashley are over here," he said, beckoning to them.

The sophomore eagerly hurried to her teacher's side. "I'm ready, David!"

"Good girl, Ashley." He glanced at Maggie, who was bringing up the rear. "How are you doing?"

"Couldn't be better," she replied, cheerfully.

"That's my girl. Good luck!" David strode off to check the progress of the team working next to them.

Ashley waded a few feet out into the cold, shallow water. She sloshed along the shoreline slowly looking for egg masses. Suddenly, she stopped. "Look! Wood frog eggs," she gushed, pointing to a gelatinous glob clinging to a branch floating in the dark water. "How cool is that?"

Maggie waded out and inspected the eggs. Immediately, she realized the girl's mistake. "These are salamander eggs," she said.

"They look like wood frogs to me," Ashley replied, with an indignant sniff.

"I think not."

"How would you know?" the student challenged.

Maggie scooped up some of the goopy mass, cradling it in her bare hands. The frogs' eggs were slippery and cold. They were definitely salamander eggs. She held the dripping egg mass out to Ashley.

"Eew!" the girl exclaimed, pulling back.

"Sorry. I thought you might like to hold them."

"Gross!"

"I know they're salamander eggs because I've hatched mudpuppies before—that's what we call them in Maine." Maggie delicately probed one elongated, kidney-shaped black egg with her fingernail. "See how this coating around each individual egg looks like an uncooked egg white? Wood frog eggs don't have that; they sort of goop together. Let's find some of those and you'll see the difference."

But Ashley refused to budge. "Well, I still say they're wood frog eggs."

"Check your handout," Maggie persisted. She remembered David saying that spotted salamander egg masses counted twice as much as wood frog eggs. Correctly identifying this one egg mass might be a big step toward saving the vernal pool. Besides, if they couldn't identify the eggs correctly, what was the point in counting?

Ashley, either miffed at being wrong or simply wanting to be with David, waved to get his attention. "Maggie says these are salamander eggs, but they look like wood frog eggs to me," she called, loudly. She tossed back her long blonde hair. "Come tell us who's right."

David, now wearing hip waders, quickly joined them. He glanced at the lumpy gelatinous mass in Maggie's palms and pronounced her identification correct. "These are spotted salamander eggs, Ashley. Where's your PowerPoint presentation?"

Secretly pleased and gratified by David's confirmation, Maggie carefully returned the egg mass to its home. She rinsed her hands in the cold water. "One spotted salamander mass," she said aloud to nobody in particular, "and nineteen more to go." She wiped her hands on her jeans and squished back to shore. Maggie retrieved the clipboard and checked the appropriate box on the form David had given them. She reattached the pen and assumed a waiting position.

David and Ashley continued to huddle over the Power Point print-out. Realizing that the impromptu lesson could take a while, Maggie decided to continue without her partner. She wandered over to where a haphazard pile of dead sticks stuck out from the water. Didn't he say that blue spotted salamander eggs were worth even more than salamander eggs?

She stepped into the pond and moved slowly and methodically out toward the sticks, careful not to go deeper than the tops of her barn boots. Maggie reached down and gently lifted the slimy blackened end of one of the smaller sticks up out of the water, revealing gunky-looking egg masses clinging precariously to the dark wood. "Hey, I've got some blue spotted salamander eggs here," she called out excitedly.

David pulled up short. "Seriously? Are you telling me you can identify blue spotted salamander eggs, Maggie?"

"That's what I'm telling ya," she replied, happily. A fond memory popped into her head, of Peter and her as kids hatching out what they had thought were frogs' eggs—only to end up with mudpuppies. What fun they had playing with the tiny salamanders before returning the creatures to the pond!

"Do you know what this means?" David demanded, splashing out to her. He took the stick from

123

her hand, examined the eggs, and returned it to the pond. The stick sank slowly out of sight.

Maggie wiped her cheek with the sleeve of her fleece "It means we saved the vernal pool?" she asked, hopefully.

To Maggie's amazement, David knelt in front of her, still holding her hand, water nearly up to his hips. His students, who had stopped counting egg masses to watch them, whispered amongst themselves, aware that something significant was occurring. "It means I want you for my wife, Maggie Walker."

His declaration took her completely by surprise. Was David was really asking her to marry him!

"All of my life I've been looking for a woman who could identify blue salamander eggs. It's been my personal glass slipper for my very own Cinderella. And here you are! Say you'll marry me," he demanded.

Maggie stared at him stupidly. Oh, my God—he *was* proposing!

Chapter 9
To Be (Married)—Or Not To Be

Flabbergasted, Maggie didn't know what to do or say when David dropped to one knee and proposed to her. Goodness, what a sight! There he was—kneeling in the vernal pool in his tan hip waders—dark eyes demanding an answer. What reply should she give him? Did he honestly expect she would give him an answer here, at Sheldon Nutter's pond? With his students—and maybe even Sheldon—watching them!

Worse, all she could think of at the moment was that he had gotten her name wrong! She had taken Peter's last name, Hodges, when they were married, although she had still used her maiden name professionally. But after Peter's death she had dropped her maiden name altogether and certainly had been introduced to David as "Maggie Hodges." It irritated her that David had either forgotten all about her prior marriage, or, more likely, just didn't care about it.

David cleared his throat. "Maggie?"

Embarrassed, Maggie realized a minute or two had lapsed since he had proposed. She cleared her head and discovered with chagrin that his students had gathered at the pond's edge, waiting eagerly to hear the response she was to give their favorite professor. Good grief!

"Um, can I think about it?" she asked, awkwardly.

David's hazel eyes flashed with anger—and perhaps a little disappointment. "Well, that's not very flattering and certainly not the reply I was expecting." He hauled himself up—the mud reluctantly releasing his knee with a little sucking sound—and scowled at his students, who quickly dispersed. He stood in place, looking at Maggie but not seeing her, water and muck dripping from his waders. He fondled his beard.

Maggie, seeing the non-verbal sign that David had mentally moved on took the opportunity to escape. She stepped carefully back to shore. He quickly sloshed after her, however, grabbing her by the arm. "Not so fast—I'm not done with you yet." He turned her to face him, holding her fast by the wrists. "I thought from what I'd discerned over the past few months that you might not be disinclined to be my wife. Was I wrong?"

She hadn't meant to lead him on. She'd just been taken by surprise! "I'm sorry," she apologized. "It's just that Peter hasn't been gone very long."

"He's not gone—he's dead," David remarked cruelly. He dropped her wrists and tilted her chin up. "And it's been three years."

"Not three, yet. Two years and eight months."

"The bottom line is, Maggie, Peter is dead. He's not coming back. Funny, I never pegged you for the type of woman who would be satisfied to spend the rest of her life with a ghost. You either love me—or you don't. It's that simple."

Maggie felt herself yielding to the force of his logic and the magnetism of his charismatic personality. She was fond of him. She might even love him. "I ... I just need time to think," she stammered. "I'm sorry."

"Stop apologizing. I'm not asking you to walk into a gas chamber with me, after all. Take a few days to think about it. In the meantime, let's see if we can save this vernal pool, shall we?"

126

Maggie nodded, feeling somewhat dazed. She turned and stumbled over a grassy hummock. Instinctively, his right arm shot out and caught her, preventing her from tumbling into the water. "Easy," he urged, steadying her with both arms. "I'd hate to lose you just when I've found you, Sweetheart." He gave her a pat on the bottom and bent to retrieve her clipboard. He handed the clipboard to her and strode off.

Maggie tucked the clipboard under her arm so she could rub her wrists, which were throbbing from where David had held her tightly. She was sure he hadn't meant to hurt her, however. She knew he had been angered by her response and by her referral to her late husband. She was aware that she'd only used Peter as an excuse to request time to think about David's unexpected proposal, but was that fair to David?

She watched him as he pointed out several egg masses to Ashley and another student. He certainly was a wonderful teacher and instructor. "Take a few days to think," he had allowed her. What did that mean? Two days? Three? No more than four or five? How long before he was tired of waiting?

Maggie wasn't sure when she would be ready to give him the reply that he was expecting. After all, they had only known each other seven months. What if she needed more time? Would he wait? Or would he move on, searching for another woman who would fit into his blue salamander glass slipper? No wonder he had never married, with such a bizarre requirement! She certainly didn't want to be his Frog Princess, either. She had never wanted to play Cinderella for any man—not even Peter. Those caricatures of females who need to be rescued never appealed to her. Why would any woman want to be a princess when she could be a Queen?

Maggie smiled to herself as she realized the foolhardiness of her notion. Perhaps it was a bit

127

unrealistic. Two sovereigns in one household might be two rulers too many—especially in Sovereign, Maine! But … would David be open to an equal partnership?

And why had David never married? Had he ever had a long-term relationship with a woman? Lived with a woman? If so, how did that go? Why had they broken up? Hadn't he ever wanted to have children of his own? He was close—but not particularly close, Maggie had observed—with his nephew Walden. Frankly, she knew more about Nick Faulkner's inner life than his uncle did. As a biologist, a preserver of species, wouldn't David have wanted his genes to continue? She doubted very much whether he was the type of man content to let his brother's children carry the family line forward, but obviously she could no longer have children. Men like him typically took up with much younger women, squiring around Trophy Wives for the world to admire and envy. What did he see in her? Was it simply the blue salamander glass slipper? If so, how foolish was that!

But had she never made any foolish mistakes in her life, based upon similar foolish notions?

"Hey, Maggie," the blonde girl yelled, interrupting her reverie. "Bring the clipboard over."

How annoying to be addressed by her first name! Perhaps more annoying to Maggie, however, she had forgotten the student's name again. Oh, well, this was David's life. If she was going to join forces with him, she had better get used to such familiarities from his students—and pay attention when she was introduced to them!

By four-thirty it was apparent to all that the vernal pool would be saved from the donut shop, its future protected by the Maine Farmland Trust's Forever Farm program. The group of students and Maggie under David's direction had recorded the presence of twenty-two spotted salamander eggs masses, forty-seven wood frog egg masses, and at least nine other blue spotted salamander egg masses in addition to Maggie's find. "Good job, everyone!" David said, when announcing the tally. "There won't be a new donut franchise in Troy. The pond meets the criteria—exceeds them, actually—for a Significant Vernal Pool under the Natural Resource Protection Act. We could have stopped counting an hour ago, but I wanted to gather as much data as possible."

Cheers and clapping greeted his announcement. Maggie clapped along with the rest, thrilled to have played a small part in preserving the vernal pool, protecting the frogs and mudpuppies that she loved. How happy Peter would have been could he have seen this day!

But David was right. Peter was dead; he was not coming back. She must go forward alone, unless she could bring herself to give David an affirmative response to his marriage proposal. She had deeply offended the environmentalist by not falling into his arms immediately upon his offer. She knew, however—or thought she knew—that David was a reasonable man and a reasonable man wouldn't want a wife merely because she couldn't say "No" with the social pressure of six or seven sets of eyes upon her.

To her relief, he dropped her off first before returning the students and the van to Unity College. Maggie wanted some time to think, to give serious consideration to her future. She also wanted to consult with her daughter, Nellie, and a few friends, before giving David a definitive answer.

"I'm busy tomorrow, but I'll call you soon," he said, leaning over and opening the door for her from inside the van. He glanced over his shoulder, most likely wondering whether his students were watching him. They were.

"OK," she replied, aware that the eyes had shifted to her, much like the gaze of spectators at a tennis match.

"I'll look forward to it." She slid down out of the high passenger seat and gathered her things from the dashboard and floor. She hesitated before closing the van door, her stuff crushed against her chest. "Thanks for a lovely afternoon, David," she added, venturing a smile.

"You're a trooper! See you soon—Sweetheart."

To Maggie's relief, David winked at her. He wasn't angry! She slammed the door and stood back. David put the vehicle in reverse and backed out of the driveway. The puddle of water from the rain had dissipated and the mud was beginning to dry out. Once in the roadway he paused to switch gears, taking the opportunity to smile and salute her. She smiled and waved back.

Maggie, still hugging her gear to her chest, watched as the van's taillights disappeared up the hill. Suddenly, she realized the dew had fallen. She was cold, damp, and tired. She went inside, hung her waders on their hook and removed her barn boots. She doffed her jacket and stepped into the kitchen, retrieving her fleece-lined flannel shirt from the back of a chair. The house was already chilly as she had let the fire go out that morning. There was no central heating in the old schoolhouse, which wasn't well insulated and was heated by the two woodstoves—one in the kitchen and one in the living room. Without a fire in at least one of them tonight the place would be very cold by morning.

As she built a fire in the kitchen woodstove, scrunching newspaper and layering kindling in Boy Scout fashion, it occurred to Maggie to wonder where she and David might live if they married. Would they stay in Maine? Or would he expect her to sell out and follow him around the world where ever his career might lead them?

She was aware that David had been invited to teach at Unity College for one year as special Environmental Professor-in-Residence. His year would conclude at the end of August and she was a little fuzzy about what was to happen after that. Would the college renew his contract? Or did they select a different environmentalist every year to fill this particular position? Was David still under contract with Harvard? If so, even considering the possibility that Unity College would renew his contract or offer him a full-time teaching position, would he leave the prestige of Harvard for a small, relatively obscure college in Maine? Surely he must have thought of all the contingencies before he proposed to her? Or was his proposal truly spur of the moment?

But maybe David was ready to retire? At sixty-two, he was old enough to take early retirement, to travel and lecture, to focus his energies and attentions on individual environmental causes, such as saving the vernal pool today. If so, did that dovetail with Maggie's own life vision? What was her current life vision?

She realized they had never spoken about what would happen when this semester was over. She didn't even know if he wanted to make his home in Maine. Could she (and Maggie shuddered at the thought) be happy anywhere other than in her home state? David currently resided in a log cabin on Unity Pond, a rental property. She had heard him mention in passing that his lease expired at the end of August. What would happen after the lease expired? If they were engaged—or married—wouldn't David naturally expect to move into the old schoolhouse with her? Sleep with her in the big bed upstairs?

The thought of another man inhabiting the same space where she had snuggled with her late husband was unsettling to think about. Why, David would probably also put his shaving kit on the same shelf in the bathroom that Peter had built to house his comb and razor! He would hang his clothes from Peter's hook on the back of the bathroom door!

Could she sit cheerfully and comfortably with David at the kitchen table every day—the very same table over which Peter had slumped and died while folding clothes? Worse, could Maggie bear the daily comparison between the two men, which comparison would naturally occur to her treacherous, traitorous mind? She knew herself only too well and could already hear the little voices in her head: "Peter did the dishes this way." "Peter stacked the wood like this." "Peter always paid the bills." "Peter kept the roof shoveled." Peter, Peter, Peter!

Her fire-laying complete, Maggie touched a match to the newspaper. Greedy hot flames licked her fingertips and she quickly grasped the coiled metal handle to the cast-iron stovetop lid and screed the black lid back over the hole, leaving it open a couple of inches to provide the necessary draught. The pleasant scent of smoke drifted up as the fire roared to life. She returned the cardboard matchbox to the wall holder and absently opened the refrigerator, searching for something to eat for supper.

And ... were they ethically compatible? Maggie had her doubts in this regard. Last week after explaining to David her dilemma with the financial advisor, the man who was using her name without her permission to gain access to potential prospects, David had shrugged the situation off. "It's not your job to take care of your neighbors," he had said. "Better let them mind their own business, especially when it comes to their money."

Not her job to look out for her neighbor? Why, that was the very basis of Christianity! "Love thy neighbor as thyself." Even if she wasn't their pastor—but only one of the flock—it would still be her duty as a Christian to alert the others to the presence of a wolf among them. If the situation were reversed, Maggie knew that all of her friends and neighbors (Wendell and Rebecca, Ryan and Trudy, etc. etc.) would certainly give her a heads up. In fact, Henry had already given her a warning about Bill Gagnon!

Unfortunately, Ryan had yet to get back to Maggie with official information about the financial advisor, but she knew how busy he was. Still, she must contact the lawyer soon to find out if he had discovered anything. She felt guilty being remiss in notifying her neighbors. Henry's visit had shown that Bill Gagnon wasn't wasting time contacting them! But in her defense, the times when she had remembered she needed to give her friends a heads-up had never been conducive to such a private communication.

She snapped the refrigerator shut without making a supper selection and appropriated her rocker in thoughtful contemplation. There was some truth to David's hypothesis that each individual was ultimately responsible for his or her own financial decisions; however, why hadn't she pushed him further on this? She should have spoken up, explained her position and asked him to justify his. Perhaps David had misunderstood the potential seriousness of the problem? What if one of her neighbors lost a lot of money simply because he or she hadn't been informed of the presence of the wolf? How could that transgression be justified?

She had learned long ago—through her personal life and through her quarter century in the ministry—that partners, married or otherwise, must share the same code of ethics in order to remain happy together. Ethics gave one a jumping off point, a point of reference from which one weighed decisions (consciously or unconsciously) about how one interacted with others. If partners didn't share the same jumping off point—if they were on different bridges, metaphorically speaking, one a little upstream of the other—over time the one downstream would lose respect for the one upstream (or vice versa). Without mutual respect, Maggie knew that love would perish. A happy and healthy married life must be built upon a foundation of respect. "My child, let me not have the grief of seeing you unable to respect your partner in life," Lizzy Bennet's father had counseled the spunky heroine of Jane Austen's classic novel, *Pride and Prejudice* and Maggie had never forgotten Mr. Bennet's advice.

And then there were obvious ontological differences between David and her. How they were in the world was poles apart. David was a 'do-er' and she was a 'be-er.' David loved to buckle on his armor, pick up his sword, and sally forth on his white horse to save the world. She, by contrast, was at her best when invited to be present with someone who was sick or suffering. When she simply sat and shared another person's pain or grief, she felt complete and in perfect harmony with the world. During such times of ministry, she had occasionally been rewarded with glimpses of Heaven— particularly at the moment of death, when a spirit rose up to be delivered by the angels into God's hands. Then, she had experienced a sense of a peace beyond compare, knowing that she—that all of them—were not one, but part of the One, the amazing circle of life.

There was no reason why do-ers and be-ers couldn't come together and be perfectly happy; however, Maggie had her reservations about the two of them. Could she sit down with David and have a serious ontological discussion? Wouldn't he just raise his dark eyebrows satirically? Laugh her questions off? In seven months, they had never had a truly meaningful conversation or deep dialogue, she realized. Their conversations, even those of a personal nature, mostly centered around David and what he was doing or planned to do or wanted to do. Discussions between them were always on an intellectual and factual level, such as how many frogs' eggs were in the pond; what was the best way to assess porcupine damage in a woodlot; and what was for dinner.

"Oh, dear Lord!" Maggie exclaimed aloud with a heartfelt sigh. She sank back into the comfy chair and began to rock. "Why did I ever think life would be easier when I was sixty?"

Maggie awoke at five a.m., shortly before sunrise. The first blush was greeted with glorious bird songs—mating calls, she recognized—and she was tempted by the cheerful racket outside to pull on her sneakers, throw on a jacket, and join them. She paused on the door stoop to inhale the delicious scent of growing things. Flowers, weeds, shrubs, trees—everything was growing, sending out shoots and swelling buds, perfuming her little world with divine ambrosia. The spongy grass on her front lawn would soon need mowing and a previous check of her rhubarb nubs had convinced Maggie that she would have rhubarb sauce and pie by the end of the month.

The day was so glorious she felt as though she wanted to share it with someone. David, she knew, didn't arise until six-thirty or seven o'clock. She glanced at her wrist to check the time before remembering she had somehow misplaced her grandmother's watch. She made a mental note to search for the cherished timepiece. It was certainly too early to call David, however.

Maggie set off up the hill, knowing that Wendell, a notoriously early riser, would be up taking in the world with his coffee. She hiked along in silence, enjoying the smells and sounds of spring. In ten minutes, when Maggie turned onto the Russell Hill Road, it occurred to her that Nellie might be up. Perhaps she should stop and tell her daughter of David's proposal and see what Nellie had to say. When she reached Nellie and Metcalf's house, formerly the home of Miss Hastings, the town's music teacher, she searched the quaint cottage for lights and signs of life, but found none. Well, Wendell would serve as her first sounding board, then.

She found Wendell sitting, as expected, on the granite steps leading up to the porch. He and Rebecca's cat, Mr. T, were basking in the early-morning sun. Wendell cupped a mug of coffee and the fat tabby was splayed across the bottom step. Maggie saw her neighbor watching her approach up the driveway, but per usual he made no sign or sound of greeting; he simply moved over so she could join them on the steps. Maggie gingerly stepped over the cat and appropriated her designated seat. Several minutes passed before either spoke as the odd little trio enjoyed their silent camaraderie in the sun and birdsong.

"Coffee?" Wendell asked, finally.

Maggie nodded. She reached down to fondle Mr. T's ears while Wendell went into the house to fetch a cup of coffee. The cat rolled over and offered up his rotund belly for scratching. Maggie obliged.

Wendell returned handing her a hot cup of coffee fixed just the way she liked it. She took a satisfying swig and swallowed, feeling that life was good—very good. She felt grateful to live in such a warm, caring community, much like that into which she had been born on the Garland Road in Winslow.

Maggie soon found herself confiding her marriage dilemma to Wendell. True to form, she presented a case to her friend and neighbor as to why she shouldn't marry David, hoping that Wendell would rebut her argument. "Well, what do you think?" she inquired, after she had listed off all the reasons why she shouldn't marry the environmentalist. "You know me better than anyone in Sovereign, except maybe Rebecca, and Leland, of course. Don't you think it would be a mistake for me to marry again?"

136

Wendell hesitated, turning the bone-colored coffee cup round and round in his rough, weathered hands. "Course 'tain't good to be alone," he offered. He tossed the coffee remnants onto the grass, careful not to shower an eavesdropping chickadee that hopped on the ground nearby.

Maggie immediately latched onto the ray of hope. "So you think I should marry again?"

"'Tain't 'xactly what I said."

"Hmm. Why do I get the feeling that what you're *not* saying is what I need to hear?"

Before Wendell could reply, the tabby rose to its feet and stretched magnificently. The chickadee, feeling threatened, fluttered off. The rays of the rising sun highlighted Wendell's honest face and Maggie thought she could read his thoughts. "Ah, I get it! You think it's OK for me to marry again—you just don't think David's the right man." Wendell's eyes revealed Maggie had guessed correctly. "Don't you like David?"

"Wal, you know, 'tain't who I likes as is important."

"Yes, it is," Maggie corrected her neighbor. "I need to know my friends and family are on board with my decision. For what it's worth, Shirley Palmer has given me permission to have sex again," she added with a wry smile.

The old chicken farmer chuckled. "Thet don't surprise me none."

"But you know very well, Wendell Russell, that what you and Rebecca think is more important to me than anyone else, except maybe Nellie. You're my best friends."

"Didja ask Leland?"

"Leland? No, I don't think that would be a good idea."

"Why not?"

Maggie took a sip of her coffee. Should she tell Wendell of David's disdain for Leland? Or should she let sleeping dogs lie? If she expected honesty from Wendell, shouldn't she be honest with him in turn? "David doesn't like Leland," she admitted. "For all I know the feeling is mutual."

Wendell passed his coffee cup to his left hand and clasped the wooden hand railing with his right. "Wal, Leland ain't the shaapest tool in the shed, so I don't expect he's picked up on thet lettle fact yet," he said. He hoisted himself up.

"Are you going in?"

"Thought I might."

"But you didn't give me your opinion, yet!"

"Kin I give it to you later?"

"When? Tomorrow?"

"Nope. Jest as soon's I go in and ask Rebecca what 'tis." Wendell grinned and winked.

Maggie burst out laughing. "Well, I might as well book the wedding chapel now! You know how romantic your wife is." She handed Wendell her empty cup and stood up herself. She brushed off her pants. "Thanks for the coffee. I guess I'll go up and see if Nellie's up yet. She'll at least tell me what I want to hear."

"Wal, you know, if you hed told me what 'twas you wanted to hear in the fust place, I'd probbly hev obliged."

"Smarty!"

Maggie departed and the old chicken farmer watched the minister stride away from the stone steps. When she reached the road, he returned to the kitchen. Rebecca, still dressed in her cotton nightgown and bathrobe, moved around the large, eat-in kitchen preparing breakfast. "Did Maggie have any news?" she inquired. "I hope nothing's wrong. Why didn't she come in?" She tossed some bacon onto the fry pan and the

138

meat sizzled and hissed. Rebecca expertly twizzled the strips of bacon around the cast-iron frying pan with an old two-pronged fork.

"You were right. David's popped."

"Oh, my!" Rebecca exclaimed, dropping the fork. She rushed to the window to see if the minister was out of sight, altogether disregarding the frying bacon. But Maggie had disappeared up the hill and she had to be satisfied with plying him for the particulars of the engagement.

At her daughter's house, Maggie peered in through the kitchen window. She spotted Nellie at the table and rapped on the glass window. "Hello, honey!"

"Mom!" Nellie jumped up to answer the door. "To what do I owe the pleasure of this unusually early visit?" She was a tall, attractive girl, with poise beyond her twenty-six years. Nellie had left Sovereign at a fourteen, winning a full scholarship to a preparatory school in New Hampshire. After graduation, she had studied at Columbia in New York and also traveled extensively. For many years she had carried a chip on her shoulder for the small town she had left behind. Following the death of her step-father, however, Nellie had returned to Sovereign, where she had discovered the meaning of unconditional love in her childhood friend, Doctor Bart, who was now her husband.

Maggie appropriated Miss Hastings' rocker and unbuttoned her wool coat, one of Peter's old Pendleton jackets. "I can't seem to find you free any other time!"

"Don't be silly! You know all you have to do is tell me you want to talk and I'll make myself available." Nellie absently twisted her long blonde locks up and fastened them into a loose bun with a pencil from the table.

"Do you know how that sounds to a mother? No you don't, because you're not a mother."

"Please, Mom. Don't start with the baby thing again. We've only been married a couple of years."

"This is not the 'baby thing.' What you just said sounds as though I have to make an appointment to see you—my own daughter."

Nellie gave her mother a quick hug. "Mom, you know Metcalf and I are here for you anytime. But you're here now, so tell me—what's up?" She pulled a chair close to her mother and sat down, giving Maggie her full attention. "He's in the shower, but you can tell me."

"David has asked me to marry him."

Nellie clapped her slim hands ecstatically "That's wonderful," she gushed.

"You really think so?" Maggie entreated, as though she was the child and Nellie the mother.

Realizing she might have erred by being too enthusiastic, Nellie tempered her tone. "Don't you want to marry him? You do love David, don't you? You've been dating him quite a while now."

"I think I do. I admire him and like him a great deal."

"Mom! That's hardly a ringing endorsement."

"OK, so maybe I do love him. I'm just, well, I think I'm afraid." She fondled the tail of Peter's jacket, enjoying the feel of the rough wool against her thumb. Memories of her beloved childhood chum flooded her head.

"Afraid of what?"

"Afraid it might be too soon," she whispered, as a tear rolled down her right cheek. Maggie quickly brushed the tear away.

To Nellie, the nearly three years since her step-father had passed away seemed an eternity. "Too soon? Why, I know women who have remarried less than a year after their husbands died!"

140

"I guess I'm not one of those women," Maggie replied sadly.

"Obviously not. Listen, Mom. Let me ask you this—what would Uncle Peter say? What would he want you to do? I think that should be your guiding star."

"That's not fair," Maggie protested. "You know what Uncle Peter would say. He always thought of me first. Of course he'd want me to find someone who could make me happy."

"Right! And does David make you happy?"

"I'm happy when I'm with him. Yes, he makes me happy."

"Then ... what's the problem?"

Maggie frowned. She had come to see her daughter because she thought she had wanted to be talked into marrying David and Nellie had obliged, but now, perversely, she felt as though she wanted to be talked out of the relationship with David. "I guess there really isn't a problem," she conceded.

Nellie laughed. "Mom, why don't you just admit it—you love the guy and you want to marry him. It's not a crime! You're not too old to get married again."

"Too old! For your information, Shirley Palmer has given me permission to have sex again," she replied tartly. "And I'm looking forward to it. Very much."

"Geez, Mom," Nellie cried, covering her ears. "Too much information."

"What? You don't want to know old people still have sex? Just remember, you'll be old, too, one day. I'd think you'd want to know. I did, when I was your age."

"No, I do not want to know. Not now, anyway."

"When, then? After I'm dead? How are you going to know? Unless you read my journals. Are you going to read my journals?"

"No way! I'll give them to my daughter to read someday."

141

Maggie pounced. "Ah, ha! So you do intend to have children."

"Nice try. But don't change the subject. What are you going to tell David?" Nellie pushed. "Are you going to put that poor guy out of his misery or what?"

"Well, if I can't shock you—and Shirley has given me permission to have sex again—then there's no reason to hold out any longer. I might as well marry David and have a grand time in my old age." As soon as she said the words aloud, Maggie knew she was committed. For better or for worse, she was going to become David Faulkner's wife.

Nellie hopped up and gave her mother a warm hug. "Wonderful! I know this is what Uncle Peter would want. I'm so happy for you!"

Maggie felt a sense of relief that she had finally made her decision. Nevertheless, she feigned a frown. "You married people are always happy when someone else takes the plunge," she grumbled.

"There's a simple solution to that—become one of us!"

"Looks like I'm headed that way. I guess I'd better go give David the bad news."

"You know he'll be thrilled with your answer, Mom. But why don't you wait and give Metcalf the good news before you go? Have breakfast with us."

"Oh, you tell him for me, honey."

"You could just pop your head in the door. I think he's out of the shower—I don't hear the water running."

"I bet he'd love that. Besides, I really think protocol dictates I should tell my husband-to-be before I tell your husband."

"Confess, Mom! You're ecstatically happy right now, aren't you?"

Maggie did indeed feel a growing sense of elation. "I think so. But if you tell anyone else that I'm human, I'll disinherit you."

Chapter 10
Twin Piques

Maggie let herself out her daughter's quaint cottage, wondering what her late friend Miss Hastings would have said about this morning's work and about her impending marriage to David. That Miss Hastings would have liked the environmentalist, Maggie accepted as a foregone conclusion. Miss Hastings liked everyone. No doubt Miss Hastings would have urged her to marry again, too. After all, the former music teacher was the one who had encouraged Maggie to wed Peter years before she finally said "I do."

Back in the warm breath of the May morning air Maggie set off at a good clip up the hill. She inhaled deeply the scent of springtime. Several varieties of bulbs popped up from grassy spots along the roadside and bobbed their colorful heads in the light breeze—peachy-colored jonquils, yellow daffodils, and white narcissus— all planted by a mysterious, unknown hand, perhaps by Miss Hastings' mother, Helen Hastings. As Maggie hiked along, she felt the sheer joy of being alive. She realized in a flash of inspiration that surely God was wise to give the gift of companionship. Without companionship—true caring and sharing for another individual—it would be all too easy for her to live a life of selfishness and self-centeredness.

She slipped her phone from her jeans pocket and quickly dialed David's number. After a few rings, however, her call deferred to voice mail. A bit piqued, Maggie disconnected without leaving him a message.

Why didn't David answer? Where was he? How could he not know she was calling to accept his marriage proposal!

Maggie laughed at her own foolishness. Yes, she was happy! She recollected now that David had said he would be busy today, but couldn't recall with what. No doubt he had told her and she had forgotten. He would see her call and get back to her. If he was to become her husband, she must pay more attention to him!

The question was—what was she going to do today? She certainly wasn't going to work! If ever there was a day for playing hooky this was it. Serendipity was rising like a full moon in daylight. Maggie performed a little dance step on the side of the paved road. She felt light-hearted and effervescent. By the time she turned the corner onto the gravel Cross Road she was practically skipping. She glanced around to see if anyone was watching her and, spying nobody—and hearing no on-coming traffic—she appropriated the center of the road and expanded her repertoire to include some tap dance steps her feet remembered from her childhood lessons. How she had loved tap! Most of the other little girls in the class had preferred ballet, dressing up in their glittering tutus, but Maggie had been mesmerized by the sound of the metallic clicking of the taps against the polished hardwood floor of the studio. When their dance teacher set the needle upon the flat black disc of a 33 RPM jazz record and a catchy tune crackled through the giant speakers, nothing could prevent Maggie's feet from tapping.

A musical riff floated through her head and Maggie did a little shuffle ball change, toe-step-toe in time to the music. The song was from the hit musical play *Showboat*. An image popped into mind of her lively and light-hearted mother singing and dancing to this tune in their rustic farmhouse kitchen in Winslow. Maggie hummed a few bars of the song and then, with a flourish of twists and turns, loosened her limbs and her fine soprano upon the refrain:

> *Fish got to swim, birds got to fly,*
> *I gotta love one man till I die,*
> *Can't help lovin' dat man of mine.*

A blue jay intrigued by Maggie's performance flew from tree to tree announcing her presence as she sang and danced her way down the hill. Finding herself with at least an audience of one (and an occasional chattering red squirrel) Maggie gave herself up to the intoxication of the morning and the joy of singing. She sang several of her mother's favorite songs, including *A You're Adorable* and Maggie's personal favorite, *Orange Colored Sky* by Nat King Cole. Finally, running out of steam—and memory— Maggie paused to catch her breath. Morning dew dripped loudly from a nearby tree arresting her attention. Beautiful! Life was so beautiful. How wonderful her childhood had been—at least until her mother had died.

Funny, she hadn't thought of her mother in years. Rose Aberdeen had been a vivacious and talented artist who Maggie's very staid father had met when taking his first ever vacation the summer after graduating from college. It had been love at first sight for them both on Old Orchard Beach although they couldn't have been more different had they been born on opposite sides of the Atlantic rather than both in Maine. Her father hailed from a family of conservative teetotalers; her mother from a fun-loving family of people who—knew how to have a good time. Maggie had always thought her mother had played a minor role in her life, having died when she was six. Now, however, she wasn't so sure. Rose's premature death had prompted her father into making a big life change, from dairy farmer to professional, initiating the sale of their family farm. It had almost broken Maggie's heart to be torn from the family 'nest' in Winslow, where her grandparents and great-grandparents had remained on old family homesteads until they too, passed. How hard it had been for her to leave the cows, the scent of fresh-cut hay, the barn cats, the home-cooked meals—and her mother, who was buried beneath the black rich sod and thatch of grass in the cemetery overlooking the Sebasticook River.

Their little family—Maggie, her father, and her younger sister (sadly, now also deceased)—had moved around the country from one college community to another, without settling down, until her father received his PhD and was offered a teaching position in New Hampshire. Two years after graduating from high school, Maggie had elected to return home to Maine to live with her last remaining parental figure, her grandmother—Rose's mother—whose influence had largely shaped her life and eventually her career. Maggie's grandmother had been a professional career woman who had lifted herself from teaching in a one-room schoolhouse at age sixteen to become Supervisor of Elementary Education by the time she retired. Unlike the Aberdeen family into which she had married, Gram abhorred alcohol, dancing, and singing, and was usually the only sober person in the room during holidays when the Aberdeen clan celebrated.

Yet was Maggie not also an Aberdeen descendant? Didn't she enjoy a glass or two of wine? And didn't she also enjoy all the good things that life had to offer? Hadn't she early-on in her life thrown off the chains of the stern Calvinist theology to which the Walker family was wedded, deciding that she didn't need to suffer her life away? When the Aberdeens and Walkers sang *Joy*

148

to the World, the difference was—the Aberdeens really meant that the world should be joyful.

And what about those times in her life when Maggie had thrown caution to the wind and enjoyed just being human without worrying about the consequences or what the neighbors might think? Wasn't that the Aberdeen philosophy?

Maggie smiled as she recalled that first sublime August afternoon when, with sun blazing and honeybees buzzing, she had thrown off her clothes and run naked through the radiant and musky-scented field of goldenrod next to her house. Yes, running naked through the goldenrod as she now did annually every August was something her mother might have done. Or what about those summers when she sought out the nearest frog pond in the neighborhood? She recalled one afternoon in particular when she slipped into the lukewarm, pine pollen-covered pond in her birthday suit and the pollen parted like a prayer from her skin as she glided through the water. She didn't need to read Alan Watts to know she was one with the universe, because she had discovered this truth cavorting with the frogs as a child. Her personal experiences with the divine in nature had heightened her awareness of God and the goodness of all things; therefore, when her call to ministry had come, she had been prepared to receive and answer it.

And what about now? Surely her father's Calvinist ancestors wouldn't be caught dead performing this open-air musical recital on a back road in Sovereign, Maine! No, this little al fresco concert was the result of her mother's genes taking a rare turn at the helm of Maggie's life. It was only fair, after all. She couldn't and shouldn't be in rational Walker mode all the time. So what if she always felt slightly unsettled, much like Alice in Wonderland, whenever she was under the influence of the Aberdeens? Given the light-hearted joy she was feeling today, she should be grateful for those genes and allow them to take charge more often!

The feelings of doubt that had nagged Maggie for months—since she first sensed David might be serious about their relationship—evaporated. In their stead, a strange and wonderful world was unfolding like a blooming rose. It was the same world she had experienced while walking up the hill to Wendell's house—the same birds, the same birches and balsam trees—only now Mother Nature seemed to play an active role in her life. The trees stretched down to shake hands with her. (Congratulating her on her engagement, no doubt!) The blue jay introduced her. Wild flowers popped up beside the road as though a flower girl was passing before her strewing blossoms before a bride.

Maggie was shaking hands with a group of grasping balsams, thanking them for attending her impromptu performance and accepting their accolades for her engagement, when she suddenly spotted a movement deep in the woods. She stopped in her tracks and instantly reverted to cautious Walker mode. "Good grief! Who's that?"

From a distance she discerned a man threading his way through the woods over the old logging road, carefully picking his steps along the muddy, rutted way. Thanks to the work of some Unity College students that particular logging road had been joined to a series of connecting trails leading to the major points in Sovereign—the Millett Rock (a popular picnic spot), Ma Jean's Restaurant, Gilpin's General Store, and the church—so that one could get 'there' from almost any 'here' in town without ever having to travel over a public way. But the only person she knew who would take to the woods this time of year was Walden—because he lived there. For the past three years her young protégé Nick had been repairing, in exchange for rent, an abandoned

Jennifer Wixson

house on Wendell's woodlot, about a half mile up the trail in back of her house. She knew the youth hoped to purchase the early nineteenth century homestead from Wendell and she and he had had many conversations on the topic. Most likely Walden was just stopping by for a morning snack.

On closer inspection, however, Maggie realized her mistake. The man was much too small for Walden. Why, it must be David! Her new fiancée-to-be must have stopped in for an early breakfast with her before going to his appointment. Finding her gone, however, he had hiked out for a quick visit with his nephew. What good luck! She could give David the answer to his marriage proposal right here and now.

Heart racing with anticipation, Maggie hid behind the grizzled gray trunk of an ancient maple, waiting for David to exit the trail so she could jump out and surprise him. She tried to hold her breath, but he was taking too long. Did he see her through the trees? Was he planning a counter attack? Maggie suddenly heard the loud snap of a broken branch and knew he was close.

When David finally stepped out onto the gravel road, she could barely contain her childlike excitement. She jumped out and threw her arms around his trim waist, giving him such a bear hug that she almost lifted him off the ground. "Yes!" She proclaimed happily. "I'll marry you!"

Startled, he jerked away and whirled around to face her. When he caught sight of Maggie's face, however, he relaxed and laughed heartily. "My goodness, you scared me!"

"What! You didn't expect Alice in Wonderland to leap out and accept your marriage proposal?"

"Apparently not. I do apologize. Of course I should have been ready for anything from *you*."

151

Maggie felt her cup overflowing with love. She drew close to him and tenderly placed the flat of her hand upon his upon his cheek. She stroked his smooth, shaven face. Now, that was very curious! "You shaved your beard," she cried. "Why did you shave your beard?"

He collected her hands, holding them within his warm, comforting clasp. He smiled, his expressive hazel eyes sending out signals of empathy and rapport. Maggie allowed herself to meld into the harmony offered by his eyes. She no longer heard the harsh cry of the blue jay nor smelled the spicy scent of the mayflowers in the woods or the sweet, delicious scent of dried pine needles. She was in that heavenly zone of love where time has no meaning and joy surrounds the happy couple like an infinite protective barrier, separating them from the outside world.

"Ah, I knew it was too good to be true," he said in a rueful tone. "Alice would never want to marry me. I think you must be confusing me with that other White Rabbit."

Maggie stared at him somewhat stupidly. "What other White Rabbit?"

"My brother, David."

"What!" She yanked away, almost losing her balance in the process.

He reached out and steadied her. "I'm sorry—I didn't mean to embarrass you. But I see I have embarrassed you."

Maggie quickly regained her balance, but not her equilibrium. "I'm not embarrassed. But I am a bit confused."

"All of which leads me to suspect that my brother has failed to inform you of the Awful Truth."

Maggie swallowed hard. "The Awful Truth?"

"That he's one of two—a twin. I'm Duncan Faulkner."

David was a twin? Why hadn't he ever mentioned this to her before? How embarrassing!

"Not that I'm not flattered to have been asked to marry you," Duncan rambled on, obviously giving Maggie time to collect herself. "Wait—was I asked? I don't remember." His brow furrowed. "No, I think you said Alice was accepting his proposal, leading me to conclude that my brother—the world wanderer and confirmed bachelor—is finally going to settle down. Congratulations, Maggie! You are, Maggie, aren't you?"

Bemused, flustered, and deeply embarrassed, Maggie let Duncan reclaim her hand and press it in a brotherly fashion. "I had no idea ... a twin?" she muttered. Really, this couldn't be happening!

"We're both down the same rabbit hole, then. It never occurred to me you wouldn't know."

"Why didn't he tell me?" Maggie wondered aloud, thinking how much embarrassment David's honesty would have spared her.

"That's something you'll have to take up with my brother." As Duncan spoke, he avoided her eyes. He casually brushed two or three rust-colored pine needles from the arm of his V-neck navy pullover. "I have my pet theory, of course."

"And that is ...?"

"Sorry, that was small-minded of me. Forget I said that."

Her mind illuminated by what she knew of David's character, Maggie felt everything fall into place. "Let me guess—David doesn't like to admit there's a replica of his DNA. He's special; he wins all sorts of awards for his environmental work. But he's not that special, because he's one of two. You're fraternal twins, obviously."

"We are."

"You look just like him," she concluded. But even as she said these words, Maggie realized that Duncan was actually very different from his brother. He was thinner and his face was more drawn than that of his twin, making his cheekbones stick out. His skin was whiter, no doubt from spending less time out-of-doors. In addition, Duncan's shoulders were rounded and slightly stooped, where David's were square and muscular. Altogether there was an air of lightness and frailty about Duncan which was certainly not present in his robust, tanned twin, who appeared at least five years younger. If she had not been expecting to see David, she would have noticed the difference immediately.

"I look just like him except for the wrinkles, the gray hairs and the beard, or lack thereof," Duncan pointed out in a lightly self-mocking tone.

"Yes, that was rather a clue—the lack of a beard. I'm sorry I startled you. You must think I'm a lunatic, jumping out from behind trees and talking about Alice in Wonderland."

"Don't forget your song and dance number down the hill," he said, mirth dancing from his soft hazel eyes. "What was that? A traveling buffalo step you were doing?"

"Oh, Lord!"

"I don't think you're a lunatic. I think you're a charming and delightful woman, everything I expected to find, given what my son has told me about you over the past two years. I've often felt envious of your relationship with Nick, in fact."

Of course! In addition to being David's brother, Duncan was Walden's father. "Envious? I'm sorry for that," she apologized. "I didn't mean to step on your parental rights."

154

He laughed; an open-hearted, honest laugh. "I'm not jealous of your relationship with my son. I'm envious you adopted Nick and not me!"

Maggie felt herself blushing—actually blushing. He saw her confusion and quickly continued his chatter. "So ... we're to be related now? My brother is a lucky man. Welcome to the family!"

"He doesn't know, yet."

"So I concluded. Don't worry, I won't tell a soul," Duncan said, placing his hand over his heart. "Pastoral privilege, remember?"

"It's OK if you tell Nick, though," she qualified. "I don't think David would mind that, either."

"Thanks. That's very thoughtful. I admit it would have been difficult for me to keep this a secret from my son. By the way, don't wait too long to tell David his happiness. Patience has never been one of my brother's strong suits."

Thinking it was high time to turn the focus away from her and David's relationship, Maggie cast about for a new conversational course. She recollected Walden mentioning that his father was planning to retire from the ministry soon and hoped to make his first visit to Sovereign. It appeared as though that day had finally arrived. "Nick said you're an Episcopal priest?" she inquired politely. They naturally fell into step with one another, walking down the hill toward Maggie's house. Except for their ages, they could have been a pair of neighborhood children strolling down to school.

"Yes, although I prefer the term 'minister' or 'pastor.' Priest sounds a bit too high church for me and my ministry, not that I have anything against them, of course. I simply followed in my father's footsteps. He was also ordained in the Episcopal Church, but considered himself a minister, not a priest. David took a different path, obviously. And you?"

"Ordained Unitarian Universalist, although I'm Quaker at heart and my ancestors were Calvinists. I tried to become recorded in the ministry with New England Yearly Meeting when I was in seminary, but when it appeared it would take the Friends thirty or forty years to figure out whether or not they wanted to record ministers again, I decided to seek ordination elsewhere."

"Smart move. Well, that settles it; you're quite sane." The sun poked golden fingers through the dense green branches of the tall pines, creating shafts of light that impaled the pointed shadows of the trees. "You know, I think you're just what this family needs," Duncan pronounced, with frank appreciation.

"Thank you," Maggie murmured, flattered. "I'm very fond of Nick. And David too, of course," she added hastily.

"We Faulkner men need a good woman in our lives. I think you're just what the doctor ordered." He inhaled deeply, held his breath for a moment in satisfaction, and then exhaled. "Ahhh! I love this time of morning, don't you?"

"I do."

"I feel connected and disconnected at the same time. Connected to the natural world: the birds, the trees, and those pretty white flowers on that very strange tree there." He gestured with his free hand toward a spindly, multi-stemmed shrub tucked in amongst some taller trees. The shrub's leaves weren't out yet, but the bush was in full bloom. "Do you know what that is?"

"It's a shad bush—one of the earliest bloomers in Maine. I always watch for shad in the springtime. Then I know winter's really over."

"I thought shad was a fish?"

"It is, and that's actually where the bush gets its name—or one of its names. The old-timers in Maine nicknamed the bush 'shad' because when they saw the white blossoms they knew the shad were running in their favorite streams."

"A very pretty signal to go fishing! But you said shad was only one of its names. What else does my picturesque friend go by?"

"You'll like this nickname, being in the ministry— 'serviceberry'."

"As in Robert Service?"

"As in when you see the bush in bloom, you know the ground has thawed out enough to bury those who died over the winter."

He laughed. "Time to get the Bibles out rather than the nets! Or perhaps they buried their dead in the morning and went fishing in the afternoon?"

Maggie smiled at the imagery. "Perhaps."

"Reminds me of Jesus telling his followers to let the dead bury the dead, but 'go thou and preach the kingdom of God'."

"Another form of fishing."

"Exactly! See how quickly two ministers can turn a pretty bush into a theological discussion? David would never stand for that. He's always telling me to get out of my head and connect with Mother Nature."

"Probably good advice," Maggie agreed. "You said something earlier about feeling connected and disconnected at the same time. Is that the disconnect part?"

"No, I was alluding to the sense of relief I felt hiking over here through the woods. For the first time in a long while I felt disconnected from all the pain and suffering in the world, the evil, the hatred and mistrust. On days like this I just can't understand why we humans can't get along. It seems so easy to love one another, doesn't it?"

"It does."

"For example, there's probably a thousand things upon which you and I disagree …"

"I doubt that!"

"… and yet we can walk here pleasantly as though life were a musical interlude that was never going to end."

"Isn't that rather a contradiction? I thought an interlude was a break between whatever was going on?"

"I told you there were a thousand things upon which we'd disagree!"

Maggie rewarded her future brother-in-law with a sideways smile. "If that's what you call disagreeing, our friendship seems pretty certain."

"I hope so," Duncan replied. "Nick has told me so much about you I feel as though we're already chums. Do you know Cowper's poem on friendship?"

"Nick has recited it to me—several times."

"I was afraid of that. Nick does go a bit overboard on Cowper and Emily Dickinson. I'm more into Thomas Merton and Simone Weil myself."

"Too bad Cowper and Emily never met," Maggie mused. "Perhaps she might not have spent so much time in her room with a friend like William Cowper!"

"Maybe not," he said with a grin. He quickly returned to his thread, however. "Cowper tells us friends should be prepared to disclose their true selves to one another, which Emily certainly did in her poetry. Is that your house?"

"Yes." Maggie glanced at the rustic set of buildings now less than a hundred yards away, as though seeing her home for the first time. What must the old place, cobbled together with so many sheds and outbuildings appear to this stranger? There were indiscriminate windows and doors, all obscured by flowers and bushes, and herbs growing every which way like witch grass. But she needn't have worried for Duncan was too much engaged in recollecting Cowper's poem on friendship to pass judgment on her modest, ramshackle abode.

"Very quaint! I like it. Let's see—here's the first part of Cowper's poem, I think:

> *Who seek a friend should come disposed,*
> *T' exhibit in full bloom disclosed*
> *The graces and the beauties,*
> *That form the character he seeks,*
> *For 't is a union that bespeaks*
> *Reciprocated duties."*

"Reciprocated duties!" Maggie repeated, laughing out loud. "I think I've exposed myself enough for one day, thank you very much." She recalled her song and dance number down the hill and felt a renewed rush of embarrassment. She unbuttoned her wool jacket, allowing some of the superfluous body heat to escape.

"You mistake me, my friend," he replied gently. "You've come to me in full bloom, like the shad bush. Now it's my turn to reciprocate."

"Please don't think you need to do something silly just because you saw me acting out!"

"But I've waited years for the opportunity to step off this merry-go-round; to step out of my role as minister and be completely human. And now you want to take it away from me?"

"Don't worry. You'll have plenty of opportunities to step off the merry-go-round during your visit to Sovereign."

"I hope so! I wouldn't want to miss my one opportunity to play croquet with the Queen of Hearts."

"Careful, you might lose your head," she cautioned him.

"What matters if I lose my head but gain my life?"

An Eastern Tiger Swallowtail suddenly flew between them, her black-tipped yellow wings fluttering like miniature flags. Instinctively, Maggie and Duncan stepped away from one another to allow the butterfly freedom of movement. Two sets of eyes followed the beautiful creature as the butterfly weaved her way via a circuitous route to the blooming shad bush and then proceeded to flit from white blossom to white blossom.

Stillness descended upon the remote stretch of road and woods. As if by unspoken agreement, Maggie and Duncan walked the remaining distance to the old schoolhouse in companionable silence. When they reached her house they paused just outside the shed door.

"Thank you, Maggie. I'm going to enjoy having you for a sister. I haven't felt so content and hopeful since—since I lost my wife." That last part came rushing out, like a beaver dam breached.

Maggie felt Duncan's pain. She knew only too well what it was like to lose a beloved spouse. Still, what could one say to the bereaved except for the commonplace remarks one always said? "I'm sorry for your loss," she said. "Nick has told me about his mother. She sounds like a wonderful woman."

"She was. Thank you." He rested the arch of his mud-stained hiking boot upon the granite step and leaned an elbow against his knee, offering up a sympathetic smile. His was a commonplace pose, a pose Leland or Wendell might have struck. But this simple act seemed quaint and antediluvian to Maggie coming as it did from someone from Away and an Episcopalian minister at that!

"Geez, Dad! I hope you're not embarrassing yourself," Walden cried, as he emerged from around the back side of Maggie's house. "Or worse—embarrassing me!" He was dressed in jeans, work boots, and a flannel shirt. His long, thick hair was pulled back in a ponytail at the nape of his neck. "What took you so long to get here? Did you get lost? I've been here ten minutes!"

Duncan smiled and straightened up, obviously pleased to see his son. "Did you reach Uncle David?" He pulled Nick Faulkner forward, creating a little family grouping.

"Finally. I had to climb the Millett Rock to get cell service, though. He'll be home later this evening. I told him you were in town."

"Great! Maybe we can all go out to dinner tonight, to celebrate?"

"Good idea! I'm so happy you finally made it here, after all these years. Let's go out whether Uncle David is free or not, OK?"

Duncan offered up a dry cough. "We're going out to celebrate your uncle's engagement."

"Uncle David? Engaged?" Walden's gaze immediately shot to Maggie. "To whom?"

Maggie smiled weakly. Even though she had told Duncan it was OK for him to share the news with his son, she felt awkward hearing her engagement announced in person. Walden dropped his eyes without making contact with hers.

"Maggie has agreed to become your uncle's wife," Duncan continued gently.

The youth didn't even attempt to hide his dismay. "Seriously?"

Maggie felt her cheeks grow warm. In all of her 'should I's' and 'shouldn't I's' she had never considered how her protégé might feel about her joining the Faulkner family. She knew Walden was fond of her; certainly that wasn't it. So what was his problem? What was going on for him?

"I know how much you care about Maggie, Nick. So I hope you'll join me in welcoming her to our family."

Walden ran a hand through some short hairs that had escaped the ponytail. "Sorry, yeah. Welcome to our crazy family." He bent down and gave Maggie a kiss. His full beard brushed against her cheek, feeling like duck down. "I suppose I can call you 'Aunt Maggie' now?" he continued.

She searched his bright blue eyes, reading in them Walden's sincere affection for her. "I'd love that," she replied, relieved. "Aunt Maggie sounds so nice."

"I hope you'll be happy, then, Aunt Maggie—*if* marriage to Uncle David is what you really want."

If that's what she really wanted?! Walden's final words sounded like an admonition to her to rethink her decision. Why wouldn't a life with David Faulkner be what Maggie wanted? Did Walden—this young, sensitive and perceptive adept—see something in her future that she hadn't seen? If so, what was it?

Chapter 11
The Engagement Dinner

A nd that's how I learned Maggie had accepted my marriage proposal," David concluded cheerfully. "Good thing Nick let it slip or I might have heard it first from the old timers at Gilpin's General Store." The environmentalist bestowed an amused smile upon the other dinner guests—friends and family of Maggie's—who had gathered late Saturday afternoon at the old Russell homestead to celebrate their engagement. Although there had been no official announcement, by early June word of Maggie's impending second marriage had percolated throughout the little community of Sovereign. "Any more of those fried potatoes, Wendell?" David inquired, resuming his fork.

"Ayuh," Wendell replied, handing his guest the big bowl containing delicious herb-encrusted, golden fried potatoes. "'Tain't the usual way of goin' about love-making, that's for shore," he added.

"Heavens, how can you talk so, Wendell," exclaimed Rebecca. "Love-making! Nobody says that anymore."

"Ain't thet what 'tis called? Sparkin' 'n such?"

Rebecca laughed. "In a Jane Austen novel, maybe!" She shook her head; her loose brown curls bounced prettily against her shoulders. "Sparking, indeed." She turned her gaze somewhat fiercely upon Maggie, who was sitting at the opposite end of the table.

"You're very quiet, Maggie. This dinner is for you, too, you know. Don't let the men hog all the conversation, as Jane would say."

In response, Maggie smiled. "My grandmother always told me that when you're wondering what to say, it's probably best to say nothing at all."

"Sage advice," said Hannah Trow, delicately cutting her portion of meat.

Doctor Bart, Nellie's husband, reached for the salt. "Seems like you told everyone in town you were engaged to him before you told David, Aunt Maggie," he pointed out.

Maggie was quick to respond. "I didn't tell *you*, although Nellie did encourage me to go in while you were showering to give you the news." She grinned wickedly at her somewhat staid son-in-law, who still called her 'Aunt Maggie' despite having married her daughter. The nickname had been in use since Metcalf was a little child.

"Thank you for restraining yourself," he said gravely.

The evening sunlight splashed a glorious rose-gold color across the great room, a combined living-dining room. The scent of freshly-mowed grass wafted in on a light breeze through the open windows. The boisterous chirping and purring of the tree frogs and spring peepers could be heard from as far away as the pond. The little group happily helped themselves to a variety of locally-grown dishes, for which Rebecca and Wendell were known.

"When I mentioned something to Bub—sorry, that's my pet name for my brother—anyway, after Nick's slip, Duncan went on and on about how great my fiancée was and what a lucky man I was," David continued, helping himself to more of Wendell's just-picked asparagus. "Thus I concluded Bub must be speaking of

Maggie. I haven't been going around proposing to any other women lately."

Rebecca laughed. "I hope not! One woman is more than enough."

"Especially this one," David contended, giving Maggie's thigh a possessive pat. "I have a feeling she's going to make me—make all of us Faulkner men—toe the line. Although Bub declares she's an angel."

"Perhaps not quite that," Duncan interjected, correcting his twin. "But I do think Maggie is very special." He smiled down the table at his future sister-in-law.

"Well, I've seen Maggie's wild side," David added. "And let me tell you—I like it!"

Embarrassed, Maggie wanted to protest the excessive praise, but held her tongue. She glanced anxiously over at Walden, wondering how he was receiving his uncle's declaration about Faulkner men. The young poetry lover and woodsman remained unusually silent.

"More apple juice, Maggie?" Rebecca pressed her honored guest, holding up a blue pottery pitcher. The homemade bottled juice had been brought out from the cellar in lieu of celebratory champagne since Wendell and Rebecca abstained from alcohol. "I made it myself. Wendell gave me a juicer for Christmas—the old cider press quit, you know—and I processed the last of our Ida reds in February."

"I'd love some more apple juice," Maggie replied. The pitcher made its way down to her. "It's just right. Not too sweet—not too sour."

"Thank you," Rebecca replied, pleased. "I'm going to try pear juice this year. We should have plenty of fruit—the pear tree was loaded with blooms. That is, if the blossoms got pollinated. May was so cold and wet Wendell is afraid his honeybees didn't fly much."

Maggie refilled her glass with the apple juice. "I'm glad we finally got some sunshine today. I was starting to feel a bit mildewed." She offered the pitcher to Doctor Bart, who was sitting to her left. Wordlessly, her son-in-law accepted it. "What do you think, Wendell? Will the sun keep shining?"

"Always has," Wendell replied. Everyone laughed, everyone, that is, except Henry's granddaughter Kate. She was seated between Walden and his father and knew nobody at the engagement party except for her grandfather and his wife.

Kind-hearted Leland Gorse had noticed Kate's discomfort, however, and made an awkward stab at drawing her out. "Yer kinda quiet, gal," he remarked, as his left hand instinctively fished for a third slice of homemade sourdough bread from the basket, which Ryan had mistakenly placed near his plate. "Kinda nervous—like a long-tailed cat in a room full o' rockers."

"Father!" Trudy admonished. "Kate is a guest."

Kate shrugged. "It's OK; I can take it," she replied. "I've been called a lot worse."

"See!" Leland crowed to his daughter.

"Actually, I like the imagery—a long-tailed cat in a room full of rocking chairs," Kate repeated. "That cat has a right to be nervous and I guess so do I."

"I could tell jest by lookin' atcha you was my kind o' gal!" Leland declared.

Kate rewarded Leland with the smile of a kindred spirit. She was a tall, thin girl, casually dressed today in jeans and one of her grandfather's flannel shirts over a scoop-neck tee. She wore her dark-blonde hair in a single neat plait down her back.

"Careful your tail isn't the one that gets rocked on, Leland," Henry advised, taking pride in his granddaughter. "My Kate can give it right back. She takes after her grandmother, God rest her soul."

"I ain't scairt," said Leland.

"I'm so glad you came this evening," Rebecca said warmly to Kate. "It's such a pleasure to have a young person among us old fogies."

"Amen to that," seconded Ryan.

"Thank you for including me," Kate replied sincerely.

Rebecca glanced at Walden. "Oh, dear! Except that you and Nellie and Doctor Bart aren't old fogies, are you, Walden?"

"I was wondering about that," the youth replied, showing a set of even white teeth through his thick black beard.

"Me too," said Nellie, helping herself to more baby salad greens. "Although some days I feel old, especially after a full day at the clinic."

"Whereas I on the other hand just assumed I've been lumped in with the 'old fogies' for years," Doctor Bart said drily.

"Likely 'cause yer sech a serious fellar, Doc," Leland replied. He rapped his spoon roundly against the tablecloth two or three times, getting his host's (and everyone else's) attention. "Got any more of thet venison down they-ah, Wendell?"

Wendell regarded the white ironstone platter containing the venison, which had been fried up fresh in a cast-iron pan with some of Ryan and Trudy's Jersey butter, chopped bunching onions, and some of Walden's chanterelles. "Yep."

"Pass 'er down! By the by, you ain't told us yet how you got yer June deer."

"June deer? Did you just shoot this?" Hannah interjected, as the platter was passed hand-to-hand down to Leland.

Ryan coughed loudly, interrupting. "Perhaps this story had better wait until you and Wendell are alone,

Leland," he advised. "Since we all know hunting season doesn't officially open until the end of October." He held the platter for his father-in-law, who generously helped himself to the illegally-gotten game.

"Possibly a good idea, son."

"I do have one occasionally." Kate giggled; Walden chuckled; and even David smiled at the notion of the Harvard-educated Ryan McDonald, a former Boston attorney, having a good idea "occasionally."

"More apple juice, Duncan?" Rebecca asked, proffering her neighbor the pottery jug, which she had just refreshed from the kitchen.

"Thanks. This apple juice hits the spot," Duncan said. "I agree with Maggie—it's definitely the best apple juice I've ever had. I didn't know you could make apple juice at home, just cider. I see I've got a lot to learn about how people live in Maine."

Leland snorted. "You ain't nevah hed no hard cider if ya think apple juice is good stuff," he allowed. "Ain't nuthin' better'n hard cider, 'specially in wintah. A good swig o' hard cider will cure what ails ya."

"Yes, it's much like drinking 100-proof cider vinegar," said Ryan. "The beverage will kill you, cure you, or permanently curl your hair. Pass me the butter please, Doctor Bart."

Leland scoffed. "Vinegar my ar..."

"Ahem!" Ryan interrupted loudly, in the process of securing the butter. The flame on the pair of candles flickered.

"...my hat," Leland concluded, catching himself just in time.

"I've had regular cider, but I'm sorry to report I've never tasted hard cider," Duncan replied good-naturedly. "I'll try to remedy that obvious deprivation while I'm here. Maybe you could help me with that, Leland?"

"Possibly," Leland agreed. "Fer a price."

"Father!"

"Cain't make a livin' if we go to giving everythin' a-way," the old woodchopper groused, stuffing his mouth with potatoes. He chewed loudly with his mouth open. Trudy frowned at her father and he quickly shut his mouth.

"I'd be happy to buy a bottle of your hard cider," said Duncan. At the offer, Leland guffawed and Wendell chuckled. The Episcopal minister glanced around the table. "Did I say something funny?"

Maggie took pity on her future brother-in-law. "Hard cider isn't bottled like juice or wine," she explained. "Regular cider is mixed up with sugar, yeast, raisins, and spices in a big wooden barrel—preferably an old Jack Daniel's barrel, right Leland?"

He thumped the table with his right hand. "Yessir, by gawd!"

"And the mix is allowed to ferment several months until the cider has just the right flavor and alcohol content."

"Then ya un-bung 'er," Leland added.

Confused, Duncan appealed to Maggie for a translation. "Un-bung?"

"You take the cork out," she clarified.

"Of course! I'm such a simpleton. Have you ever tried Leland's hard cider?"

"Not lately. I wouldn't advise you to, either. Not unless there's an outhouse handy."

"Ah! Then I'll be sure to keep my eyes peeled for an outhouse. I might be able to cross two items off my bucket list at the same time."

The Episcopal minister's sagacious reply was rewarded with hoots of laughter. When the mirth melted away, a companionable silence fell over the little group of friends. A large, cut-glass vase in the center of the table overflowing with orange-red poppies captured and reflected the flickering flames of the candles and their happy, smiling faces.

Wendell broke the silence first. "Wal, I got a backhouse attached to the shed. 'Tain't bad, if you ain't too particular."

"Wendell!" Rebecca said, shocked. "Duncan's not serious about using an outhouse."

"Oh, but I am serious," the minister corrected his hostess. "I'll be very pleased to visit your backhouse later, Wendell."

Wendell nodded. "Make yoreself to home. Jest be shore 'n leave a quartah in the coffee can."

"Now he's definitely not serious!"

Wendell grinned.

The conversation once again flagged as the guests returned to the delightful business of eating and drinking. Leland spied an opening and thrust himself forward. "Speakin' o' hard cider—did I evah tell ya 'bout the time Pa sent me 'n Clyde down to fetch a jar o' cider, Wendell?" A quick eater, he pushed his empty plate away and settled his forearms on the table. Leland regarded his audience intently.

"Don't think you evah did," Wendell obliged his friend.

Maggie, who had been pleased to see David enjoying himself amongst the easy camaraderie of her friends, felt her fiancée stiffen in disapproval. She gave him a sidelong glance and noted he had set his fork down. He was frowning. What could she do? If she tried to head Leland's tale off at the pass, her maneuver might backfire. Wendell already knew David disliked Leland and she might end up being so obvious and heavy-handed about shutting down the octogenarian woodchopper that all the rest of her friends would start to suspect the truth, as well. There was nothing for it but to let nature—in this

170

case, David's nature—take its course and to trust that everything would come right in the end.

Leland fondled the salt shaker. "Clyde's Pa was workin' on the railroad thet year so Clyde spent a good deal o' time with us," he continued. "He was ten o' eleven 'n I was jest knee-high to a grasshopper. 'Twas hard wintah time—must'ave been 'bout four o'clock in the arternoon 'cause Ma hed gone into the kitchen to lay suppah—'n the old cider barrel was gettin' pretty low by then. Pa's knees was actin' up, too, with the arthritis. Soon's Ma left the room he fetched himself up from his chair 'n hobbled ovah to the quart cannin' jar he kept hid in the Grandfather clock. Pa told me 'n Clyde to creep quiet-like downstairs 'n fill thet jar. He give Clyde the jar 'n me the lid, 'n I felt quite proud 'bout havin' my share o' the responsibility." Leland paused to take a sip of apple juice. He grimaced at the taste and Kate laughed out loud. Leland, who appreciated a responsive audience, rewarded the young woman with a look of approbation. Walden regarded his tablemate thoughtfully, as though seeing Kate for the first time.

"Then what happened?" Rebecca prompted Leland.

"Like I said, the barrel was mighty low, 'n we had an awful job gettin' a siphon stahted. Fust Clyde sucked on thet rubber hose 'n then I give her a good suck, 'n we kept takin' turns. But we couldn't git the cider to run into thet jar no matter what we done. Course we had to swaller every mouthful o' thet hard cider we sucked in. Upstairs Pa was gittin' nervous 'cause we was takin' so long, so he called down to us 's quiet 's could: 'You boys all right?' which set us both to gigglin' as we was certainly feelin' no pain. Pa stuck his head down to assess the sit-u-ation 'n seed us both drunk 's skunks. "Niver mind the cider,' he barked. 'Git your arses back upstairs!' Clyde tried to take the stairs, but he missed the bottom step 'n fell down. He howled with lafftah 'n stahted rollin' round on thet dirt floor like a dog with fleas. I nearly wet myself I was laffin' so hard."

David pushed back his chair abruptly. "Excuse me," he interrupted, laying his cloth napkin on the table. "There's an important call I need to make." Before anyone could reply, he arose and strode out of the great room.

Rebecca started up, as if to go after David, but Wendell stopped her. Maggie glanced around the table and saw Ryan and Trudy exchanging glances. She hung her head, becoming aware that her daughter and son-in-law were watching her anxiously. Even Henry and Hannah seemed cognizant of the fact that David's departure had something to do with Leland.

Leland, however, remained oblivious. "Ma come lookin' fer us when we didn't show to suppah—course Pa pretended he didn't know nuthin' 'bout whar we was. She found us curled up like hedgehogs at the bottom o' the cellar stairs, too drunk to clumb back up. She marched down them steps, took us by the ears, 'n hauled us up to the kitchen. Clyde 'n I figgered arter 'twas a good thing we drunk 's much hard cider 's we did 'cause by the time Ma got done with us our backsides was raw. Pa was pretty scairt o' Ma so he disappeared out to the hay barn, whar he kept 'n emergency stash o' whiskey. I guess he figgered this was an emergency. 'You ain't gonna git away thet easy!' Ma hollered arter him, 'n the next thing we knew we heared her slide the bolt on the back door. 'Twas a pretty cold night Pa hed in thet barn, let me tell ya!"

Everyone laughed but Maggie. She had heard the kitchen door close quietly and knew that David, like Leland's father, had absconded.

Rebecca took a sip of sweet spring water and set down her glass. "I take it your grandmother was a teetotaler?"

Jennifer Wixson

"Fust rate. She was one o' them wimmen bound 'n dee-termined to rid the world o' alcohol. She fixed Wendell up good—dinn't she, Wendell?"

The former chicken farmer grinned. "Ayuh," he agreed. "She did."

"I don't believe I've ever heard that story. Now, that would be a tale worth hearing, Wendell," Ryan encouraged."

"Yes, do tell," Hannah echoed.

"Wal, t'ain't much to tell," Wendell replied agreeably. "Old Ma Gorse got a-holt o' me one day when I was home on leave from the Navy. She come to see Grammie Addie and found me passed out in the bahn instead. She set herself down on a bale of hay and tolt me how horrid 'twas when alcoholics git sick 'n die—two of her brothers and her father died drunks. Ain't a quick death, neither, 'tis a lingerin' demise, she said. Old Ma Gorse shore liked to drug her story out, worse than Leland even. She scared the bejesus out of me thet day and I never drank agin."

"Thank goodness for that!" Rebecca exclaimed, tears in her eyes. She gave her husband's hand a reassuring squeeze.

"But if your mother was so good at drying out drunks, how come it didn't work for you?" Kate queried Leland. "Not that I'm saying you're a drunk, Mr. Gorse," she amended hastily, "but you do seem to prefer hard cider to apple juice."

The old woodchopper shrugged. "I jest flyed undah Ma's radar, I guess. Once she got to savin' souls she run the roads like a dog catcher runnin' arter loose hounds. She dropped in on the fellars at their clubs all hours o' the day 'n night. She warn't a welcome sight when she come marchin' in, neither, I kin tell you!"

173

"Haaha," Kate chortled. "A dogcatcher chasing after loose hounds! And while she was away, the home dogs would play?"

Leland rewarded Kate with another grin. "Something like thet."

"What happened to your father, Mr. Gorse? Did he fly under the radar, too?"

"Nope. Pa niver could get away from Ma after thet wintah. She stuck to him like a burdock burr to a sheep's wool. She wouldn't let Pa outa her sight durin' the day 'n made him drive her 'round at night so as she could keep her eye on him. Toward the end o' it, Pa even become a crusader himself. On Saturday nights he 'n Ma used to stand outside The Cotton Candy—'twas a notorious waterin' hole 'n girly club in Waterville— passin' out fliers 'bout the dangers o' alcohol. Ma also took the opportunity to give the fellars hell fer goin' to a girly show."

"I bet they loved that," declared Nellie. "Not!"

Doctor Bart, who had been listening intently, leaned back in his chair and folded his arms against his chest. "Thank goodness for women like your mother, Leland," he spoke up. "They helped bring attention to the devastation alcohol can have on people's lives. I wish there were more like her today. It's not just alcohol, nowadays. Now we have the opioid epidemic to contend with. I find it disgusting that gangsters and hooligans make money by preying on the weaknesses of others."

Ryan leaned forward into the conversation. "Unfortunately, this is nothing new. I'm not excusing your hooligans and gangsters, Doctor Bart. But those criminals are simply providing a means for their clients— if one can call them that—to wash away their pain. We need to take a look at the underlying social, economic, and spiritual issues causing the pain in the first place.

Until that's addressed, I'm afraid the abuse of alcohol and drugs will always be with us."

"My mother believed that if we took care of our friends and neighbors—helped them through their difficult times—they would be less likely to seek solace from a bottle," Trudy added quietly. "She lived out her vision here in Sovereign, helping others, caring for everyone in need regardless of their income or social status. Unfortunately, she left us way too young."

Ryan, seeing that his wife was close to tears, threw an arm around her shoulder and hugged her. After exchanging loving glances, Ryan handed Trudy her napkin, which she used to daub her eyes. She gathered herself together and straightened up in her chair, smiling at the rest of the little group of friends, who were obviously concerned about her. "Sorry about that," she apologized. "Somehow no matter how old you are you never get over the loss of your mother." Trudy, like Maggie, had lost her mother when a young girl.

At Trudy's words, Maggie felt her heart squeeze in painful empathy. *Somehow no matter how old you are you never get over the loss of your mother.* She realized Trudy had hit the nail on the head. She had never truly gotten over her mother's death; she had simply put her mother out of her head, as though she'd never had a mother. Maggie wished now that her father, after her mother's death, hadn't gathered her and her sister up like so many remaining eggs in a despoiled bird's nest and relocated the family from one college town to another. Maybe then, in her beloved home of origin, on the farm with her grandparents and great-grandparents to comfort her, she would have come to understand and appreciate the circle of life at a much earlier age. Instinctively, her right hand sought the comfort of her fiancée; however, she realized, with a little shock of disappointment, that David had not returned to the table. Her hand dropped back into her lap. Where was he? What was taking him so long?

"Don't feel as though you need to apologize, Trudy," Rebecca urged. "We all understand and we're here to support you—that's what friends are for."

"Here, here," Henry Trow seconded. "Hannah and I are always on the look-out for young people to take under our wing. Isn't that right?" he said, seeking confirmation from his wife.

"I'd love to adopt Trudy," Hannah replied, as her calm, quiet eyes sought out the young woman's across the table. "Perhaps you'd like to come for tea and cookies when school lets out?" In addition to farming, Trudy worked in the library for the consolidated school district.

"I'd love that."

"Wonderful! Bring the children, too."

"That's why I love Sovereign," Rebecca gushed. "There's so much genuine goodness here—neighbors helping neighbors. When Lila and I first arrived, people came out of the woodwork to help us get our egg business up and running. In fact, you couldn't pay me a million dollars to live anyplace else on earth. I even used to hate going into Waterville to the doctor's office. Thank goodness you opened your clinic, Doctor Bart!"

"Don't thank me; thank Miss Hastings for leaving her place to me. We couldn't have done it without her, could we, Nellie?"

But his wife hadn't heard him. She was gazing out the large, east-facing picture window enjoying the view of the lush green pasture in back of the old Russell homestead. Splotches of white, expired dandelions—old soldiers, as Leland called them—contrasted sharply in the gloaming with the mysterious sea-green waves of meadow grasses. "Look! There's a lightning bug," Nellie cried. "That's the first one I've seen this season. It must be a sign!"

176

"Maybe it's my mother," said Trudy, smiling. She rotated in her seat and caught sight of the twinkling firefly. "I see it, too! She's winking at us."

"Maybe 'tain't yore Ma," Wendell interjected with a gold-toothed grin. "Maybe it's yore grandma—Old Ma Gorse—comin' after Leland." Everyone laughed.

Contentment settled down among them like a cat lying beside a warm fire. The gathering dusk drew them closer together. Everyone had finished eating, yet no one was in a hurry to bring an end to the meal, fearing perhaps to break the spell.

Wendell offered up a little "ahem," as though about to make an announcement. His wife looked at him and gave him a nod of approval. "We hev some news," the old chicken farmer disclosed. "We sold the Nutt place to Walden. We passed papers last Friday."

"Oh, that's wonderful!" Hannah exclaimed, instinctively reaching over to pat Nick's hand. "I'm so glad we'll be permanent neighbors, dear."

"Thank you, Aunt Hannah." Walden had already become one of Hannah and Henry's unofficial adoptees.

"Congratulations, Walden," Doctor Bart added. "I know how hard you've been working on the old Nutt place. Now it's legally, as well as emotionally and spiritually, your own."

"I couldn't have done it without Dad's help," said Nick, rewarding his father a warm smile. "He's the one who put up the cash. He sold his house in Massachusetts and is coming to live with me."

"More wonderful news!"

"I'm afraid I come with the property," Duncan added in an apologetic fashion. "At least until I can find a home of my own."

"Dad's determined to make me miserable by saying he's going to leave me all alone out there in that big old place!"

Doctor Bart smiled at the young woodsman. "It seems to me you've come a long way from the young man I treated for a gunshot wound at the clinic a couple of years ago. Back then you wanted to be left alone in the woods."

"Oh, don't mention that horrible accident," Nellie cried. She recollected that day only too well. Although she and Doctor Bart had not been an item then, she was helping at the clinic at the time when Walden had been accidentally shot by Henry.

"He's just telling it like it was, Nellie," Henry replied gruffly. "I was an old grouch when I first came to town, although Nick knows I only meant to scare him when I shot over his head. He knows how sorry and ashamed I was and Nick and I are good friends now."

"We certainly are, sir. And I've changed, too, thanks to the kindness of folks like you and Hannah, and Doctor Bart and Nellie. And Maggie, too, of course."

Maggie felt several sets of eyes upon her and realized her friends were waiting for her blessing upon the real estate transaction. "Nothing could make me happier than to know you have your heart's desire," she said sincerely to Walden. "I know what a labor of love the restoration process of the old Nutt place has been—still is! We're all rooting for you."

"And helping me," Walden added. "You're not just encouraging me from the sidelines, Maggie, you're all helping make my dream a reality. I couldn't have done what I've done to the old place so far without you or Wendell or Leland. And Ryan did the legal work for us, free of charge."

"I think there was something unwritten but understood about taking the kids mushroom hunting," replied the attorney.

"Yes, but, please don't let them eat every mushroom in sight!" Trudy added. "I'm afraid they'll get sick."

"Pshaw! Ain't like Walden don't know one mushroom from 'nother," Leland said. "Why, he sells 'em down to New Yock City! Don't think he'd be in business long if he kept sendin' down poisonous 'shrooms."

"And speaking of thanking friends, Wendell and I should thank, Maggie, too," Rebecca interjected hastily, recognizing the signs that Leland was winding himself up for another story. "Maggie referred her financial advisor to us at just the right time. We've given the money from the sale of the Nutt place to him to invest. Hopefully, by the time both Wendell and I go to claim our Great Reward, there'll be enough money built up in the account so Tad and his descendants will be able to keep the place in the family for another two hundred years."

"Marvelous!"

"Good for you!"

At Rebecca's pronouncement, Maggie felt the ice-cold hand of fear grip her heart. Her financial advisor? Oh, Lord! That could only mean one thing—Bill Gagnon had gotten to Wendell and Rebecca before she had been able to warn them! What if her best friends lost everything? Was it possible that because she had been dragging her feet about Bill Gagnon they might lose the old Russell homestead? What a nightmare scenario! What could be done to rectify the situation now? Could they get their money back?

Maggie quickly glanced over at Ryan. He was frowning down at his plate, nostrils dilated in obvious consternation. Henry, Maggie noted, was quizzically assessing her face, wondering, no doubt, how she could have failed to alert her friends to the wolf in sheep's clothing.

179

Where was David? Why hadn't he returned to the table? She needed her fiancée's love and reassurance right now. She had failed her friends, failed herself, and failed her little community. What's more, she felt it. She was nauseated by her failure and felt sick to her stomach. Certainly, it was more than she could—should—bear alone!

Chapter 12
The First Quarrel

Maggie, desperate for support and advice, accosted David after the party ended, when they were alone together in his vehicle. "Why were you away from the table so long? What on earth were you thinking?"

Unfazed, David put the Land Rover in gear and backed out of the Russell's driveway. "I was thinking that muttonhead Leland might ramble on for half an hour or longer. So I made myself scarce. I did have some calls I needed to make, actually."

"Well, it was very rude," said Maggie, miffed. "Plus, I needed you!"

"You needed me?" he questioned, slipping the Rover into forward gear. "With all your friends and Nellie there? Somehow I doubt that."

Maggie felt her hackles rise. "Are you doubting my word?"

"Calm down, Sweetheart. I simply said you had quite a support group present. Did I miss something?"

"You'd know if you had remained at the table," she retorted. "Wendell and Rebecca gave all the money from the sale of the Nutt place to that shady stockbroker to invest!"

"So?"

"So they could lose everything! Don't you realize what a dreadful position this puts me in?"

181

"Not really." He slowed the vehicle in order to make the turn onto the Cross Road.

"It's all my fault! I should have given them a heads-up about Bill Gagnon, yet I didn't."

"Aren't you taking a little too much on yourself? After all, you're Wendell and Rebecca's friend, not their financial advisor. You're not giving them much credit for being financially astute."

David's response infuriated Maggie. Obviously, she wasn't going to get the comfort and support she needed from her fiancée! When they reached her house, she deliberately popped out of the car and bade David goodnight without a kiss or without even inviting him in.

Early the next morning, before heading for the church, Maggie drove over to Scotch Broom Acres to see Ryan. She found the attorney cleaning out the cow barn. The acrid smell of ammonia from the urine mingled with the sweet scent of hay greeted her as she entered the superannuated tie-up. Maggie, never knowing where the lawyer might be working—in his office or in the barn— had fortuitously brought along one of Peter's flannel shirts to throw over her church dress. She'd also worn footgear appropriate for the barn.

The lawyer lifted his hand in greeting when she pushed through the swinging door. "Be right with you," he called from across the center aisle. He briskly finished scraping manure into the wooden gutter. When he was done, he flipped on the switch and the heavy iron chain of the antiquated gutter cleaner ground into action. The rusty contraption inched steadily forward, scraping the loose manure, hay, and other debris toward the far end of the barn where the refuse dropped off into a waiting manure spreader. The Jerseys had already been milked and had been turned out into the green pasture for the day.

182

"What are we going to do, Ryan?" Maggie lamented, as he approached her. "Can we get Wendell and Rebecca's money back from Bill Gagnon, do you think?"

The tall attorney paused and leaned against his hoe. He thoughtfully pushed his red barn cap back on his dark head. "I doubt it. At best, he's probably got the money invested already and most likely there would be hefty penalties and fees for reversing those investments. At worst—well, we won't go there, yet. Have you said anything to Wendell and Rebecca?"

"No, I never got around to giving them a heads-up before last night. I wanted to speak with you first, before going over there and worrying Rebecca sick. You can't think how I've been kicking myself!"

"You're not the only one," Ryan replied, knocking the heel of the hoe against the edge of the gutter cleaner. Loose manure dropped off into the steadily moving gutter cleaner. The cows had been gorging themselves on lush, high-protein grass and as a result the manure was dark green and loose. "I've been doing a lot of self-flagellation since last night, too. I told you I'd check into Mr. Gagnon, Maggie, and I've been so busy on the farm and with my law work that I haven't contacted the Office of Securities or FINRA or anybody about him."

"What if Wendell and Rebecca lose all their money!"

"That's a possibility. But let's not panic, OK? I'll make some phone calls soon and get back to you when I know anything definite. In the meantime, let's not alarm Wendell and Rebecca until we know for certain whether this stockbroker is a scoundrel or not. It's possible he's legit."

"Possible. But not probable. What can I do?"

"Keep your fingers crossed. Better yet—pray. My mother used to say, 'When all else fails, try praying'!"

"Now, why didn't I think of that?"

Maggie wasn't sure whether she was relieved or disappointed when David didn't show up for church. After their disagreement the night before, she hadn't really expected him. Upon mature reflection, she thought she had been a bit short with him. She had learned from experience, too, that David was sensitive and his feelings were easily hurt. Probably she should call him later and apologize.

Maggie relaxed back in her Bishop's chair, turning her attention to the church choir, which was warbling out the anthem that Hannah, the organist and music director, had selected. The members of the choir averaged seventy-five years of age and relied heavily upon Hannah's strong soprano—and the loud pump organ—to buoy them up.

No, she wouldn't call and apologize. Why should she apologize? Women were too quick to try and make things right, Maggie decided. She would give David a day or two for reflection. If she didn't hear from him by Tuesday then she would call him. (But she wouldn't apologize!) She couldn't let the rift continue throughout the week because David was slated to receive a prestigious award for environmental excellence from the Grassroots Environmental Transformation Society (GETS) on Saturday evening. The dinner and awards ceremony were being hosted by Colby College, the historic liberal arts college in Waterville. Maggie, as David's fiancée, had received her own personal invitation to the event in the mail. David had been jubilant when he described to her his phone conversation with the GETS President of the Board of Directors, who informed him he was one of three national recipients. Maggie didn't want to ruin David's special night simply because of a minor disagreement between them.

As it turned out, David phoned Maggie on Monday night and apologized to her. "I'm sorry I brushed off your concerns," he said. "It's just that Leland gets under my skin. I'm not sure why; I just know he bugs me and I lose my patience. After that, it's all downhill."

Maggie, who had not expected her fiancée to apologize, was quick to return the favor. "I shouldn't have been so harsh with you, either, David. I expect there will be plenty of times where we aren't on the same page as each other. We'll have to learn to deal with it, that's all. I'm glad we've made up before the award ceremony."

"Me too. I wasn't looking forward to having just Bub and Nick as my date. They're not much to show off to the guys."

"Are they going, too?" Maggie asked, surprised.

"Of course they're going—they're not much, but they're my family. Thank goodness we finally have a woman to offset some of our male testosterone. Since Gail died—she was Duncan's wife—we've been a pretty rough-and-tumble bunch of bachelors. I think you'll keep us in line, though."

Maggie wasn't so sure about that statement, but she held her tongue. "Is it a fancy affair?" she asked, concerned that her wardrobe might be a bit thin. "It's not black tie, is it?"

"Black tie for a bunch of environmentalists? No way!" David replied, laughing. "They'll be lucky to get us out of hip waders. I'm wearing one of my favorite sports coats."

"Not the one with the elbow patches, I hope."

"I was going to wear that one, but now I suppose I can't," he replied, in a mocking tone. "You should probably wear a dress, if you own one."

"Of course I own a dress! Haven't you seen me wear dresses to church?"

"I don't notice what you wear under that robe. For all I know, you're butt naked."

"David! You're impossible."

"You'll discover I'm not too observant when it comes to people, just frogs, birds, insects, and the like."

"We should make a good couple then. I'll do the people part and you take care of the environment." If Maggie had secretly hoped to get David to second her pronouncement about their relationship, her hopes remained unfulfilled. David's focus was elsewhere.

"We'll pick you up around five o'clock," he continued.

"Why so early? My invitation said six-thirty?"

"I thought we might have some pie and coffee before we go. To be honest, Sweetheart, I've been bragging your pies up to Bub. You don't mind, do you? We probably won't get dinner until eight."

Maggie was pleased—and surprised—that David had touted her baking to his brother. Obviously, her homemade pies had made quite an impression on him. She only hoped she could impress Duncan, as well.

Chapter 13
"We're All Family Here"

Saturday was a gorgeous day, seventy-five degrees and sunny. Maggie rose early to bake the pie. When she was finished—and the pie was cooling on the pie rack in the pantry—she sat down at her antique oak desk to finish writing her sermon. She reviewed the draft she had sketched out the day before on a pad of yellow-lined paper, listening to the loud serenade of the red-eyed vireo, whose melodic birdsong was a summertime favorite in the neighborhood. The living room windows were open and a fresh breeze blew into the room bearing the delicious scent of her mock orange bush. Maggie could hear the fierce buzzing of two ruby-throated hummingbirds as they fought over the bush's satiny white, orange-scented blossoms.

She finished her sermon around three o'clock and put her books and papers in order for the next day. Then she headed to Nellie's old bedroom, which she had been using since Peter died. She donned her outfit, a light-weight, lavender-colored cotton skirt and sweater set. She chose a sleeveless, ivory-colored scoop-neck silk blouse to wear under the sweater so that if the banquet room became hot, she could remove the sweater and still be comfortable and yet fashionable-looking. The sweater's lavender color highlighted her sky blue eyes and Maggie, after finishing a light application of make-up and twisting her hair up into a becoming bun, decided that she still "cleaned up good," as the locals would say. An antique necklace with Maine amethysts and matching earrings that she had inherited from her grandmother completed her outfit. Maggie wished she could find her grandmother's gold watch to wear, however, she had misplaced the watch a while ago and so far it hadn't turned up.

In the kitchen, Maggie donned an apron and set out plates, forks, and napkins in preparation for her guests. The tea kettle was whistling on the propane stove when, at five o'clock on the dot, David arrived with Walden and Duncan in tow.

Maggie was disappointed when David failed to offer her a compliment. Instead, the environmentalist made himself at home, per usual, selecting the chair at the head of the table as a matter of course. Nick and Duncan hesitated, politely awaiting an invitation to sit down.

"Sit anywhere you like," she encouraged them, her heart swelling with quiet joy. She loved to entertain guests and frequently hosted small dinner parties to which she invited her special group of friends. But this—this was something different and special. Duncan and Nick would soon be part of her little family. How wonderful it was that at this time of her life her family was increasing, not decreasing! "Who wants tea?" she inquired cheerfully, pouring hot water onto some dried herbs in her yellow, six-cup ceramic teapot. The boiling water released a minty-licorice scent, which bouquet soon seeped throughout the old-fashioned kitchen.

"Smells great," said Duncan. "Where do you buy your tea, Maggie?"

Nick laughed aloud at his father's question. "Maggie makes her own tea, Dad! She grows and dries her herbs and everything." The bearded youth gestured at the exposed hand-hewn beams overhead, from which a variety of brightly polished copper pots hung and where bunches of green herbs dangled from a braided twine clothesline. "Cool, huh?"

Maggie, pleased by Walden's homage, nevertheless felt a pang of uneasiness. Why didn't Nick refer to her as 'Aunt Maggie,' which he had previously asked permission to do? Was there still something bothering him? If so, what was it? Or was Nick simply so used to calling her by her first name that he couldn't change horses in the middle of the stream?

Duncan examined the herbs hanging from the ceiling. "Very cool," he agreed, bobbing his handsome dark head in approval.

"You like?" his twin said, with proprietary pride.

"I like everything about this place; it has a special feel to it." Duncan turned his attention back to his hostess. "The beams are hand-hewn, aren't they? How old is your home?"

Maggie placed the hot teapot on a cast-iron trivet situated on the table, leaving a potholder on the lid. "Early nineteenth century, I believe. And yes, the beams are hand-hewn." She adjusted the tie on her apron. "This used to be a one-room schoolhouse where all the kids in the neighborhood attended."

"An old schoolhouse! I never would have guessed." Duncan leaned forward with interest, elbows on the blue and white checked tablecloth.

"If you look at the floor you can see where the desks were bolted down. I filled in the holes, of course, but they're still visible."

He glanced at the battle-scarred pine floor, which despite its age and obvious defects nevertheless was lovingly polished and shone a warm pumpkin-color. "Remarkable! You've turned the old place into a comfortable and welcoming home, haven't you?"

Pleased at the compliment, Maggie appropriated her chair at the table. "Thanks. It was a lot of work, but I

189

spread it out over many years. My late husband helped me and so did Nellie." She lifted the lid of the teapot to check the tea's progress, allowing the minty-licorice bouquet to escape. "This is peppermint tea, with some anise hyssop thrown in for good measure," she disclosed. "It's one of my favorites."

"Mine too," Walden chimed in.

David shot his nephew an amused glance. "You're hardly an unbiased judge, Nick. You like everything Maggie does. Bub is going to think you're a teacher's pet."

Maggie saw Walden frown and tense up in his chair. She wished David hadn't sounded so critical of his nephew, knowing as she did how sensitive Nick was. "So what if I am?" the youth replied, defensively.

"I guess it's a good thing I'm going to marry her, then, so nobody else steals her away from the family," David continued, lazily.

"Yeah. Good thing."

"I think the tea is ready," Maggie interjected quickly, anxious to pour oil on what could be troubled waters. "Who's first? Duncan? Why don't you pass me your cup?"

The Episcopal minister moved his mug across the table. "Thanks," he said. Maggie placed the stainless steel strainer over his cup and carefully poured out the steaming tea.

She proceeded to fill the other three cups and returned the teapot to the trivet. "Try some of this," she encouraged Duncan, passing him Wendell's golden honey, which maintained a place of honor in the center of the table. "It's Wendell's—and it's wonderful." Duncan's teaspoon clinked against the side of the china cup as he stirred honey into his tea.

"Aren't you forgetting something, Sweetheart?" David asked with a mocking smile.

Jennifer Wixson

"Oops!" Maggie cried, leaping up. "You've distracted me so much I forgot the pie," she scolded the three men in general. She departed for the attached pantry, but not before overhearing David inform his brother that she was "a bit of a scatterbrain at times." Although the epithet was true—her thoughts were a bit scattered sometimes, largely because her life was so full— she wished David hadn't shared that description with his twin. She was trying to put her best foot forward, eager for her new brother-in-law to have a good opinion of her.

Maggie needn't have worried, however, for when she returned with the pie Duncan was suitably impressed. She had decorated the golden, flaky piecrust with dozens of miniature birds, cut from the dough and tacked to the pie with milk. The birds were baked to a dark biscuit color. "Wow! I've never seen anything like that," Duncan declared.

"Didn't I tell you, Bub?" David said, gloatingly. "Wait 'til you try it, too. Maggie knows how to cook."

"Please, now you're embarrassing me," Maggie protested. She resumed her seat and picked up the pie server. Adeptly, she cut the pie into six pieces.

"I almost—but not quite—hate to have you cut the pie up; it's such a thing of beauty," Duncan remarked, holding out his dessert plate. "You must have learned at your mother's knee?"

Maggie served Duncan one of the larger pieces of pie. "My grandmother's knee, actually. Gram was a great cook. She gave me her recipe, but it took years for me to perfect the pie crust. Either I had too much water in the dough or not enough."

"Obviously, you resolved your issue," Duncan said. He waited politely for everyone to be served before taking a bite of pie. "How did you do that?"

"I begged Gram to tell me her secret, but she said good pie crust couldn't be taught—it was something I

191

had to learn to 'feel' for myself." Maggie plated pieces of pie for David and Nick, and then served herself. A momentary silence ensued as all four of them enjoyed their first piece of pie.

Nick spoke first. "This is great stuff," he said.

"Really good," Duncan echoed. "I might have to have a second piece. But excuse us for interrupting—you haven't finished your story, Maggie. How did you figure out the crust? I'm curious."

"Well, Gram told me I was overthinking it. She suggested I stop worrying about how to make the crust and let my hands take the lead, which is a lot harder than it sounds. One day—ages ago now—I was having company over and I wanted to serve fresh raspberry pie for dessert. My first crust was awful. Way too sticky and gooey! So I threw it away. The second crust was too dry. The flour and lard wouldn't stay together at all. I kept trying and trying—I think I went through about eight or ten crusts—until my left hand suddenly felt the moment the crust was right, the moment when the flour mix had exactly the right amount of water in it to make a perfect crust. After that, even though I'm right-handed I always let my left hand take charge. And I've never thrown away a pie crust since."

"Remarkable," said Duncan. Unfortunately, he was gazing intently at Maggie while also ferrying another piece of pie into his mouth. Some of the juicy filling dropped from his fork onto his light blue Oxford shirt. A blackberry bounced off and dropped to the floor, but the juice remained, staining the cloth.

"Geez, Dad!" Nick cried.

Duncan ruefully beheld the dark blue stain on his shirtfront. "That was clumsy of me." He picked up the errant blackberry from where it had fallen on the floor and set the fruit on the edge of his plate. "Now I'm done for," he said, wiping his fingers on his napkin.

"Great. Just great," David said, a bit testily. He glanced at his watch. "We don't have time to get you home to change, either."

"Can't you just button your jacket over the spill, Dad?" Nick asked anxiously.

"I don't think so. I'm sorry, David. Don't worry about me. I'll walk home through the woods and you can tell me all about the ceremony tomorrow. Better yet, Nick can take pictures on his phone and text them to me."

"You always find a way to screw things up, don't you, Bub?" David groused.

Maggie wished David hadn't added the last condemnation. Duncan, she could tell, felt badly enough about the situation. "Let me see if I can get the stain out," she offered, rising up. She flicked on the gas under the tea kettle of hot water. "My grandmother taught me a few other tricks besides making pies. We need to do it quick, though, before the juice sets. Take off your shirt," she instructed Duncan.

The Episcopal minister leaned back in his chair, slightly taken aback. "Take off my shirt?" he repeated, abashed.

"Well, I can't clean it with you in it," Maggie pointed out.

"Come on, Bub. Don't be shy," urged his brother. "We're all family here."

"She doesn't bite, Dad," Walden added.

Reluctantly, Duncan rose and removed his suit jacket, draping it over the back of his chair. He slowly unbuttoned the top button of his Oxford shirt. David glanced at his watch a second time. His twin, taking the hint, picked up speed and finished unbuttoning the shirt in short order. He untucked his shirt, shrugged out of the light blue cotton cloth, and placed the shirt in Maggie's waiting hand. She politely averted her eyes as she took the shirt, sensing that Duncan was embarrassed at his state of undress, but not before noting that the hair on his chest was still thick and dark, and that he wore the same kind of white, V-neck tee-shirt that Peter preferred. She spied a small hole near his left armpit and mentally decided that Duncan, like his twin, was also in want of a wife.

Maggie stretched Duncan's shirt over a strainer in her wide farmhouse sink, holding the fabric in place with a large rubber band. Using a pot holder, she removed the steaming teakettle from the stove and slowly poured boiling water directly onto the stain, careful not to douse the rest of the shirt. In less than a minute, the stain appeared to evaporate, leaving only a small wet spot behind. She released the rubber band, shook out the shirt, and handed the cotton cloth back to Duncan. "There! I think the shirt will dry before we get to Waterville," she assured him. "No one will ever know you spilled blackberry pie on it."

"You're amazing!" Duncan declared. His warm hazel eyes shone with admiration. "I'm surprised nobody snapped you up before David found you," he added, hastily re-buttoning his shirt.

"Don't tell me—now you're in love with Maggie, too?" David wisecracked. "First the son and then the father?"

"And the uncle," his brother pointed out, smiling. "Who knows? If I had met Maggie first, I might have given you a run for your money."

David's eyes flashed, but his face remained inscrutable. "But when did you ever outrun me, Bub?" he asked lazily.

His twin was quick with a rejoinder. "There's always a first time!"

Maggie glanced over at Nick and noticed that the youth was frowning. His father and uncle's banter was obviously distasteful to him, although for the life of her she couldn't figure out why. Over the past few years she and Nick had developed a close relationship, almost like that of mother and son. Surely he couldn't feel resentful that she was joining the family?

David pushed away from the table. "Speaking of time, we've got to run," he declared. "As one of the guests of honor, I shouldn't be late."

Forty-five minutes later Maggie found herself as a peripheral satellite hanging around David as he laughed and joked with a constantly changing crowd of well-wishers and colleagues. She was amazed at how many scientists were in attendance that evening. The banquet room seated five hundred comfortably and she estimated there must be close to that number present. Some of the environmentalists had travelled from as far away as California and Alaska. David had told her the GETS awards were held in a different state every year and that it was by sheer coincidence Maine had been selected as the site for the presentations of this year's awards, which were for projects completed in the previous year.

With the exception of one or two of David's Unity College colleagues, Maggie knew nobody present, other than their little party. She had nothing to add to the conversation, either, which was all science talk. She felt completely out of place.

When another biologist came up and slapped David on the back, Maggie decided enough was enough—she would slip away. Nobody would miss her, certainly not David. She glanced around the room and spied Duncan sitting by himself at one of the round banquet tables, which had been decorated for the evening with green linens, fresh floral arrangements, and flickering candles. The tables were set for a three course dinner. David had been right. They probably wouldn't eat until eight, at the very least.

Duncan rose when Maggie approached the table and pulled the chair out for her. "Thanks," she said. She tucked her skirt behind her and gracefully seated herself. "Where's Walden?" she asked.

He retrieved his chair. "Over at the bar, holding court."

"Oops," said Maggie, realizing her mistake. "I guess I should have called him 'Nick.' It's just that we've all gotten so used to calling your son by his local name."

"I know all about it. That was a thoughtless trick Nick played, introducing himself in Sovereign as Walden Pond."

"Well, before we knew what Nick's real name was we used to call him the Mushroom Man, so you see, we weren't much better than he was," Maggie replied, disarmingly. "Frankly, I'm surprised Nick is getting along so well this evening. I thought he was rather shy of crowds?"

"He is. But apparently word has gotten around that Nick is an expert on mushrooms. He was spirited away to the bar before he knew what was happening. I think one or two beers might have helped the situation, too. Speaking of which, may I get you a glass of wine?"

"That would be lovely." Maggie removed her dress purse from her lap and hooked the brass chain over the back of her chair. "A chardonnay, if they have it."

Duncan departed for the bar and soon returned with a chilled glass of white wine. Maggie took a sip. "Very nice, thank you."

An awkward pause ensued. To fill up the empty space, Duncan unbuttoned his jacket and instinctively tugged his shirt into place.

"Is it dry?" she asked.

"Just about, thank you." They fell into silence again.

Maggie took another sip of wine. "Do you know anybody here?" she spoke up.

"No. Do you?"

196

"Not really. I've met one or two of your brother's colleagues, but I wouldn't exactly say that I know them." She fingered the round stem of her wine glass.

"Who does know anyone, really?" he moralized.

At this remark, Maggie felt the awkwardness evaporate like the stain on his shirt. She bestowed a coy smile upon her companion. "You're not going to go all theological on me again, are you?"

He laughed. "Not if I can help it! But I can't promise not to stray occasionally. Set me straight if I start to wander again, OK?"

Maggie made a wry grin. "I don't know how much help I'll be. I have a tendency to wander in the same direction myself."

"We're two peas in a pod, aren't we? Not so very different than they are." He gestured toward the milling environmentalists.

"I'm a better dresser," Maggie felt obliged to point out, taking another sip of wine.

"You are indeed," Duncan agreed. "In fact, I would have complimented you earlier, when we were back at your house, except I didn't want to step on my brother's toes."

She sniffed. "David wouldn't have noticed if you did step on his toes. He certainly didn't notice my outfit," she complained. She regretted the complaint the instant the words left her mouth. "Forget I said that, please," she entreated her future brother-in-law.

Duncan opened his eyes wide. "Forget what?"

"Thank you." A waiter came by and offered Maggie a tray of hors d'oeuvres. She shook her head and the waiter passed on to Duncan, who liberally helped himself.

"Will you be joining our outing to Sovereign Gore Thursday?" Maggie continued. "I know Henry invited

Nick, because he told me he did, but I wasn't sure whether or not Henry included you."

Duncan did justice to a bacon-wrapped scallop and wiped his mouth with a napkin. "Nope, I wasn't invited. I just assumed the expedition was for the young people." He gestured toward Maggie's nearly-empty wine glass. "Ready for another?"

Maggie regarded her glass ruefully. "I better not. I might have to make meaningful conversation with someone I don't know."

"Perhaps the wine would help?" he suggested.

Maggie laughed. "Perhaps. In that case…" She held out her glass.

"Say no more. I'll be right back."

When Duncan returned with her second glass of chardonnay and a fresh ginger ale for himself, Maggie repeated her invitation to Sovereign Gore. "Please join us," she urged. "Henry asked me to round up a few more bodies for our outing. There aren't many young people available during the middle of the week. Most of us are over a certain age. Plus we're going with Leland and he's not exactly a spring chicken. Leland's team of oxen will be ferrying us in the hay wagon."

"Where is this place we're going?"

"Sovereign Gore is very close to Unity Pond, where the first settlers landed more than two hundred years ago. It's in the extreme southwest corner of town. Nowadays, however, the old road to the Gore is so bad you can't get there by car. Hence the oxen and wagon."

"The outing sounds like a lot of fun. I'd love to go."

Maggie lifted her wineglass. "Here's to Sovereign Gore!" she toasted.

The two of them clinked glasses. Duncan took a sip of his ginger ale and set down his glass. "I'm not sure how well I'll get on, though."

"What's the matter? 'Scairt' of riding in Leland's wagon?" she teased.

"Not exactly. It's the movement I'm afraid of. I get motion sickness, " he admitted, sheepishly.

"No need to worry about that! Leland's oxen only go two or three miles an hour, and that's on a good day. If worse comes to worse, we can always go Shank's mare and get there just as quick."

"I'm afraid I don't ride horses, either."

"Good! Because Shank never owned a horse—he walked."

Chapter 14
Outing to Sovereign Gore

More than a week had passed and Maggie still hadn't heard back from Ryan about whether or not Bill Gagnon was to be trusted with Wendell and Rebecca's money. She hated holding back information from her friends; however, she realized it could take the attorney some time to ascertain the truth about the financial representative. She couldn't go about making unsubstantiated charges against Mr. Gagnon just because she didn't like his cheap looks or the slimy way he spoke—or even that he was taking advantage of the slimmest pretexts of a relationship for drumming up new business in the neighborhood.

The longer the issue dragged on, the more frustrated and angry Maggie became, not with Ryan but with herself. How could she have been so lackadaisical about cautioning her friends—her best friends, too!—about this potential wolf in sheep's clothing? When thoughtful reflection on her part revealed the answer to her question it turned out to be even more painful than the failure itself, for it revealed to Maggie her ignorance and prejudice. The truth was—she had never expected Wendell and Rebecca to have extra money to invest in the first place, thus she had subconsciously reasoned there was no need to give them a heads up.

How wrong her assumption had been! Her blindness in regard to Wendell and Rebecca made Maggie question herself and her relationships with others. How well did she really know her friends and parishioners? What other ignorant prejudices might she not unknowingly harbor? Was she guilty of discriminating against others—either consciously or unconsciously—based upon their apparent incomes and social standing? How many others in Sovereign had she misjudged?

"You're very quiet today, Maggie," Duncan remarked, interrupting her meditation. He and she were sitting on bales of hay in the back end of Leland's hay wagon while the cart bumped along over the old abandoned road. That morning, several of their little group of friends had rendezvoused at Scotch Broom Acres for the outing to Sovereign Gore, the site of the town's first settlers. Abandoned early in the nineteenth century, not long after the settlement was founded, the Gore nowadays was home to little more than old stone foundations, rock walls, scraggly lilacs, and a few heritage rose bushes.

"Sorry, ethical dilemma," Maggie replied. "You know how it is." She grasped the side of the hay wagon as the cart lurched to one side. Despite the ruts and potholes in the woods road, Leland's team of oxen trudged steadily onward and upward. Henry and Hannah, Kate and Walden, and Rebecca and Wendell were perched on hay bales closer to the front of the wagon. Alice Rose, on loan from her parents, and Tad Russell sat up front with Leland, clinging to the wagon seat. Leland had an arm around each of the young children, harness reins held confidently in his calloused hands. David had opted out of the field trip at the last minute, of course.

The idea for the outing had first been floated at the engagement dinner. Wendell had made an off-hand remark about this forgotten historical section of Sovereign and Henry, a former teacher and history buff, had pressed his neighbor for more information. When no actual date was set for the visit to Sovereign Gore, Henry had taken it upon himself to follow up. While he and Hannah were both interested in history—especially local history—her neighbor admitted to Maggie later that he particularly wanted the outing for his granddaughter. "Kate needs to get out and be with other young people. All she does is mope around the house," he declared. "You know how important it is to get her interested in something besides herself." As a result, Maggie agreed to help organize the outing and after some phone calls to the family at Scotch Broom Acres, and to Wendell and Rebecca, a week from Thursday was selected. Since Sovereign Gore was inaccessible by motor vehicle, except four-wheelers, Leland had offered to take them via this old road with his team of oxen. The end result was the outing to the Gore, where the little group planned to leisurely explore the old ruins and feast on box lunches.

"Can I help with your dilemma?" Duncan offered quietly. "I'm pretty good with ethics." He kept his voice low to prevent the others from overhearing their conversation.

Maggie relaxed her grip. She hesitated before replying. She did long to unburden herself! Particularly since she and David had not yet discussed her problem in any great detail. Yet she knew it would be improper to confide in Duncan. He was not the Faulkner male whose love and support she had a right to expect. "Thanks, but it's something I have to work out for myself."

"I understand. Well, I'm here if you need me. You know where we live," Duncan concluded with a warm smile, his hazel eyes twinkling. For a moment, he looked so handsome, so much like his twin that it took Maggie's breath away.

The June air was warm, bursting with the rich, astringent scent of pine. Cheerful birds darted among the trees and bushes lining the abandoned roadway, which was used now mainly by hikers and horseback riders who wanted to explore the Sovereign backcountry. The old-fashioned hay wagon creaked and groaned as it jounced along.

"Hey, Maggie, explain this 'gore' thing to us," Henry entreated cheerfully from the front of the cart. The retired teacher was looking younger than his seventy-something years today, dressed for the outing in wide-wale corduroy pants, a spruce-green turtleneck, and Scotch plaid wool jacket. He wore a jaunty tweed driver's cap on his head. The day had started out cool—in the low fifties—but the sun had gradually warmed the air and Henry, feeling hot, unbuttoned his jacket. "Finally! Some sun," he exclaimed. "What a damn cold spring we've had, eh?"

"Please do educate us, Maggie," Hannah encouraged. Like Henry, she was a history buff. Both were active members of the Sovereign Historical Society. Today Hannah was looking the picture of mature, married contentment. The wagon jounced again and Hannah grasped her husband's arm for support. He smiled at her fondly and patted her hand.

"Yes, Wendell is having a hard time making us understand," Rebecca declared.

"Might not be all Wendell's fault," Walden allowed, grinning through his beard. "I get poetry, but not history. What the heck is a gore? I thought it was a verb, not a noun. As in—'the ox gored the farmer'."

"Ouch," said Kate, who was sitting on a hay bale opposite the young woodsman. "Poor choice of words, don't you think?" She bobbed her blonde head in the direction of Leland, who was happily—and obliviously—instructing his three-year-old granddaughter how to handle his precious team of matched oxen.

"He can't hear us—the wagon makes too much noise."

"Gore is both a verb and a noun," Maggie interjected hastily, anxious to avoid further altercation between Kate and Walden. For some reason, the two young people had been at loggerheads since rendezvousing at the farm. "In this case, gore is a surveyor's term for a piece of land that's created through a mistake when the land is first surveyed. When town lines are later discovered to not match up—or come out right—a small piece of no-man's-land is accidentally created. The creation of gores actually happened a lot in the northeast since most of the land was surveyed in the seventeenth and eighteenth centuries using rudimentary equipment and under harsh conditions. In fact, Sovereign Gore was accidentally created by Ephraim Ballard in 1789, I believe. He didn't quite lay out the lines correctly between Sovereign and Unity, which was then 25-Mile Pond."

"Ephraim Ballard? Wasn't he Martha Ballard's—the famous midwife's—husband?" Hannah inquired excitedly.

Maggie nodded. "He was."

"Martha was an amazing woman! She delivered hundreds of babies and never lost a mother. I read that Ephraim was quite a character, too."

"I think he was. He spent some time in jail for uncollected taxes—not his, but the taxes of other residents. Back in those days," Maggie explained, "the Tax Collector, which Ephraim was as well as a surveyor, was legally responsible for collecting the assessments of others. When Ephraim didn't get their money, he was jailed."

"That doesn't seem fair," pronounced Walden.

"Hardly," echoed Kate.

"Fair or not, that was the way things were back then," Maggie continued. "I'm not sure he minded very much. They fed Ephraim pretty regular in jail. I understand there was plenty of ale around, too."

"I didn't know Ephraim Ballard did any surveying work in this area," said Hannah.

"He was hired by the Kennebec Proprietors, the descendants of Plymouth Colony who owned much of the land in central Maine, to survey their territory." The cart bounced again and Maggie instinctively grasped her hand-hold. "Ephraim had some difficulty surveying here, however, since there were hard feelings between the absentee landlords and those who had squatted around 25-Mile Pond, the settlers who cleared the land, and built the homes, schools and churches. In fact, Ephraim and his surveying crew were set upon one night by a group of settlers disguised as Indians. They beat him up and burned his surveying equipment. I guess he can be forgiven for this little mistake that created Sovereign Gore, which, perhaps not coincidentally, was the first area in town to be settled since it's the only section of Sovereign that touches up against Unity Pond."

"I thought you said it was called 25-Mile Pond," Walden interposed.

"Well, that's what the early settlers called the body of water because it was situated twenty-five miles—by water—from Fort Halifax."

"Lake Winnecook," Henry interjected brusquely. "That's the Native American name for Unity Pond. Means 'at the portage' in Abenaki."

Maggie picked up on Henry's thread. "Remember, in those days, waterways served as roads—because there were no land roads. After the Indian Wars ended, a Quaker named Stephen Chase, and his family, set out by bateaux from Fort Halifax in Winslow. They paddled up the Sebasticook River to the outlet of what was known as 25-Mile Stream, and then slogged upstream through the dense underbrush and overgrowth to Lake Winnecook—25-Mile Pond."

"Wow! You are one history machine, Maggie," Walden exclaimed, impressed.

"Machine? Seriously?" Kate retorted, slipping off her light-blue cotton sweater and draping it over her knees.

"Geez, I can't say anything right today! At least, not as far as you're concerned," Nick replied testily to the young woman opposite.

"Try thinking before you speak, why don't you?"

"Children!" said Hannah, clapping her hands to get Walden's and Kate's attention. "You're acting like children. I'm going to have to read you the book, *No Fighting, No Biting* when we get home—if you don't straighten out."

"Sorry," Kate mumbled.

"Yeah, me too," echoed Walden. "Truce?" He held out his rough paw to the sullen young woman. Kate hesitated, and then accepted his peace offering. They shook hands.

Henry, who had been observing the exchange anxiously, visibly relaxed. "So the old-timers like me who settled Sovereign Gore didn't make it, eh?" he asked Maggie, steering the conversation back to its original course. A red-tailed hawk circled low overhead. The falcon caught a current and soared off out of sight over the tall tops of the pines.

"No, unfortunately not," she replied. "When roads were developed and the stagecoach came through those original settlers discovered, too late, they were too far out from civilization. They ended up abandoning their farmsteads, moving closer to town, and starting over. Many others had followed the Chases to 25-Mile Pond, not just Quakers, either, although most of the old brick houses still standing in Unity were built by the children of

Stephen and Hannah Chase. In fact—you probably know this, Hannah—the brick building that houses the Unity Historical Society was built by Lemuel Bartlett for his wife, Hannah Chase, Stephen and Hannah's second daughter, who was an itinerant Quaker minister. Like Martha Ballard, she was another remarkable woman. But that's fodder for another tale. In the meantime, all that's left today as a reminder of the first white settlers to Sovereign are the old stone cellar holes where their houses and barns used to be. I hope you won't be disappointed when we get there."

"I know I won't be disappointed," Hannah said. "Gives me goose bumps just thinking we'll be walking in the footsteps of those early settlers. Poor creatures! Wresting those homesteads from the land, attempting to keep the woods and the wild animals and the bugs at bay—only to discover later they were too far away from town."

"I'm just enjoying the ride," added Walden. "I love to watch Leland work his team. He's a pro." He glanced over at the old woodchopper, who was now clucking and encouraging his sweating beasts. "Looks like the oxen are having a hard time, though. Maybe we should walk up this hill?" The young woodsman directed a meaningful glance at Kate.

"Sure. Why not?" Kate replied. Both young people rose from their respective hay bales and jumped down into the road. To everyone's surprise, the couple set off at a good clip up the hill ahead of the team and wagon, chatting as they hiked in what appeared to be amicable camaraderie.

Wendell scratched his head. "Well, don't thet beat all."

Henry smiled sideways at his wife. "Now, don't get your hopes up, Hannah! She's an incurable matchmaker," he added, for the benefit of the others, quite unnecessarily as everyone but Duncan was familiar with Hannah's penchant for pairing people off.

"Mother Nature is a much more successful matchmaker than I," Hannah replied, good-humoredly. "Ah, smell those dogwood blossoms! Aren't they deliciously sweet? What a wonderful outing! I hope we'll run across a forgotten rose or two when we get to Sovereign Gore. I love old-fashioned roses and the early settlers were known to bring their heirloom roses with them."

"Maybe we should walk," Rebecca said worriedly. "The oxen do seem to be struggling up this hill."

Wendell put his arm around his wife gave her a reassuring squeeze. "I seen Leland's team pull at the Skowhegan Fair and you got nuthin' to worry 'bout. I know how much weight they kin pull."

"Well, I'm certainly not going to walk," Henry declared. He thumped his cane against the wooden floorboards. "My knees are in worse shape than those two oxen."

Suddenly, Maggie decided she would rather walk. "It is a beautiful day for a hike. Why don't I meet everyone up at the Gore? Don't worry if I don't keep up with the wagon. I might linger a bit."

"Walk alone 'n you might git et by a bear," Wendell teased.

"You know very well Wendell Russell that a black bear would turn tail and run the other way if it saw me, even faster than me," she retorted. Maggie stood up and effortlessly let herself down onto the ground. She had spent many years helping Peter hay on their family farm in Winslow and was no stranger to hay wagons. She calculated that a short hike in the delightful verdure of the woods might be just what the doctor ordered. Perhaps she even might be able to find some clarity and peace regarding the situation with Wendell and Rebecca's investment money.

"I'll walk with you," Duncan offered.

Before Maggie could reply, he jumped off the end of the wagon and joined her in the road. She eyed him anxiously to discern whether or not he was experiencing motion sickness and was relieved to see he was fine. "I might not be the best company," she cautioned her future brother-in-law, at the same time waving goodbye to the others as the wagon pulled away from them.

"I'll take my chances." Duncan shaded his eyes from the slanting south-eastern sunlight and watched as the old wooden wagon lurched from side to side. Leland whistled and called to his team, urging the oxen upward. In a minute or two, the wagon crested the hill and disappeared from sight.

Duncan dropped his arm and turned to his companion. "I'm glad you know the way, because I'd be lost out here."

"I'm pretty sure I do, although I haven't been to Sovereign Gore in years," Maggie added honestly. "If all else fails we can always follow the ox droppings."

"Well, I'm not worried. It's a beautiful day for a hike, no matter where we end up. Although we did leave our box lunches on the wagon," he added, ruefully.

Maggie laughed. "Didn't you have a donut?" Jessica Gould, the proprietor of Ma Jean's restaurant, had included a large bag of sugared donuts with the group's order for a dozen box lunches.

"Yes, but that was over an hour ago."

"Well, if we don't catch up with our lunches, I can rustle up something for us to eat, probably mushrooms and wild strawberries this time of year."

"Sounds too good to be true, although I do believe if anyone could forage a feast you could do it, Maggie."

Maggie closed her eyes and tilted her face to the sky. She felt the balmy mid-morning sun against her skin and inhaled the delicious scent of the pines, holding the sweet smell in her lungs for several seconds. When she exhaled she heard the purposeful whistle of a Baltimore oriole. She opened her eyes and craned her neck to search the tops of the tall pines, gesturing excitedly upward when a flash of orange darted between the bristly tree tops. "Did you see the Baltimore Oriole?"

Duncan looked up. "That orange bird?"

"Yes, that's the male. He's probably got a mate nearby. Orioles are one of my favorite birds. They make the most beautiful hanging pouches for nests way up in the tree tops. Every spring I lay out short pieces of string for them to use for their nest-building."

"Do the birds use your string?"

"Most of the time," she replied. "Although I have to keep my eyes peeled pretty sharp to see them take the pieces. It's thrilling to watch when the male oriole comes swooping down and retrieves a strand from my bridal wreath—that's the bush I drape the string over. He carries it off like a prize blue ribbon at the fair. Funny how small things like that can bring one so much joy," she mused.

The two of them began to walk, falling into companionable silence as they observed the antics of the oriole and enjoyed the melodic birdsong. Duncan broke the silence first. "I envy you your life here, Maggie," he said, his voice low with sincere feeling.

"You do?" Maggie immediately thought of Wendell and Rebecca possibly losing their savings because of her failure to act, and inwardly shuddered. "My life isn't as rose-colored as it might seem on the surface. Bad things happen here, just like anyplace else."

"I expect bad things do happen here. Still, I envy the way you and your friends handle your challenges—together."

Hearing this pronouncement, Maggie nearly unburdened herself to him. Duncan seemed so sincere and so trustworthy! Surely if she could tell anyone, she could tell a fellow minister? But somehow she managed to bite her tongue. She had promised Ryan she would say nothing about the situation until the attorney reported back to her with concrete information about Bill Gagnon. She hadn't spoken to Ryan recently, but she knew he would have phoned if he'd uncovered anything. She would keep her promise to Ryan no matter what it cost her in anxious moments. Besides, she should feel anxious and apprehensive. Wasn't she the one who had caused the problem in the first place by her failure to act?

"I also envy your integration with nature," Duncan continued. "It seems so natural, so artless and effortless."

"I'm sorry; I'm not quite following you."

Duncan kicked boyishly at a loose stone in the road. "Promise you won't laugh?"

"Of course I won't laugh at you."

"Well, then—do you think trees are ... sentient?"

"Speak up. Or do you think they're eavesdropping?" she joked.

"You tell me."

Maggie surveyed the host of young saplings that over time had managed to creep away from the thick, deep woods: baby birches, youthful-looking balsams, a stray maple or two. The young seedlings had risen up and now crowded the edges of the road, pushing and jockeying for position. The trees were definitely listening!

"I thought you'd be a good person to ask, since ... since, well, you know."

She understood exactly to what Duncan was alluding. "Since you saw me shaking hands with some of the trees the day we met," she finished for him.

He nodded. "I confess I watched your spontaneity with some envy. When I saw you shake hands with the trees I realized there are many things I don't know—and want to know—because I've been so busy helping others get through their lives that I've forgotten to live myself."

Duncan's words propelled Maggie into a state of thoughtful contemplation. Her step automatically slowed. Likewise, Duncan followed suit.

Certainly, Duncan was nothing like his brother! David would never wonder why she affectionately greeted trees, probably wouldn't even 'see' such an action. But David's twin seemed genuinely interested in her fondness for her rooted companions. But if she related her own experiences to Duncan, how would he be learning his own reality?

"If I tell you what I know—or what I think I know—you'll still be living vicariously through me, won't you?" Maggie pointed out.

"Yes, but ..." he broke off.

She glanced over at him, curious. "But what?"

Duncan gave Maggie a sheepish grin. "I do think I need a leg up here. I'm sixty-two not twenty-two, remember?"

Maggie burst out laughing. "In that case, a good place to start is with Peter Wohlleben's book *The Hidden Life of Trees*. You won't look at a tree the same after reading that book, I guarantee you."

"Did the book change your thinking about trees?"

"I suppose not. Wohlleben rather validated what I had experienced as a child growing up on the farm in Winslow."

"Where's Winslow? I'm not familiar with the different towns and cities in Maine." Duncan kicked away a slightly larger stone, which had been loosened by one of the ox's hooves.

"Winslow is outside of Waterville. Do you remember where that is?"

"That's where Colby College is, right?"

She nodded. "Our family lived about twenty-five miles from here, on the Garland Road in Winslow. I was born into a multi-generational dairy farming family. We all had farms contiguous to each other. At ours, we raised the young stock for my grandparents down the road, who milked a registered herd of Jerseys."

"Sounds like the perfect childhood. What was it like?"

"It *was* perfect. My mother allowed me to run free like one of the wild creatures of the woods. Peter—that's my late husband—he and I explored every nook and cranny of the forest, fields, and meadows along the banks of the Sebasticook River. We didn't see ourselves as separate from the natural world, rather part of it."

"Your mother sounds like an amazing woman, to have allowed you such liberty."

"She died when I was six. Cancer."

Duncan was taken aback. "Such a loss for a little girl!"

"She's buried there in a small cemetery. The Crosby Cemetery," Maggie added thoughtfully. "Not the neighborhood cemetery, where the Walkers and the Hodges—Peter's family—are buried. The Crosby Cemetery is actually several miles away."

"Isn't that rather unusual? Not being buried in the family cemetery?"

"Well, Mother was only a Walker by marriage, not by birth. She always loved the little cemetery in back of our house, the Crosby Cemetery. When she knew she was dying, she asked to be buried there instead of in the bigger, neighborhood burial ground. My father loved her and promised he'd lay her to rest where she wanted. The Crosby Cemetery faces west, on a ridge of land overlooking the Sebasticook River. Mother used to stand there on the ridge gazing into the setting sun, musing aloud how it must have looked to the Native Americans when they saw the first white people sailing up river. I haven't been there in years, but lately I've been thinking about going to visit her again."

"I would if I were you. It's obvious you love the place, too."

"I do. It's one of my favorite places. Such a lovely, peaceful spot! On hot summer afternoons, before she knew she was sick, Mother and I would stroll down the access road to the cemetery. She'd open the iron gate and I'd dart inside and play happily amongst the Crosby headstones. Mother would read her book or sit quietly, reflecting on life, I suppose. Funny, I've been thinking about my mother a lot lately."

"You really should go to visit your mother, then. Tell me more about her," Duncan urged.

"She used to sing and dance around the kitchen as she cooked supper. Mother was so full of joy! Despite the backlash from my father's family, the Walkers, who wanted to tame me up, Mother allowed me to run free. She taught me to love the flowers and the birds and the trees. She had a special affinity for trees in particular. After her death, trees seemed to take a special interest in me, too. I felt as though they were always there to support me whenever I was depressed or offered me a shoulder to cry on whenever I felt lonely. I'm very grateful for the kindness of trees. And now you probably think I'm crazy," Maggie concluded, realizing she had run away with herself.

"Far from it! Shall I tell you a story?" The two of them crested the hill and Duncan halted to tighten the laces on his hiking boot.

"Please do," Maggie encouraged. She paused, politely waiting for him. A variety of green mosses and short grass had crept into that part of the abandoned roadway and felt spongy beneath her feet. She wanted to kick off her sneakers and thrust her toes into the moist warm moss, but resisted the urge, fearful that if she did she wouldn't be able to resist a further urge to throw off her clothes and run naked through the woods. Maggie had a history of appearing in her birthday suit on fine summer afternoons and exceptionally balmy evenings. The naturism began, she realized now, when her mother had occasionally liberated her from her stiff and starched Walker garments as a young child.

Duncan straightened up. He took Maggie's arm and they resumed their stroll. "My wife and I used to walk regularly in a park near our house. After she died I continued to walk there alone. One day I noticed that the trees and bushes appeared to lean out as I passed them by. My first thought was that they were in league with the tick population. But then I noticed the trees weren't leaning down in a threatening manner so much as rather compassionately, as though trying to console me for … for," he broke off.

"For the loss of your wife," Maggie finished for him. She gave his hand an empathetic squeeze. "I lost my husband nearly three years ago. It does get easier, I promise." She dared not look him in the eye, however, lest the thread of eternity, the similarity of the human condition—the pain of loving and losing that love—connect their unspoken thoughts. She experienced in his unsaid words the awful, aching sadness she had felt after Peter's death. How very strange it was that it was David's brother, the minister—and not David, the environmentalist—who shared her special connection with trees!

"The trees take pity on us, I think," she continued in a voice barely above a whisper. She felt like tip-toeing around the topic, so sacred was it to her. "They feel for us because we walk around ignoring them. Trees attempt to reveal a bigger picture, open our eyes to our place in eternity, but most of us never notice the benevolent endeavors of trees because we're too self-absorbed. We hardly spare any attention for the people we love, let alone for these tall queer things that never go anywhere but proudly rise themselves up from the ground. It seemed so obvious to me as a child. How did my father and grandparents not notice that trees were connected with one another and with us? How could they not see the trees stretching up toward the heavens? Or reaching down to comfort us? God only knows we need their comfort, too! We humans have such a limited capacity for understanding the natural world because we think we're separate from it or control it. We see a flaming orange maple tree in the fall and snap a photo to post on Instagram. But we don't care about the tree—the post is just to glorify ourselves, not the One Who Calls Us Into Being. 'See what I've done! See where I am!' the photo cries out, like a wounded deer. Pathetic creatures, that's what we humans are. No wonder trees feel sorry for us," she concluded sadly.

"But if God gave trees the gift of awakening us, I wonder ...?"

"Why does God allow us to sleep? I think we both know the answer to that. So we can escape our pain—until the day comes, and pray God that it does come!—when we can allow ourselves to feel again." Maggie felt a hot tear roll down her cheek before she knew she was crying. Instinctively, she brushed the tear away.

"I'm sorry—I've put a damper on the day," he apologized. "You see what happens when two ministers get together? Our conversation always returns to theology, in this case, the problem of why a loving God allows pain and suffering."

"Please don't apologize. We have a saying in Maine," she said wryly. "'The worse the winter—the more we appreciate the spring.' There's no joy without suffering; no Heaven without Hell. Do you know how I know that?"

"Because you're a minister?"

"Because the trees told me! Now, my pastoral advice to you is that you take two aspirin—a willow bark derivative by the way—hug a tree, and call me in the morning."

"Advice heard and taken!" Much to Maggie's amazement, Duncan immediately released her arm (she hadn't even realized he'd still been holding onto it) and leaped across the ditch. He paused a moment and probed the woods with his eyes as though considering his next move. He singled out a mature oak tree, about twice the diameter of his shoulders, and somewhat awkwardly wrapped his arms around the oak's thick trunk. He gave the tree a poignant hug and then patted the oak on the shoulder. "Thanks, old girl!" Duncan jumped back over the ditch and joined her in the road, proudly and a bit breathlessly. "Mission accomplished," he declared. He brushed some dirt from his pant legs and retrieved Maggie's arm. "Now, let's go find our box lunches!"

Chapter 15
The Crook in the Lot

aggie had prepared her sermon for Sunday well in advance, selecting for her main reading a passage from *A Crook in the Lot—Living with that thorn in your side*, a collection of seven sermons penned by the noted seventeenth century Scottish Puritan pastor, Thomas Boston. Reverend Boston, a self-described "minister of the gospel," was able to clearly and concisely lay out his thoughts on the nature and value of suffering and Maggie intended to expound upon his little treatise. As an ordained Unitarian Universalist minister—and pastor of a Union church—Maggie was not required to follow the Revised Common Lectionary, which provides Bible readings for the liturgical year for ministers to preach upon and is utilized by most mainline Christian churches. Thus she was free to expound upon a topic of her choice. Given unfettered liberty of choice, most preachers will select a subject for their sermon that they most need to hear (whether they are aware of it or not) and Maggie was no exception.

Boston had singled out three Biblical verses to parse in his seven sermons—Ecclesiastes 7:13, Proverbs 16:19, and 1 Peter 5:6—all of which relate to suffering and the ability of God to "make straight that which he hath made crooked." The gist of Boston's message, which was spread out over the seven sermons, is that the cross—or in Boston's case, the thorn in your side—which

God gives us to bear is providently-given, offering humans the opportunity to be humbled, and through this humility experience the love of a personal God. Boston suffered greatly in his own life, living many years with painful kidney stones and a manic and depressed wife; therefore, Boston spoke of what he knew. His personal insight enhanced the power of his sermons.

Maggie believed Boston's message was particularly relevant for the twenty-first century. In point of fact, she considered her own failure to act—to warn Wendell and Rebecca of the potential wolf in their midst—as the current thorn in her side. (She had certainly been afflicted with other thorns in her life, but most of those had long been removed.) Suffering her present thorn—having the knowledge of her failure continually chaffing her mentally and emotionally—she hoped (and even prayed, as Ryan had suggested) that she might be properly humbled. She thought by sharing her story, using general references and not particulars, she might offer an opening to others to view their afflictions in a different light. Instead of "Why me?" Maggie sought to reframe the question to one of: "Yes, me—now, what can I learn from this thorn in my side?" And, more importantly, she offered the prospect that the suffering caused by the thorn might lead one closer to God.

Maggie mentally reviewed the gist of her sermon while waiting for the closing notes of the offering music to die away. When the antiquated pump organ convulsed in its final gasp, she rose and approached the lectern. She folded her hands upon the plush, burgundy-colored cloth Bible holder (the two-hundred-year-old Bible, which had once held the place of honor, was now carefully stored away in her office) and perused the interested and hope-filled faces of her parishioners. The bright mid-morning sun shone through the tall, leaded glass windows, creating a mystical aura in the little white church. Colonnades of light saturated with floating dust particles created the effect of sitting inside a warm, bright snow globe. Sunlight splashed across the white-painted pews, highlighting faces at random. Rebecca's face was one of those brought into relief by the sun and Maggie was grateful to see her neighbor at church. She hoped Rebecca might remember her words this day and understand Maggie was speaking of herself—and had repented.

Two fresh arrangements of blue and yellow iris bedecked the altar and into each bunch Trudy had tucked white sprays of mock orange blossoms. The gentle movement of air from the huge overhead fan in the tall ceiling helped diffuse the heavenly, fruity scent of the mock orange. The candles on the altar flickered. Into the expectant hush the sharp whistle of a cardinal could be heard from a pine tree adjacent to the southern window. Asa Palmer, the local Road Commissioner, twisted around in his seat attempting to catch sight of the blazing red songbird. Shirley gave her husband a sharp elbow to the ribs. "Ow!" Asa cried out and several parishioners tittered. Maggie hid her smile and quickly reached for her reading glasses. She launched into her pastoral message before she lost the attention of her little flock altogether.

As usual, Maggie had difficulty discerning from her parishioners' faces whether or not her sermon was well-received. When she concluded her pastoral message and the closing hymn was sung—and the benediction delivered—she exited the bishop's seat and doused the candles. Maggie walked briskly down the center aisle of the nave, her solemn ankle-length black robe following her. She placed herself at the end of the pews where she could exchange a few words with each parishioner as they left. Hannah, pumping away on the organ, filled the church with the rich harmonic sound of *Abide With Me*, one of the hymns she had selected for the service. Out of the corner of her eye Maggie noted Asa dart away and disappear through the connecting door to the banquet hall, successfully giving Maggie—and his wife—the slip. Several of the ladies had departed prior to the last hymn to set out the goodies for coffee hour. Today, most of the rest of the congregants appeared in no hurry to partake of the refreshments, preferring instead to linger and chat with friends in neighboring pews.

Miss Crump, a ninety-four-year-old maiden lady and a particular friend of Hannah's, reached Maggie first. Under the care of Doctor Bart, Miss Crump's scoliosis and osteoarthritis had greatly improved, thanks in large part to the prescribed medication the impoverished spinster purchased at a great discount from the Songbird Medical Clinic. Nellie had once told her mother that Miss Crump traded chickens and eggs for her medical care. The old lady was still afflicted with a hunchback, however, and leaned heavily upon an old wooden cane as she hobbled forward. Although Maggie didn't know her well, she was aware Miss Crump still drove a car and appeared to live a fairly normal life. She greeted the elderly woman with boisterous good humor. "How are you today, Miss Crump?" she inquired loudly, instinctively bending down closer to the frail, hunched frame.

Miss Crump stuck out her neck and accosted Maggie, reminding her of a majestic old snapping turtle. "I ain't deaf," retorted the spinster. "Ye don't have to shout."

"Sorry—force of habit," Maggie apologized, offering her hand. Miss Crump passed her cane to her left hand and grasped Maggie's outstretched member with a knobby claw. Maggie lightly pressed the older woman's arthritic hand, which felt hot and dry to her touch.

"'Tain't no matter. 'Tis better to shriek than to speak so soft a body cain't hear ye," Miss Crump allowed in a more congenial fashion. "'Twas a fine sermon ye gave today, Pastor." (Miss Crump always addressed Maggie as "Pastor" or "Minister," rather than by her given name, which Maggie suspected Miss Crump had long forgotten. Or, more likely, since the spinster had lived through so many different ministers, Miss Crump no longer bothered to remember the name of each one.) The nonagenarian was dressed neat-as-a-pin per usual in a long denim skirt and starched white blouse over which she wore a dark-blue button-up cardigan. Her white hair was wrapped in braids and coiled around her head, and her feet were encased in black leather lace-up boots. A direct descendant of early English settlers, Miss Crump looked and acted the part. Her speech was sprinkled with remnants of an earlier dialect.

"Thank you," Maggie replied, surprised and not a little pleased at the compliment. "I'm glad you liked my pastoral message."

"I guess ye could say I've got my own thorn to bear." The spinster indicated her Dowager's hump with a little back thrust of her silvered head. "'Twas good to hear the Lord has a purpose for my hunchback. I always thought might be so, but could nevah figger out what thet purpose was. Ye spoke to my condition clearly. 'Tis a fact I've been brought low by my thorn many a time, which the Good Lord knew I needed. I've always hed a mighty good opinion of myself, you see. So I'm grateful to ye for the illumination today."

Maggie was smote by a wave of contrition. She had been magnifying the weight of her latest thorn (such a small thorn, too!) when Miss Crump had borne her burden in silence for years, perhaps decades! Although the elderly lady regularly attended church, Maggie, in all the years she had lived in Sovereign, had never been to her house for a visitation. When she first arrived in town, she was warned that Miss Crump had a reputation for being a curmudgeon. Unfortunately, she had bought into that epithet and as a result, the spinster had never been a favored member of Maggie's flock. Feeling guilty, she immediately offered restitution. "Miss Crump, are you going to be home later this afternoon?"

Miss Crump tottering a bit, clutched at a pew back with her left hand to steady herself. "Ayuh, I'll be to home. I'd like to know who would take care o' my chickens if-en I ain't?"

"Would you like a visit? I'd love to drop by."

Miss Crump eyed Maggie warily. "Don't git many visitors, 'cept Hannah, course. Ye got a mind to lecture me?"

"No, no," Maggie assured the elderly lady hastily. "I just thought I'd visit with you a while—if you don't mind." She floated the idea in her mind of mentioning Miss Crump's thorn as a possible topic of conversation, but decided against it. If the older woman needed to talk about her condition, Maggie would listen. She had learned the hard way in her ministry that to offer advice when none was sought was akin to such mean offenses as beating one's dog or borrowing a neighbor's lawn mower without his permission.

Miss Crump loosened her grip on the pew. She appeared pleased at the notion of a pastoral call. "Wal, now, Hannah brung me a fresh supply o' Needhams yestiddy 'n I'd be pleased to share the chocolates wi' ye ovah a cup o' tea. 'Tis a good day for ye to come, too, since the trucks don't run to Sunday."

"Trucks?" Maggie inquired, unsure as to what Miss Crump was referring.

"Dump trucks. 'Tis how we earns our keep, me 'n Abraham. I sells gravel. Most days I sit to home in my rocker 'n count on my clicker the loads they hauls out o' my pit."

"I'm sorry, I've forgotten—is Abraham one of your relatives?"

"Ha! Abraham's me cat. Afore he settled down permanently w' me, Abraham sired a tribe o' felines in the neighborhood. Thet's how he come to git his handle. Course I had him altered, after thet."

"Wise idea! By the way, I didn't know you owned a gravel pit?"

"Ye would have known, Pastor, had ye made a call earlier," Miss Crump chastised, with a satisfied gleam in her dark eye. She thumped her cane against the burgundy carpet as if to emphasize her glee. "Been sellin' gravel fer nigh onto thutty years. Every Tuesday the fellars come to pay me in cash fer what they took out the prior week. They knows I keep count so's most the time they air right on the money."

"I bet they are!" Maggie had no difficulty picturing Miss Crump sitting in her rocker by the kitchen window keeping a close eye on all the dump trucks coming and going. "Would four o'clock this afternoon be a good time to visit?"

"'Tis fine if ye don't mind Abraham beggin' fer his suppah."

"I don't mind—I love cats. I can't wait to meet Abraham." Maggie pressed the spinster's hand again. "See you around four."

Miss Crump favored Maggie with a smile. "'Twill be good to have a pastor call on me agin," she declared. For the second time, the maiden lady's words smote Maggie's heart. Obviously, Maggie's predecessor (or perhaps predecessors, in the plural!) at the Sovereign Union Church had made a regular habit of calling on Miss Crump. Why had she ever allowed her mind to be tainted by the negative opinions of others?

After Miss Crump moved past, Maggie greeted several other parishioners, exchanging civilities with each one. Her observations were commonplace, however, as her mind kept reverting to the spinster's disclosure. Miss Crump sold gravel? Why, in Maine sand and gravel were nearly as valuable as gold! Maggie thought of the elderly lady bartering chickens and eggs for her medical care and wondered if Doctor Bart was aware of the financial situation of his patient. But then, perhaps Maggie was reading too much into the elderly woman's words? Perhaps Miss Crump only sold enough gravel to pay the taxes on her house and gravel pit? Maggie wondered if Bill Gagnon had called on the spinster and felt a moment's panic at the thought. What if the shady financial advisor had gotten his hands on Miss Crump's cash, as he had Wendell and Rebecca's? Woe would betide them all if Maggie discovered the stockbroker had finagled his way into the trust of Sovereign's most vulnerable citizens!

Then she recollected where Miss Crump lived, in an out-of-the-way hamlet on the far side of town near Black Brook. She thought it unlikely Bill Gagnon would ever have ventured out on such a back road. Nevertheless, Maggie made a mental note to give Miss Crump a heads-up about the financial representative during her pastoral call that afternoon.

Henry came down the aisle with Kate in tow. He shook Maggie's hand and offered his customary compliment on her sermon in his brusque manner. Then her neighbor departed to collect Hannah from the organ. Kate lingered, appearing to want to speak with the minister further. Maggie smiled and held out her hand. "Good to see you again today, Kate. I hope you enjoyed yourself on our little outing Thursday?"

Kate accepted Maggie's proffered handshake. "Sure. It was fun."

Kate continued to chat, but Maggie's attention was instantly diverted by the watch on the young woman's wrist. Upon surreptitious inspection, she was shocked to discover the timepiece was her grandmother's gold watch! She had been missing the valuable heirloom for some time now and had looked everywhere for the watch, racking her brain for where she could have misplaced it. Had Henry's pride and joy stolen her watch? Perish the thought!

Maggie was all too familiar with Kate's spotted history, of course. Still, she cautioned herself against jumping to conclusions. She couldn't infer the young woman was guilty of theft just because she had been charged with theft before. After all, Kate had been caught shoplifting when still a teenager (as many teenagers do, unfortunately), and she had never been formally charged in the most recent fracas with the missing LL Bean boots. Maggie focused on her breathing, trying to steady herself. She would not allow prejudice to color her thinking again. Surely there was a good explanation for how Kate had ended up with the watch? Maggie forced herself to listen to what the young woman was saying in the hope of learning more.

"We found some cool stuff in that old cellar hole, too. Nick dug up some white clay pipes and a glass mug. The mug is chipped, but he says the glass is amethyst. He's going to put the mug in his kitchen window and says the sun will turn it purple. What do you think?"

"If the glass is amethyst, the glass should turn color," Maggie agreed, attempting to keep her voice even and well-modulated so Kate would suspect nothing was wrong.

Kate absently toyed with the watch, twisting the gold band around and around on her wrist. "How well do you know Nick, Mrs. Hodges?" she spoke up suddenly.

Maggie was startled by the question. She had thought that the two young people disliked one another. Now, however, she wasn't sure but what the opposite might be true. "I know him very well. Nick is an honest, sincere young man," she replied, choosing her words carefully. "He's also very sensitive, as you've probably discovered."

"Oh, yeah—I noticed! Me too. I'm sensitive, too. Not that I go around reading poetry like he does," she amended hastily.

"Walden does have a fondness for Emily Dickinson. Did he quote some of Emily's poems yesterday? It would be just the thing Nick would do on such a wonderful day."

A smile spread over the young woman's face. Maggie, who was observing Kate closely, was surprised by how pretty she was. Why had she never noticed the young woman's looks before? Was it because she had only 'seen' Kate colored by the reputation that had preceded her? Was she as guilty with Kate as she had been with Miss Crump? Good Lord!

"Nick quoted me the one about roaming in Sovereign's woods," Kate replied shyly. "He told me that's how he came to be here—he followed Emily's poem to Sovereign."

"I know that one—it's one of Nick's favorite poems."

"Don't you think Nick is awfully brave? I mean, how many men—especially as macho-looking as he is— go about reciting poetry?"

"Not enough men, that's for sure! I do think Nick is very brave. He's a true Original." Too late, Maggie wondered whether it was a wise idea to encourage the pairing of Kate and Walden. Would it be good for the two young people to get together if Kate still had mental health problems that resulted in her stealing? Abruptly, she dismissed these negative thoughts. She was all done acting upon unfounded prejudice. "You couldn't find a better young man than Walden," Maggie declared. "If you're asking me in a roundabout way what I think about him as a potential boyfriend, I say—go for it." To reinforce her words, she gave the girl a quick hug. All smiles, Kate departed.

Duncan, who had been hanging back until Maggie had greeted her parishioners, came forward to shake her hand. "Nicely done," he said, as the young woman exited the church in pursuit of her grandfather and Hannah. "I don't know what you said to Kate, but obviously your words hit their mark."

"It was nothing. Just a little girl talk."

"Hmm. Girl talk? I won't press you for particulars, then. Instead, I'll compliment you on your sermon. By the way, Boston's little book is one of my favorites. Nice choice. But ... " Duncan paused, as though searching for the right words.

"But you would have followed the Lectionary," Maggie finished for him.

"I would have followed the Lectionary, yes. But I wasn't going to say that. I was going to say I wouldn't have expounded upon Boston's work half as well as you did."

Maggie felt her face grow warm, not because of the compliment—although coming from a fellow pastor the compliment was very flattering—but because once again she had jumped to the wrong conclusion. When would she ever learn!

"*Abide With Me* was one of my mother's favorite hymns, too," he continued, giving Maggie time to recover from her blunder. "Mother was music director of our church, even though she never officially joined the Episcopal Church. She remained a Baptist all her life."

"Your mother was a Baptist?" Maggie asked, surprised. "And your father was an Episcopal minister?"

"Yes, Mother was a Bible-thumping, hymn-singing, old-fashioned Baptist. Her father was a Baptist minister, you see. She used to tell us about the Thursday evening prayer meetings she attended when she was a child. She was the only young person there because she tagged along with my grandfather. The meetings began with fifteen or twenty minutes of quite enthusiastic hymn-singing. Mother loved the songs so well she naturally brought the hymns she loved into Dad's rather staid church. He tried to subdue her, subtly of course, but Mother stuck to her guns. As Music Director she was in charge of picking the hymns every Sunday and she always selected songs like *Brighten the Corner Where You Are* and *The Old Rugged Cross*. She sang when she played, too, rolling her 'r's like an Irishman—'Brrrrighten the corner where you arrre!'—to make a point about the joy and enthusiasm one should feel when worshipping God. I grew up believing Mother saved as many souls with her music as Father did with his sermons."

"She probably did. And yet you became an Episcopal minister rather than a Baptist?"

Duncan shrugged good-naturedly. "Like father, like son, I guess." He glanced around the now empty church. "Speaking of which—does my brother never attend? I'm sorry; I see I've embarrassed you again," he added apologetically, as Maggie's face reddened for a second time.

Despite Maggie's embarrassment, she felt compelled to excuse David's conduct to his brother. "He does come to church sometimes. All the little old ladies love him, of course. Sometimes adulation is too much of a good thing, though, and lately, David has found other things to do on Sunday."

"I'm sorry to hear that, but I'm not surprised. David never was a regular church-going guy."

"That's exactly what he told me!"

"I've always presumed my brother's Temple was the woods and that nature was his God."

"That's probably a fair assessment. To each his own," Maggie remarked, feigning nonchalance she didn't feel. Personally, she was saddened by the fact that David didn't share her enthusiasm for her calling.

The two of them were standing in one of the colonnades of light and Duncan, becoming warm, unbuttoned his navy blazer and loosened his tie. "And you're OK with that?" he asked. "With David doing his thing and you doing your thing?"

His question hit a sore spot and Maggie bristled. "Why shouldn't I be OK with that?" she replied, clutching her hymnal tighter under her left arm. "As long as David and I respect and support each other's calling, our relationship shouldn't suffer." As soon the words were out of her mouth, she mentally kicked herself for her misrepresentation of the truth. She supported David's career; however, she had grave doubts about his respect for and support of her chosen vocation.

"Good for you! By the way, before I escort you to coffee hour—which I see everyone has abandoned us for—I want to thank you for including me on the outing Thursday. You have no idea what a joy and pleasure it is for me to spend time with people like Wendell and Rebecca. I especially appreciate your friend Leland."

"Leland?" Maggie repeated, surprised. She was reminded of David's disdain for the octogenarian woodchopper and thought at first that Duncan was pulling her leg. Further perusal of his open and honest face, however, revealed how unworthy that suspicion was.

"Leland is so real, so down-to-earth. He's so ... *himself*—if you know what I mean."

"I do know," Maggie replied, warmly. This was exactly what she felt about Leland!

"Where I come from there aren't many opportunities for meeting people like him who are just as they were born to be. There's so much posturing and grandstanding, and trying to pull the wool over one another's eyes. Or even sadder, pulling the wool over one's own eyes. How difficult it is to be ourselves, as nature intended us to be!"

"Painfully difficult!"

"Leland's tall tales crack me up, too. They're— how do you say it in Maine?—they're 'wicked funny'."

She chuckled at Duncan's lame attempt to imitate a Mainer. "You'll be one of us soon, if you're not careful," she joked.

His hazel eyes shone with pleasure. "That would make me happy—very happy—to be accounted as one of you."

Maggie found Duncan's unaffected straightforwardness delightful and charming. He was so natural, so sincere. Gone was the solemnity that weighted him down when he first arrived in Sovereign. The Episcopal minister had been replaced by a fun-loving and hope-filled man. When he smiled, Maggie was arrested by the frankness and ingenuousness of his gaze. His sparkling hazel eyes invited her to wade deeper and deeper into their warm and welcoming depths.

Suddenly, she was alive to the primitive intimacy of the moment. He was a man; she was a woman. They were standing so close together that her eyes soaked up every detail of his face, from the scar just below his left eyebrow to the short dark hairs that crept down the nape of his neck, tempting her eyes to follow them. She found his musky scent slightly arousing. The warm sunlight cocooned the two of them, shining as it did through the church windows, further intensifying their physical and spiritual connection. Her senses extraordinarily heightened, Maggie thought she discerned faint strains of a waltz in the distance, although the old pump organ had long since fallen silent. She felt like a swimmer wading into a warm ocean. The silken water was intensely pleasurable and gratifying, tempting her to dive in and refresh herself in Duncan's being.

Warning bells went off in Maggie's head. She tore her eyes away from his face. Her breathing felt labored. Horrified, she realized what she had been about to do—she had been about to caress her fiancée's brother!

Shocked, dismayed, and abashed, Maggie jerked away from Duncan. Her hymnal slipped out from under her arm and the heavy purple book landed on the carpeted floor with a little thud, startling them both.

Duncan immediately bent to retrieve the hymnal. "Are you OK?" he asked, concerned. "When did you last have something to eat?"

"I ate breakfast at five o'clock," Maggie replied meekly. She studiously avoided looking directly into his eyes, more afraid of what her gaze would reveal to herself than to him.

"That settles it—to the cookies and coffee we go!"

Duncan placed the hymnal on one of the burgundy pew cushions and took Maggie by the arm. He steered her in the direction of the banquet hall. She was greatly relieved to note that her future brother-in-law acted as natural as ever with her. Hopefully, he hadn't noticed her near faux pas. The erotic sensibility she had experienced must have been one-sided, felt by her only. No doubt her emotional hiccup had been caused by the fact that Duncan was a near duplicate of his brother. Maggie was sure—or thought she was sure—she had simply mistaken Duncan for David, which would explain why she felt so comfortable with him. She made a mental note to be more careful with David's twin in the future. This could never, ever happen again!

Chapter 16
The Yearning

Every Monday Maggie volunteered at the Songbird Medical Clinic, giving her daughter a half-day off to run errands. She worked alongside Doctor Bart, her son-in-law, whom she had known since infancy and whose kindness, thoughtfulness, and patience she greatly respected. The non-profit clinic had been a dream of Metcalf's since he was a young man, having grown up in a poor area in central Maine and witnessing the effects of poverty upon the health and wellbeing of his friends and family. He had shared his dream with Sovereign's beloved music teacher, Miss Hastings, who was one of his favorite patients. Upon Miss Hastings' death several years ago, Doctor Bart was amazed to discover that not only had Miss Hastings bequeathed him most of her estate, but also she had left him her antique cottage with its attached music studio—specifically for the purpose of starting his clinic. Nellie had helped him get the free clinic off the ground, and after they were married she continued to work shoulder to shoulder with her husband, who was also employed part-time by a larger medical clinic in nearby Unity.

This particular morning proved uneventful at the clinic, for which Maggie was grateful. Three appointments, all follow-ups, had been scheduled in advance and passed without complications. In addition, there were two walk-ins with typical summer issues: one a bee sting and the other poison ivy. Metcalf was finishing up treating the bee sting when Nellie returned early from Waterville. After putting her groceries away in the kitchen, she made her way into the clinic section of their little home. The parlor of the cottage had been turned into the waiting area, and the music room, where Nellie herself had once taken piano lessons, was transformed into two exam rooms.

"Did I miss anything serious?" Nellie asked her mother, as she rifled through the charts and papers on the old mahogany desk, which had once belonged to Miss Hastings' father, superintendent of the town's old corn canning factory, which was now a museum.

"Not a thing, unless you consider Marybeth Kidd's case of poison ivy serious." Maggie relinquished the desk chair and Nellie immediately sat down and made herself at home. "Michelle brought her in. Apparently, Marybeth had been 'helping' her father weed his vegetable gardens."

"Poor thing! She's only four, isn't she? I hope Tom took the opportunity to show his daughter the difference between weeds and poison ivy?"

"I doubt it, knowing Tom." Maggie regretted her words the instant they left her mouth. There had been some negative history between the Organic Kidd, as Tom was locally known, and one of Maggie's favorite people, Lila Woodsum Hobart, who now lived up north with her little family. Still, Maggie shouldn't conclude that Kidd was a bad parent as a result. "I take that back. I'm sure Tom's a good father."

"I think he is. He usually brings the kids in. He even brought the children in for their shots. It was so funny. Tom was more afraid of the needle than they were and almost passed out!"

Maggie chuckled at the notion of the rough-cut Tom Kidd fainting at the sight of a needle. "I guess we

236

don't really know someone until we walk a mile in their shoes, do we? Speaking of knowing people," she continued, dropping her voice confidentially. Maggie glanced over at the closed exam room door to ensure her son-in-law wasn't able to overhear their conversation. "I had an interesting visit with Miss Crump at her place yesterday afternoon."

Nellie glanced up from her busywork. "You went to see Miss Crump? I'm so glad. She's one of our favorite people."

Maggie was taken aback by this remark. "I thought you disliked Miss Crump? You told me once she was a grouch."

"Oh, that was years ago, Mom!" Nellie protested, laughing. "I was afraid of her at first, I admit. But now that I know her I think she's a wonderful person. She's lived a remarkable life and is such an inspiration! She keeps going, no matter what. Despite her handicap, Miss Crump doesn't let anything—or anyone—hold her back. I hope I'm half as strong and brave as she is when I'm ninety-four!"

Maggie placed her hand over her heart. "I swear I will change my assessment of Miss Crump immediately. And if the truth be known, I was already changing my opinion of her. She impressed me yesterday. She was very kind, offering me tea and some of Hannah's Needhams. I was surprised to see how neat and clean her house was, too. And she obviously dotes on that cat."

"Oh, yes! She loves Abraham. But I think Metcalf runs a close second. She and he have a thing going. You'd never know Miss Crump is fond of Metcalf, however, for some of the things she says to him. But she's only teasing and I'm sure Metcalf returns her affection. I know he does, actually, because he's told me so more than once. We're very grateful for what she's done for the clinic."

"What has Miss Crump done for the clinic?" Maggie inquired carelessly. "Besides give you a few chickens and a couple of dozen eggs!" Although the clinic was free, Doctor Bart and Nellie accepted donations of money and other types of gifts to help defray the operating expenses.

Nellie rearranged several papers on the desk. She thought a moment before replying. "Well, I know you'll keep this in confidence, Mom, if I ask you ….?"

"Of course I will."

"Last year Miss Crump gave the Clinic $100,000."

"You're not serious!"

"Quite serious. Metcalf happened to mention to her one day when she was here for a follow-up appointment that we were having difficulty keeping the doors open. She went right home and brought him back a personal check for $100,000. She told him to let her know if he needed more, too, because she said she had plenty more where that came from. Apparently, Miss Crump is very rich."

Maggie processed this piece of information slowly. "Miss Crump told me she sold gravel," she replied thoughtfully. "But if she's so rich, why does she pay for her treatment with chickens and eggs?"

"I know! Confusing, isn't it? It took me a while, but I finally think I have the answer to that riddle. It's because that's how Miss Crump was raised. Remember, she was a teenager during the Depression and apparently her family suffered horribly. She was brought up to think an outlay of cash was tantamount to an outlay of blood, and was taught to barter whenever possible. I think she's proud of her reputation for Yankee thrift, too. Miss Crump's parsimony is more important to her than the actual money. She might be tight, but she's not at all stingy. Since her donation to the clinic, I've learned how generous she's been with many others in town over the

years. Aunt Hannah told me that before she married
Henry she often had difficulty paying her real estate taxes
and Miss Crump would give her the money for them, as a
supposed loan, of course, although they both knew Aunt
Hannah could never pay it back. I don't think I'll be
betraying too much if I tell you Miss Crump had no
difficulty taking Henry's money, however, when he
offered to reimburse her the balance due after he and
Hannah were married. She took the cash, naturally."

Maggie was impressed by Nellie's admiration for
the elderly lady. She was proud of her daughter for having
discerned Miss Crump's true nature where she had failed
to do so. At least she had done something right! She had
raised a benevolent and high-minded daughter. "You
paint her character so clearly, Nellie. You're obviously
very fond of her."

"She's one of my favorite people. If I've ever said
anything to make you think badly of Miss Crump, Mom,
let me correct that error now."

"Well, not only will I never think badly of Miss
Crump again, I'll try not to think badly of anyone else,
either. I've been making so many pig-headed mistakes
judging people lately! 'Judge not that ye be not judged'
should be my new motto."

Nellie's eyes dropped to the papers in front of
her. "Is David one of those mistakes?" she asked casually.

Her daughter's question startled Maggie. She sat
up straighter on the edge of the desk. "What makes you
say that?"

"I haven't heard you talk much about him lately.
And David didn't appear very thrilled at your engagement
dinner, either. Is anything wrong between you two?
Maybe I shouldn't ask," Nellie added hastily.

"No, no. You have a right to ask, dear. The
problem is—I don't know how to answer you. Something
is wrong with our relationship, although I can't put my

239

finger on it." Not wanting to worry her daughter, however, Maggie attempted to downplay her concerns. "But maybe it's nothing more than pre-marital jitters. You know how those are!"

Surprised, Nellie allowed the pen to slip from her hand and it clattered against the hard mahogany. "You've set a date for the wedding?"

"What? No, I didn't mean to imply that. We haven't even talked about setting a date yet. I guess neither of us is in a hurry to get married."

"I'm glad to hear that," Nellie said, obviously relieved.

Maggie felt slightly irritated at this pronouncement from her daughter. Wasn't Nellie one of the ones—along with Rebecca—who had pushed her into a relationship with David? And now Nellie was glad to hear they hadn't set a date for the wedding? What was going on with her daughter?

"I thought you liked David?" Maggie said. "Weren't you the one who told me to follow my heart, that Uncle Peter would want me to be happy?"

"I do like David and I do want you to follow your heart. But ... don't you feel that things have changed, now? Ever since ..." Nellie broke off abruptly, leaving an incomplete thought dangling in air like a worm dangling in water above a hungry fish.

"Ever since what?" Maggie demanded.

"Never mind. It's not my place to suggest whether or not you should love someone—or who you should love."

Never mind. Never more. Her daughter's words struck a chord, revealing to Maggie's conscious mind the deep yearning that had been silently burned within her heart like red-hot coal. But ... for what was she yearning? To what—or whom—should she look to satisfy this unfulfilled longing? To fill this hungry hole?

In the few years since Peter's death Maggie had sought relief in nature, in her sweet little home, and in the time she spent with friends and family. Now she knew that wasn't enough. She wanted more. She needed more.

For some reason, Edgar Allan Poe's poem *The Raven* popped into her head, as it had done unexpectedly back in February when she had been scrutinizing the activity of her Corvidae pair from the comfort of her kitchen rocker. David had been present, she remembered, because he had been sitting in the spot where Peter had died. Was it possible the yearning was her unrequited desire for a soul mate? Was she longing for someone to love and cherish even as he would love and cherish her?

Maggie recollected how she had envied the ravens their affection for one another that winter's day. The birds had seemed so content with one another!

Back into the chamber turning,
All my soul within me burning,
Soon again I heard a tapping,
Something louder than before,
"Surely," said I, "surely,
That is something at my window lattice.
Let me see, then, what thereat is,
And this mystery explore.
Let my heart be still a moment,
And this mystery explore.
" 'Tis the wind, and nothing more."

All my soul within me burning. Was David the answer for the yearning in her soul? Would he satisfy the longing? Did she truly love him—love him as a soulmate?

Maggie knew she admired David. Maybe she loved him on some level. But ... her soul didn't yearn for him, nor did her heart burn for him.

She frowned as the truth began to percolate up into her consciousness. Abruptly, she pushed the truth back down. Now was not the place or time to see it! She must go home where, alone, in the safety of her little cottage, she could take the unvarnished truth out and examine it with all its warts. Then she could think about what she must do—if anything.

Nellie placed a hand on her mother's arm. "Is everything OK? You're pretty quiet all of a sudden."

"What? Oh, I'm fine, dear," Maggie replied. She arose from the desk. "In fact, I just remembered something I need to do this afternoon. I have to run."

"Aren't you going to wait and say goodbye to Metcalf? He can't be much longer with ..." Nellie glanced down at the appointment calendar, "... with Shirley."

"No, I need to go. Say goodbye to him for me." Maggie gave her daughter a quick hug and kiss. "I'll see you soon, dear. Don't worry—everything's fine."

Once home in the security of her kitchen, Maggie poured herself a frosty glass of herbal iced tea. Although the mid-July day was characteristically warm—eighty-eight degrees in the sun—she had closed the windows and pulled the shades before leaving home so the country kitchen was cool. She didn't want to sit in the dark, however, so she took her drink out back under the old apple tree where she often sat and reflected on life and where the temperature was ten degrees cooler in the shade. In addition, a dry northwest breeze blew up from the pond making the site a delightful place to seek repose.

She broke off some fresh horsemint growing in one of her herb gardens and stuck the stiff, square stem of the sweet herb into her tea. Her back lawn had been nearly taken over by various herb and perennial gardens, but there remained a small section of lush, spongy grass in which Maggie liked to dip her toes. She kicked off her sandals and placed the frosty glass down upon the little white end table. She stretched her toes in the grass luxuriously and then settled herself into her padded lawn chair. She closed her eyes and relaxed, listening to the soothing purring of the gray tree frogs, which emanated from the tall mixed hardwoods nearby. Several songbirds sang out their musical melodies and the "rhuum" of a bullfrog added a bass to the disparate chorus. The tall, stalky valerian root with its frothy, white blooming head, reminded her of the sixties model Twiggy. The herb's florets issued a sweetly pungent scent and Maggie drank in all the fragrances, inhaling deeply the refreshing essence of her flowers and herbs.

She held her breath for as long as she could, and then exhaled slowly. Ah, this was felicity! This was life at its fullest!

Why wasn't this enough? This—and a relationship with David? What woman could possibly long for more?

Since the debacle more than a quarter century ago with Nellie's father, who had abandoned her pregnant and penniless, Maggie had jettisoned her dream of finding a soulmate. She berated herself back then for building castles in the air, assuring herself that such silly dreams existed only in fairy tales. True, she had loved Peter—had always loved him since the first time she'd seen him as an insecure little boy waiting for the bus—but she had never felt for Peter the passionate heart-pounding, waves crashing on the beach kind of love like Heathcliff and Catherine felt for one another in Emily Bronte's *Wuthering Heights*. She had never sensed that Peter completed her. She and Peter had been partners, good friends, and lovers. Surely, if there had been more to love, they would have found it? Wouldn't they have?

Now, while she certainly didn't feel raging passion for David, she did enjoy spending time with him. Her lack of passion could be easily attributed to her post-menopausal state. But what about *his* lack of passion?

Perhaps that could also be attributed to age? Perhaps David had physical difficulties with sex and was embarrassed to speak of it?

Not for the first time Maggie wondered why David had asked her to marry him. Was the spur-of-the-moment proposal really due to such a simple thing as her being able to identify blue salamander eggs? Would a confirmed bachelor change the course of an independent life for something so silly? Probably he had already realized his mistake and regretted the offer. Perhaps he was hanging back, keeping aloof, hoping that she would recognize the mistake and break their engagement so he wouldn't have to do it?

And why had she agreed to marry him? Was it because she had been flattered by David's proposal? Because he was a world-renowned environmentalist? Or was it that he had proposed to her at a time in her life when she felt vulnerable, lonely, and desirous of a helpmate?

Maggie's hand shook slightly as she reached for another drink of iced tea. A Great Blue Skimmer landed on the sweet Williams in the perennial garden in front of her, which was then in multi-color bloom—hot pinks, bright whites, deep burgundies—but she didn't notice the bold, beautiful flowers. Instead, her eyes remained glazed over, her vision obscured by thoughtful fog. When a second dragonfly zipped past her nose and joined the first, however, she awoke. Her eyes followed the darting dragonfly that joined his mate and fell on the bower of blooms. Such beauty! And all hers for the pleasure and enjoyment—hers and the darning needles!

Observing the dragonflies reminded Maggie of how much she enjoyed going on natural outings with David, adventures such as rabbit hunting and counting frogs' eggs. But then, she had always enjoyed being out-of-doors. When the two of them were at home together—alone—things definitely took an awkward turn. It seemed to her as though neither knew where to look, then. And when they did talk, they never said anything meaningful. In fact, Maggie couldn't remember a single conversation in which she shared with David either a joy or a concern. The closest she had come to confiding in him had been when she had told David her fears about Bill Gagnon making off with Wendell and Rebecca's nest egg. And then, he had dismissed her concern out of hand!

Why was she going to marry David?

Good grief! Was she—*settling*? Settling for a man whose work she admired, but whose person she didn't really love!

A chipmunk rustled some dead leaves nearby. He peeped out from a blanket of stiff brown oak leaves considering his next move. "You're safe," Maggie assured the little creature. "I'm too wrapped up in my own concerns to think of you." Despite her assurance, the chipmunk disappeared back into the nest of dead leaves and from this safe harbor began an incessant monotonous chipping.

Irritated, Maggie rebuked the chipmunk. "I'm not leaving. Get over it." Abruptly, the creature quit.

Once the chipmunk was silenced, it seemed to Maggie as though a screen had been removed from her eyes and she was face to face with the truth: she didn't love David! Not in the way a woman should love a man, and especially the way a wife should love her husband. She liked him and respected him for his work—and even admired him a great deal—but beyond that her affection for her fiancée was of a garden variety fondness. Why, the love she felt for him was more like that of a sister for a brother, than a woman for a lover!

Without warning, a face similar to David's—but to her mind very different—popped into her head. It was a shaven face, less tanned and more gaunt than David's, with a set of sparkling hazel eyes so unlike his brother's that it was hard to believe she had once thought the two of them looked alike. Strange how these two twins could be so alike and yet so dissimilar! How could that be possible?

She would much rather spend time with Duncan than with David, she realized. She and he had much more in common.

Idly, Maggie began to contemplate what might have happened had she met Duncan first. Wondering this, a bright light illuminated her soul. The light was carried on unseen wings like a runner carrying a pine pitch torch up the mountaintop on a moonless night. She felt very fluid, as though her body had become one with the water of which it was made. A thrill of hope rose up from the depths of her being, shooting to the surface like a divine thread tugging her in a new direction, out of the maelstrom of the deep and into the peaceful water of the shallows.

No! She could not allow this to happen. Too many lives would be affected!

Maggie flipped a mental switch and an internal mechanism instantly shut down her giddy fantasy. She berated herself for her childish foolishness. She must live in the real world, the world as it was, taking her lumps as they came. She couldn't trifle with hearts as though they were a child's toy, plastic and throwaway, simply because she was lonely, confused, and maybe even a bit bored with her life at sixty. What kind of woman was she!

Maggie, forcing herself to be practical and pragmatic, realized she needed to break her engagement with David as soon as possible. Calling it off was the right thing to do. Neither she nor he would be happy in a marriage together, she was sure of that.

Before she lost her nerve, Maggie picked her up cell from the white lawn table and dialed David's number.

246

The phone rang three times and defaulted to voicemail. Maggie wasn't sure what to say, so she rushed out a breathless, "We need to talk," and hung up. She probably shouldn't have said anything. Nobody ever said "we need to talk" nowadays unless he or she was thinking of ending a romantic relationship. Well, at least David would know she had something important to say to him. Maggie knew she needed to be painfully honest with her fiancée, at least about the not loving him as a husband part. What happened after that was anybody's guess.

She was not going to chase after chimeras, or *ignis fatuus*. She had been down that road before with Nellie's father and had gotten her heart broken. Certainly, she didn't need to repeat that experience!

The set of sparkling hazel eyes slipped up into her consciousness a second time. Maggie pushed the haunting eyes back down, but not before lingering a moment to gaze fondly upon the sweet face that harbored them. She must be careful not to break *his* heart, either.

Chapter 17
Detective at the Door

Maggie's musings were brought to an abrupt end by the loud clanging of the old cast-iron school bell, which was attached to the shed next to the door. She sighed and arose from her lawn chair, slipping her feet into her sandals. The bell clanged again, louder this time, and Maggie realized the caller meant serious business. She hurried inside, hoping it wasn't a salesperson interrupting her for no better reason than to try and sell her a vacuum cleaner!

A middle-aged man wearing nondescript business attire stood on her doorstep, his back to her. At the sound of the shed door opening, he turned around. "Mar-gar-rett Hod-jez?" he asked, in a thick Acadian accent.

Maggie, who always had difficulty understanding Maine's French-speaking Acadians, felt unreasonably irritated with the man. "Yes?" she replied in what she hoped was a discouraging tone.

"Pardon me for interrupting. I am Detective Adrien Bérubé with the Maine State Police. May I come in? I have some kest-tions for you." He fished an identification badge from an interior pocket and held the photo ID out to her.

Maggie felt the shock as though she had unexpectedly grasped a live electric fence with her wet hands. She leaned forward to examine the policeman's badge, but in reality her eyes saw nothing. Jumbled thoughts tumbled together in her head. Was this it? Was the other shoe now going to fall? Was what she had feared to happen for Wendell and Rebecca—happening? Her stomach knotted in dread.

The detective coughed. Maggie, awakened to the situation, instinctively stepped back and opened the door wider. "Please, come in, Detective."

She led Detective Bérubé into the kitchen and offered him a seat at the table, quickly going around to the three windows and flipping up the shades so that the room was no longer in darkness. He glanced around, as though reconnoitering the situation, before pulling out a chair and sitting down. The detective was a short man, about Maggie's height, with dark skin and discerning brown eyes. He wore his thick black curls a little longer than the general hairstyle favored by most of the men that she knew. Under other circumstances Maggie would have considered the detective an attractive man; however, today she saw him only as the potential bearer of bad news. Aware that she had been rude to him, she forced herself to be polite. "How about a cup of coffee?" she proposed.

Detective Bérubé offered her a faintly ironic smile, as though Maggie might be attempting to bribe him with the coffee. "No, non. I am here on business." He waved a hand in the direction of the chair opposite him. "Please, sit down."

Maggie bristled at being offered a seat in her own home. She bit back a retort and, as majestically as she could, considering the fact that she wore only cut-off jeans and scoop-neck tank top, appropriated the designated chair. "Is there a problem, Detective?" she asked, adjusting the hair clip on the back of her head. She felt a tickle on her skin and carelessly brushed a small tree spider from a tanned shoulder.

The detective reached into the left pocket of his light-weight summer suit coat and withdrew a 3"X5" notebook. He flipped over a few of the white, narrow-lined pages, perused some penciled text, and returned his gaze to Maggie. "Do you know a man by the name of William Gagnon?"

Maggie's heart sank. "I met him once," she replied. She felt her right eye twitch, as it always did when she was overly-anxious, and knew the twitch must make her look as though she was hiding something.

Detective Bérubé's hand returned to his pocket. He pulled out a stubby yellow pencil and flipped to a clean sheet in his mini notebook. The pencil hovered expectantly over the page. "Yes?"

The detective's one-word reply demanded further details from her, and Maggie complied. "Mr. Gagnon was the agent who delivered my late husband's life insurance money to me," she explained.

"I see." Detective Bérubé scribbled a sentence or two, certainly more words than Maggie had uttered. "So, Monsieur Gagnon is your insurance agent?"

"No, he was my late husband's agent, that is, he was the agent sent here by the company to give me the check. I'm not sure that Peter ever had dealings with him." Detective Bérubé smiled again and Maggie found herself longing to wipe what appeared to be a knowing smile off his face as she had done with Nellie once when her daughter was young and had back-talked her. Instead, she picked up the long spoon with which she had stirred the iced tea and pressed the wet, curved end of the stainless steel into her palm to relieve some of her angst.

"But you? You 'had dealings'—as you say—with Monsieur Gagnon?"

She decided it was useless to try to explain the minutia of the truth. It was probably not relevant, anyway. "Yes," Maggie said firmly. She laid the spoon

251

sideways onto the blue-and-white checked cloth between them like a line in the sand. "I did have dealings with him. Please tell me what's going on, Detective. Is there a problem?"

"Sorry, but I cannot talk about the investigation. I am here to collect information only." The detective made another scribbled note. "Did you know Monsieur Gagnon used your name to solicit biz-ness in your neighborhood?"

Maggie's heart dropped to the balls of her feet. "Yes," she whispered. Her mouth was dry; her palms, sweaty. She felt like a criminal. Why? Why did she feel so much like a criminal, when all she had done was fail to warn her neighbors of this potential wolf in sheep's clothing? "I ... I did know that, yes. One of my neighbors told me."

More scribbling. "Who was the neighbor?"

"Henry Trow. He lives in the old Lovejoy place."

"Pardon?"

"I'm sorry; I forgot you're not from around here. Henry lives at the top of the hill, in the brick house to the right."

"I see. And he told you—what?"

Maggie wrinkled her brow, trying to recollect her neighbor's exact words. Her fingers rippled lightly against the cloth-covered table. "Henry said that Mr. Gagnon had stopped by, introduced himself as my financial advisor and then suggested that he might be too old to handle his own investments. Henry didn't like that—or Mr. Gagnon's looks—so he sent him packing."

"So, this Henry—he did not give Monsieur Gagnon any mon-nee?"

Maggie shook her head vehemently. "No, he did not."

More scribbling. "Did you give Monsieur Gagnon any mon-nee to invest?"

252

"No, never!"

"But some of your other neighbors did?"

At this question, Maggie felt her palpitating heart begin to move up her chest until it felt as though it was squarely lodged in her throat. "I think so, yes," she croaked. "Excuse me," she added, with a little cough. She hopped up from the table and fetched a small glass from the cupboard over the old farmer's sink. She opened the cold water tap and poured herself a glass of fresh water. She didn't bother to offer the detective a glass. Probably he would refuse that, too.

Instead, Detective Bérubé, who had rotated slightly in his chair to observe Maggie, was fascinated by the old sink's three, chrome-plated faucets with porcelain cross handles. "Why are there three?" he asked. "Three faucets?"

Maggie leaned back against the counter, glass in hand. "The third faucet goes to a field well. The well is spring fed. That's what I usually drink." She held up her glass as though it was Exhibit A. "Would you like to try some?"

"No, non. Merci. Which one is for the field well?"

"The one on the far left," she replied, pointing to the faucet in question. "See how it sets a little ways apart from the other two faucets?"

"Ah, oui! Ver-ree in-ter-rest-ting." The detective turned back in his seat and, at the sight of his notebook and pencil on the table, recollected his official business. He picked up the notebook and perused his writing. Maggie returned to her chair. "Now, Madame Hod-jez," he continued, "which neighbors gave Monsieur Gagnon mon-nee?"

Detective Bérubé offered her a friendly smile as he pronounced her name and Maggie realized that the three-faucet sink—an interesting anomaly—had softened him up. She might as well tell him as much as she knew in the hope that he would do the same by her. They were on the same side, after all. "Wendell and Rebecca Russell. Turn left at the top of the hill and they live in the old farmhouse just below the cemetery, the one with the big maple trees out front."

"And how do you know they gave Monsieur Gagnon mon-nee?"

"Because Rebecca told us that she and Wendell had given Mr. Gagnon ..."

"Excuse me," Detective Bérubé interrupted, pencil poised mid-air. "Us—who?"

"All of the friends who attended my engagement party. Wendell and Rebecca hosted the party for my fiancée and me recently."

"Ah, you are getting married again? Congratulations! I wish you and your fiancée a long life together."

"Thank you." The detective seemed so genuinely sincere and pleased about her engagement that Maggie couldn't help wondering what Detective Bérubé would think of her if she informed him that the engagement was soon to be off. Probably he would think she was unstable and scribble something else down in his notebook.

"Did Madame Russell say how much mon-nee they gave to Monsieur Gagnon?"

"No. But the money came from the sale of a piece of real estate, so I'd assume it was fairly substantial."

Detective Bérubé made a sad little tsk-tsking noise, which sounded to Maggie's ear much like the vocalization of a disgruntled bird. "Please, can't you tell me anything?" she beseeched him.

The detective shook his head. "Alas, non. But ... this is too bad." By the particular way he spoke and the way in which he sadly shook his head, Maggie knew Detective Bérubé was signaling to her that Wendell and Rebecca's money was lost. She closed her eyes, trying to hold back the hot tears that welled up upon this disclosure.

"Would you be so kind as to give me the names of your friends at the party?" he continued, gently. "I must discover if any of them gave Monsieur Gagnon mon-nee, too. Unfortunately, they might have taken Madame Russell's announcement as a recommendation to use his financial services."

"Oh, no! I never thought of that," Maggie cried. She closed her eyes, squeezing away the tears. She attempted to revive in her head a picture of those who were sitting around the table when Wendell and Rebecca made their announcement. She recollected that David had not been present and felt a pinprick of anger for her soon-to-be ex-betrothed. She listed off the little group of friends present at the engagement party. "Nellie is my daughter," she added, for clarification, "and Doctor Bart—Metcalf Lawson—my son-in-law."

The detective duly recorded this information, checking back with her several times for the correct spellings of various names and how everyone could be contacted. In five or six minutes he appeared satisfied with his notes and flipped the little notebook closed. He carefully returned the notebook and pencil to his left pocket.

"That's it?" Maggie asked, surprised he was done with her so soon. Somehow, she had thought there would be more questions. She wanted to tell the detective that she and Ryan had been worried about Mr. Gagnon's credibility and honesty, and that Ryan, as the local attorney, was making inquiries into the financial advisor and his business dealings. She desperately wanted the detective to know that they hadn't been completely taken in by a smooth-talking salesman from the city.

"That is all the kest-tions I have, Madame Hod-jez." Detective Bérubé arose and bobbed his dark respectfully. "Merci—thank-you for your time. I hope I was not too intrusive."

"Not in the least," she assured him. Maggie realized it was useless to attempt to gain further information from the detective. She ushered him out to the shed, where Detective Bérubé paused on the door stoop. He reached for her hand and pressed it warmly. "Congratulations on your engagement," the detective said sincerely. "Marriage is a bless-sed state. Pardon me for asking a very rude kest-tion, but what happened to your first husband?"

"Heart attack. He died three years ago. It was quite unexpected."

"Ah! Ver-ree sorr-ee," he said, giving Maggie's hand a reassuring squeeze. "I am happy to see you are moving on. My best wishes for a long life together with your new husband."

The detective dropped her hand, bobbed his dark head again, and exited. Maggie remained stationed at the door in order to learn which way the detective went out of the driveway. Her spirits drooped when she saw Detective Bérubé's car turn and motor up over the hill in the direction of Wendell and Rebecca's house. Soon, her dear friends would likely know all. They would know about the loss of their nest egg—little Tad's future inheritance! Nearly as bad, they might learn of Maggie's failure to warn them of the wolf in sheep's clothing. She had little hope at this point that Bill Gagnon hadn't absconded with their money.

She was standing there dully, stupidly, absently swatting mosquitoes away, when her wall phone, the line for the church that many of her friends used to contact her, jangled shrilly. Startled, she darted back into the house to pick up the receiver. "Maggie Walker," she answered, forgetting for a moment that she had formally taken Peter's last name three years ago.

Ryan MacDonald was on the other end of the line. "Maggie? I'm afraid I have bad news for you," the attorney continued in a somber voice.

"How bad is it? A Detective Bérubé just left here, but he wouldn't say much of anything—except, 'this is too bad'."

"Bill Gagnon has absconded—left the state and can't be found anywhere. As we suspected, he never invested Wendell and Rebecca's money in any financial instrument for them. Instead, he diverted the money for his own use. It's possible they'll get their money back, but not probable. Wendell and Rebecca aren't the only victims, either."

Maggie pressed her hand to her heart. "Oh, no! Were there others from Sovereign?"

"Not as far as I could learn. Most came from other small towns in the central Maine area, though. I talked to my contact at FINRA—that's the Financial Industry Regulatory Authority—and they've been investigating Gagnon for some time now for fraud and other financial abuses. Apparently, he must have caught wind of their investigation and skedaddled. Now the Maine State Police is investigating and the FBI is on the way."

"What can we do, Ryan?" she begged.

"Unfortunately, there's not much we can do, at this point. The time for action is over. Now, we need to take a step back and let the authorities do their job."

The time for action is over. The attorney's words stung, even though Maggie knew Ryan hadn't meant them as a rebuke. The truth was—she had failed her friends, and she felt it. Now, she needed to suck it up, prepare herself for the worst; prepare for Wendell and Rebecca's anger and possibly the loss of their friendship. How could she ever, *ever* live without her dear friends?

Hot tears rolled freely down her cheeks. "Thanks for calling," she replied, with a slight sob.

"Are you OK, Maggie? I can come over, if you want. Trudy's here with the kids."

"No, no. I'll be fine—eventually. Now, I think I just need a good cry." Maggie hung up the phone, sought the comfort of her little rocker, and burst into tears.

Chapter 18
Deep Dread and Dark Night

M aggie was still in a funk of despondency and self-pity, alternately weeping and blowing her nose, when, to her surprise, a car barreled down the hill, skidding and sliding over the loose stones in the recently-graded gravel road. The car abruptly came to a halt in Maggie's driveway. Hearing the noise and seeing the dust cloud approaching, she pushed the curtain aside and spied—Rebecca!

Her neighbor tumbled out of the vehicle not even bothering to close the door behind her and dashed toward the house. Maggie half rose in her chair, limbs trembling, unsure what to do and how to receive her friend and neighbor. Panicked, she realized she was unprepared for her friend's justifiable anger. What should she say to Rebecca? How should she apologize? What should she do? How should she act?

While Maggie was muddling through this conversation in her head, Rebecca burst into the kitchen without knocking. "Maggie!" she cried, holding her arms outstretched with the obvious intent of hugging her. Maggie perceived the look of unconditional love in her friend's eyes and uttered a half-strangled sob in response. Somehow the two women met in the middle of the room and the minister found herself being comforted and petted by her neighbor, as though Maggie was the one who had suffered the serious financial loss—and not Rebecca!

"There, there," Rebecca consoled her, patting her back and pressing soft kisses onto Maggie's brow. "As soon as that detective told us he had come from your house, I knew you'd be down here blaming yourself. Please, don't! Don't blame yourself. Now, there's a good dear."

Maggie wept, unable to reply. What grace! What a blessing! To have such wonderful friends!

Rebecca maneuvered the two of them into adjoining chairs. "Sit here, dear. Now, where are your tissues?" Spying the tissue box on the chiffonier, she leaned back and snatched up three or four. "Take these," she said, pressing the soft, white wad of cotton into Maggie's hand. "I told Wendell how it would be and that I needed to see you as soon as possible or you'd think we were mad at you. He sent you down some comb honey, too. He just took it off one of his hives. Goodness! Silly me, I'm babbling."

Maggie hiccupped through her tears. "You're not … mad at me?" she begged, voice quivering.

"Of course not, silly!" Rebecca cried, with a reassuring smile. "Wendell and I are grown-ups, although we don't often act it. You're not responsible for our financial mistakes—we are."

"But I failed to warn you!"

"Warn us what? From what the detective said, you didn't know Mr. Gagnon was a crook. How could you? Nobody did! Besides, dear," she continued, affectionate stroking Maggie's arm, "I'm not sure if you had warned us it would have made any difference. The investment Mr. Gagnon proposed seemed perfectly-tailored for us. Of course, we know now that's because he listened to us and then repeated back to us everything we wanted to hear. He told us how the money would be safe and how it would keep on growing and growing year after year, until there would be plenty of money for Tad to keep the homestead in the family forever. How silly were we! When something sounds too good to be true—it is too good to be true."

"But ..." Maggie began to protest.

"No, 'buts', dear! Now, you listen to me, Maggie." Rebecca's voice became almost severe. "Wendell and I love you just as much today as we did yesterday. Maybe even more! We know you're not perfect. But we're not perfect, either, and none of us ever will be. Friends love each other unconditionally, warts, flatulence, and all!"

Friends love each other unconditionally, warts, flatulence, and all!

The phrase repeated over and over in Maggie's head long after Rebecca had left. She slept poorly that night, tossing and turning and sweating in the humid July night. She had moved upstairs, back to her old bedroom, thinking that to sleep in their bed she might feel closer to Peter, closer to his wisdom and his comforting presence. Instead, she felt small, miserable, and alone.

Rebecca's visit had made Maggie realize the true value of her best friends. Unfortunately, the flip side of the visit was that her own personal character was thrown into bas relief by comparison with Rebecca and Wendell's. She realized that since Peter's death she had become self-satisfied, complacent, smug, small-minded, and as a friend, almost worthless!

Why hadn't she acted when Ryan first told her Bill Gagnon was using her name to drum up business with her friends? Certainly she should have done something after Henry also cautioned her about him! Why had she kept silent, when so many lives were at stake? Such a little effort on her part would have changed everything! A word to the wise, a heads-up, a hint! Even a warning offered in church about an investment advisor who was using her name without her permission to get his hands on her parishioners' money would have spread through the small town quicker than any of her pastoral messages ever did. For the most part, her sermons floated off into the sunset, never to be heard from again. But a cautionary word about money in this poor, hard-working community where many folks were one-step away from losing their farms to the tax man would have been taken to the heart, carefully passed around from one to another like a precious family heirloom.

In addition, Maggie realized that as of late she had been unconsciously passing judgment on everyone with whom she came in contact, holding up herself as the yardstick by which to measure and compare. She had made assumptions about Wendell and Rebecca, Miss Crump, and even the detective of Acadian extraction, all of which had turned out to be dead wrong.

The screen on the upstairs window fitted poorly—it had been a joke between them that summer the year Peter died that he would get around to fixing the screen by mid-winter—and Maggie had revered the broken screen after his death, leaving it untouched. As a result, the mosquitoes found her and were merciless. She swatted and cursed and gritted her teeth, and eventually got up in the darkness, stumbled to the window and slammed it shut. Ten minutes later, suffocating from the airless heat in the tiny attic bedroom, she flung open the window, grateful for the buzzing beasts that at least brought in with them a breath of fresh air.

Maggie drew herself up in bed and, under the protection of the damp cotton sheet, wrapped her arms around her knees. "Oh, Peter! I hate myself," she wailed aloud. "What should I do?"

Forthwith, Ryan's advice from his mother popped into her head: When all else fails, try praying.

Why hadn't she thought of that?

Like a guilty child, she scrambled out of bed, knelt beside the rustic wooden frame, and earnestly began to pray. Maggie prayed silently for several minutes, head resting on tightly clasped hands, lips clamped together in a desperate grimace. She tried not to ask anything for herself, but rather to seek God's guidance so that she might become a better person and a better minister to her flock. In an awful moment of clarity, however, the protective screen of self-deception was whisked away and she came face to face with her naked soul—and she cringed at what she saw.

In that instant of revelation, Maggie became cognizant of the fact that underneath her concern for others was a desire to glorify her own self in the name of compassion and charity. She recollected her sermon on *The Crook in the Lot* and saw that in that pastoral message she had been raising herself up, making her picayune problem appear much greater than it was, especially compared to those with real, on-going pain and suffering, such as Miss Crump. Why, even now she was more worried about how she would be perceived in town for her failure than about the financial loss Rebecca and Wendell had just sustained!

And where was God in all of this? When was the last time she had glorified God? Hadn't she merely been glorifying herself? In fact, she had moved so far away from God she had even needed to be reminded to pray!

Maggie was overcome with a sickening, deadly dread. How could she not have seen what had been happening to her since Peter's death? Without having someone to love and cherish—someone whose needs to place above her own—it had become all too easy to put herself first, before everyone else in her life: her daughter, her friends, and her parishioners. Love, true love and devotion, had helped keep her humble and it was only through this humility—through a shared humanness with

263

others—that she had ever been able to offer comfort, counsel, and care to others.

Since Peter's death, Maggie's ego had swelled to an incredible fullness of being. Much like a tick that had engorged itself too long, her ego was ready and waiting to burst. The moment of reckoning had come. Rebecca's simple act of forgiveness and charity had revealed the true state of her soul in all its horror—a shriveled, blackened little thing that smelt like burnt charcoal and dog's hair!

Sick to her stomach at the state of her soul, Maggie dashed to the bathroom and threw up. She retched again and again until there was nothing left in her stomach. Then, she clung to the porcelain toilet basin panting, sweating, and trembling—fearful she would retch some more. Finally, when nothing happened after ten minutes, she hoisted herself up to the sink. She wiped her face with a cold, wet washcloth. The vanity mirror reflected back a ghostly, unfamiliar face, a face with sallow, bloodless skin, straggly hair, and hopeless gray-blue eyes. Everything was bleached of color—of life—in the penetrating light from the vanity. A chilly fog crept in through the open bathroom window and Maggie clasped her arms to her breast, shivering.

Who was she? Maggie Walker Hodges? What had she become!

She had tried to be a good person once—a good minister to her flock—but she had failed. Lately, the times she had 'helped' others were merely sad attempts to boost her own opinion of herself. Since Peter's death, she had lost her heart, lost her spirit, and lost her faith. She had become a weak, wretched being whose modus operandi was to save other souls in a vain attempt to salvage her own.

Maggie dragged herself back to the bedroom and threw herself face down onto the bed. Racked with guilt, shame, pain—she wept. Finally, exhausted, she slept.

She awoke the next morning to a knocking on the interior kitchen door. She glanced at the bedroom clock. Nine o'clock! She slipped into a cotton bathrobe and hastily made her way downstairs in her bare feet to open the door to—Duncan Faulkner!

Her hand dropped from the brass doorknob in surprise. He seemed almost as startled to see her as she was to see him, although obviously he had come to visit. "What's wrong?" he said, moving forward with genuine concern. Instinctively, Maggie took a step back, nearly knocking over a chair. He halted on the threshold.

Maggie, recollecting the night she had just passed, realized she must look a fright. Her right hand flew to her loose straggly hair while her left hand pulled the wrapper closer together. "I overslept," she stated, simply. "Hard night."

"May I be of some assistance?"

"I ... I think not."

"Dear friend—as friends I hope we are!—don't shut me out. If I can be of some service, please let me help you. I'm a good listener, and I promise, what you have to say to me will go no further than these walls."

She bit her lip and shook her head, turning her back to him so he couldn't read the stab of pain echoed in her eyes. Her shoulders shook with grief. He was holding her before she knew it, pulling her around and gently folding her to his chest in a brotherly embrace. "Go ahead and cry," he encouraged. "Let the poison out!"

"I don't think I have any tears left to cry," she replied, with a shaky laugh.

"No?" Duncan tenderly leaned Maggie away from him in order to peruse her face. Apparently satisfied with what he saw, he released her. "Then how about some coffee? One of us could certainly use a cup!"

Maggie nodded, grateful for the opportunity afforded to busy herself. She quickly twisted her hair up into a bun and went to work. She sought the six-cup percolator pot from the pantry and filled it with water from the third faucet, the field well. She scooped coffee into the aluminum basket and set the pot on the stove to boil.

In the meantime, Duncan removed his Red Sox baseball cap and settled himself into a chair at the table. He regarded her closely. "Why don't you go freshen up?" he suggested, when the pot was heating. "That is, if you trust me to watch the coffee."

"Thanks," she replied, eagerly accepting his offer. "When the coffee starts to bubble up, just turn the gas to low and let it perk five minutes, OK?"

"Roger that," he said, with a reassuring smile.

Maggie fled to the safety and security of the downstairs bathroom. She brushed her teeth, washed her face, and combed her hair. After rolling her shoulder-length hair back up and affixing it in place with a plastic hairclip, she contemplated getting dressed.

"Coffee's perking," he called out from the kitchen.

"OK, thanks!" Maggie regarded herself in the mirror. Well, he had already seen her at her worst. Why try to pretend nothing was the matter? She readjusted her bathrobe and returned to the kitchen, which was now filled with the rich aroma of freshly-perked coffee.

"That's much better," he pronounced. "I set the egg timer for five minutes, just like you told me."

"Thanks." Feeling overly self-conscious and awkward, she removed two mugs from the cupboard. The egg timer pinged. Maggie shut off the gas and, using a pot holder, set the coffee pot to one side of the stove until the coffee grounds had settled. Her hands shook when she attempted to pour out the boiling brown liquid.

Some of the hot coffee splashed onto the counter and floor.

Duncan came to her aid. "Here, let me," he said, gently. Maggie nodded her consent and sought the comfort of her rocker. "Cream and sugar?" he continued.

"Yes, please." She watched him make himself at home, easily finding what he needed in the fridge and cupboard. He expertly fixed her coffee. "Looks like you've had some practice," she said, without thinking.

"Lots of church suppers," he replied with a grin. Duncan handed her the mug and returned to the counter to fetch his own. He reclaimed his chair. "Now, why don't you tell me what's wrong—minister to minister. And please don't say 'nothing' because we both know what happens to our souls when we lie."

At his words, Maggie shuddered. She recollected in horror the shriveled, blackened thing she had seen in her vision last night.

Duncan noted her recoil. "I'm sorry; I was trying to be funny. Looks like I hit a nerve."

"You could say that," Maggie replied, with a weak smile. She took a welcome sip of hot coffee and rested back in the rocker, clasping the mug with both hands. "I had a dark night of the soul last night, I guess."

"Tell me about it," he urged, compassionately.

Without hesitation this time, Maggie unburdened herself. She told Duncan about Bill Gagnon, about her failure to inform Wendell and Rebecca of the wolf in sheep's clothing, about the detective's visit, about Wendell and Rebecca's financial loss, and about Rebecca's forgiveness. Finally, Maggie confessed to the personal despair she had experienced the prior night. Duncan listened without interrupting. Once or twice he arose, paced the floor a few steps, and then returned to his seat. "Now I feel like a horrible human being!"

Maggie concluded. She took a big swig of coffee as she awaited his summary judgment.

"Are you finished?"

Maggie set the coffee cup down onto the side table by the window. "And I've decided to quit the ministry. There! Now, I'm done."

At this, Duncan bit back a smile. "Well, then, congratulations are in order, I'd say."

"Congratulations?" she repeated, startled that he was congratulating her on her decision to leave the ministry.

"You enjoyed a great gift from God last night, Maggie."

"I did? Sure didn't feel like a gift," she groused.

"It never does," he said, laughing. "The dread you felt—the despair you experienced—that was an honest expression of your insecurity, a realization that we are nothing without God. When we cease believing in ourselves—and instead have faith in God—we become open to the Divine to go to work through us. As ministers, you know as well as I do we don't have the power to fix anyone or save anyone. *We have only the power to offer hope*, the hope in He Who Is the Fixer of All Things and the Giver of All Life. To experience this, to acknowledge one's nothingness, to open one's self up so that God can go to work through us—that's what it's all about. You're not only a good minister; you're on your way to becoming a great minister."

Maggie frowned, unconvinced. Was he just trying to make her feel better?

Duncan noted her uncertainty. "Let me resort to Thomas Merton if you're unconvinced," he hurried on. "When I experienced a similar dark night of the soul, I found Merton's book *Contemplative Prayer* very helpful. Merton says that such deep dread and dark night must be seen for what it is, not as punishment of us but as purification and grace. Indeed, it is a great gift from God, he says, for this is the precise point of our encounter with the Divine fullness. You've been purified, Maggie! You've been prepared by God to do His work."

Maggie's brow wrinkled thoughtfully as she considered the spiritual teaching of the famous Trappist monk. "Well, it certainly did feel as though I was being purified. I tossed my cookies several times."

Duncan burst out laughing. "Oh, Maggie! I love how human you are. No wonder your parishioners adore you. I watch you with them and I can see you're a wonderful minister. I think you're too hard upon yourself, though. And I don't believe your hypothesis that you've only been helping others to feel better about yourself. Sounds like a little too much self-reflection and self-absorption on your part."

"You mean I sat too long on the pity pot?"

He smiled and reached for his Red Sox cap. "Exactly! Why don't you go get dressed and I'll take you out to breakfast." He ran the stiff rim of the navy cap around in his hands. "Nick has introduced me to the delights of Ma Jean's Restaurant and I can already taste those eggs Benedict."

Before Maggie could reply, however, they were interrupted by a knock on the outer shed door. She peeked out the window and saw Henry Trow's vehicle in the driveway, parked next to her own car. She glanced quickly at the wall Regulator clock—ten-thirty! Where had the time flown?

"Excuse me," she said. "I should get that." The flowing hem of her pretty cotton print bathrobe brushed lightly against her bare ankles and awakened her, with a little electric shock, to the realization that she was still in her night attire. Good grief! What would her neighbor think? Finding her alone in her nightdress with a man—and that man *not* her fiancée!

She gazed helplessly at Duncan, awaiting his suggestion; however, the Episcopal minister himself appeared stricken, aware of their potentially compromising situation. "Where's your car?" she whispered.

"I walked over," he said simply. He had arisen when she got up to answer the door and now stood awkwardly in the center of the kitchen, clutching his cap in both hands.

"Of course."

The knocked sounded again. "Maggie? Are you home?" Henry called out, obviously anxious to speak with her.

"Just a minute," she yelled. Purposefully, she clasped Duncan by the arm and steered him through the living room, to the back door. The door was open, except for the screen. "Quick! He won't see you if you cut through the woods. The connecting path is near the apple tree." Maggie pointed out the ancient apple. "I'll keep him busy long enough for you to get out of sight."

"Maggie, I ..."

"Go!" she ordered, giving Duncan a little shove.

He flipped his baseball cap onto his head and pushed through the screen door—but not before Maggie had caught the look of hopeless love pouring forth from his expressive hazel eyes. Why—he loved her! Duncan Faulkner loved her!

Chapter 19
Maggie's Dilemma

Henry had no difficulty accepting at face value Maggie's mumbled excuse that she was still in her bathrobe because she had overslept. He seemed to take for granted that as the local minister she must have been out most of the night comforting a sick parishioner. Maggie didn't discourage this supposition. She led him into the kitchen, feeling a bit guilty, however, as he apologized profusely for his intrusion. Spying Duncan's coffee cup, she whipped the offending china off the table and dumped the mug and spoon into the plastic dishpan with the other dirty dishes. She stood like a conscience-stricken child, her back to the sink.

Henry heard the clink of dishes. "Maybe I should come back another time," he suggested.

"No, no, this is fine. As long as you don't mind me in my bathrobe," she qualified, moving forward. "Please, have a seat."

Henry chuckled boyishly. "I don't mind your dishabille, but Hannah might have something to say about it!" He hooked his cane over a chair and sat down.

Maggie offered a weak smile.

"I hope you don't greet all the young bucks this way, though."

She couldn't help it—her eyes turned instinctively to the living room, where through the open window she could see the verdant mass of the ancient apple highlighted by the slanting, mid-morning sunlight. There was no sign of Duncan; he had disappeared down the shaded path through the woods that led back to Walden's house—his house, now!—Maggie realized, with a little start. Now that he had sold his house in Massachusetts, Duncan was to live fulltime in Sovereign with Nick. Good Lord! She and he would be permanent neighbors. But ... she mustn't think of that now; Henry was speaking. Maggie forced herself to pay attention to the older gentleman's words.

"I came as soon as we heard. Isn't that wonderful news?" Henry gushed. "I knew in my heart all along that Kate didn't steal those damn LL Bean boots. She told me she didn't, and I believed her. So did Hannah."

Maggie was delighted by what appeared to be Kate's vindication of the boot theft. "They found the real culprit?"

"Yep. Finally!"

"I'm so happy for you, Henry! Kate is such a nice girl. You and Hannah were right to place your trust in her." Over the past few weeks she had come to enjoy the young woman's company, becoming fond of Kate, despite the mysterious issue with her grandmother's watch. A cool breeze filtered in through the open window and Maggie absentmindedly covered her bare legs with her robe.

"Thanks to your advice, neighbor. I'm not sure I would have invited her to live with us if it hadn't been for your encouragement, Maggie."

"Nonsense! You would have invited Kate even if I'd told you it wasn't a wise thing to do," she replied, brushing off the compliment. She was pleased, however, to hear that she had done something right in the past few months.

"I've got some other news for you, too—Kate's going to finish her Master's degree at Thomas College in

Waterville. She's been accepted into their MBA program. She got the news yesterday. Now, what do you think of that?"

"Wonderful! That's the best news I've had in a long while. Will they transfer Kate's credits from the University of New Hampshire?" Maggie inquired anxiously.

"Some, but not all. Skinflints! Good thing ole Grampa has plenty of cash to bankroll Kate's education."

"Now, Henry, don't try to pull the wool over my eyes. I know how much you and Hannah enjoy having Kate live with you. I'd say her continued presence is worth every penny you spend on her education."

Henry chuckled. "Caught me! Well, it's money well-spent, that's for sure. Say, I almost forgot—Hannah and I are giving a little dinner Saturday night to celebrate Kate's acceptance at Thomas College. Hannah charged me with inviting you, you and that dashing fiancée of yours."

She winced. Oh, dear! Should she tell Henry that she and David were no longer an item? But how could she disclose this information when she hadn't even informed David himself? She couldn't take the chance that David would accidentally discover the news of their broken engagement like he had learned of her acceptance of his marriage proposal!

Maggie decided it was best simply not to mention David at all. Certainly, she would have told David by Saturday that she no longer wanted to marry him; therefore, if his absence was noted at the dinner she could inform her friends of their break-up. "Thanks for the invite. I'll give Hannah a call later and see if I can bring anything."

"Excellent! One down," he fished a paper list from his pocket and peered at the paper, "and two stops to go." He reached for his cane and stood up.

Suddenly, it occurred to Maggie to simply ask Henry about her grandmother's watch. "Wait a moment, Henry. There's something I'd like to ask you."

He sank back down into his chair, holding his cane between his knees. "Yes?"

Maggie hesitated. Now that she had decided to bell the cat she was unsure how to go about doing it. She didn't want to give Henry the impression she thought Kate might have stolen the valuable timepiece, not only because it would hurt him tremendously, but also because in her heart she was sure the young woman was innocent.

Henry thumped his cane against the battle-scarred pine floor. "Out with it, Maggie," he directed in his usual manner. "I need to motor over to Scotch Broom Acres. Hannah charged me with inviting all that crowd. I must remember to pick up some fresh eggs and cheese, too."

Maggie resolved that a direct approach was best. "Do you know where Kate got her new watch?"

"Her what?" said Henry, taken aback.

"Her gold wristwatch. It's an antique. Do you know where Kate got it?"

He frowned, his bushy white eyebrows nearly touching. "I bought the watch for her. Why do you ask?"

"You!"

"Yes, I bought the watch on Craigslist."

"Why?"

"Because Kate doesn't get cell service in our neck of the woods and she kept wandering off not knowing when it was time to come home. None of these kids today have watches, you know. They all use their phones to tell time. Frankly, it's damned annoying. Anyway, Kate was late for dinner once or twice—Hannah didn't mind, but I don't like to wait for my supper!—and so I bought her the watch. Rather pretty, don't you think? Reminds me of my mother's watch; that's why I bought it. I

274

suppose you want to know where to get one, but I doubt you could find another one just like it."

"I'm sure of that," Maggie agreed. "Who did you buy the watch from?" she pressed him, eager to follow the scent to the end of the trail. "Do you remember?"

He shrugged. "A Unity College kid, Ashley somebody-or-other. She said she was selling her grandmother's watch because she needed money for text books. I felt sorry for her, so I didn't even try to beat her down on price, old fool that I am. I paid $100 for the thing."

Ashley! This time Maggie remembered her name. She was the tall, thin girl with the stringy blonde hair who had been Maggie's partner at the vernal pool the day David and his students counted frogs' eggs. The day David proposed to her! Maggie recollected she had stuck the watch into her jeans pocket before she left home—intending to place it in her jewelry box for safekeeping—when she was interrupted by Henry himself, who had come to speak to her about Kate. She quickly calculated that she must have lost the watch at the vernal pool and Ashley picked it up and offered Maggie's precious heirloom for sale on Craigslist! Maggie had known the girl disliked her. Most likely she was in love with David—which one of his female students wasn't?—and had been jealous when he proposed to Maggie. "That explains everything," she cried. "Now I know what happened to my grandmother's watch!"

The cane stopped spinning. Henry's hooded eyes opened wide. "Your grandmother's watch?"

"Yes! I lost the watch in May and I've been looking for it ever since."

"Say, you didn't think...?"

"No, certainly not. I knew there was a perfectly logical explanation for how Kate came to have Gram's watch. That's why I didn't hesitate to ask you about it."

Henry was obviously relieved. "I'm glad to hear you didn't suspect her, Maggie. I'll have Kate return the watch to you as soon as I get home."

"Please don't! I'd love for Kate to keep the watch."

"You know I can't allow that."

But Maggie was firm. "Listen, Henry, my grandmother would be proud to know Kate had her watch. Gram worked hard to get her own Master's degree. She taught school full-time while she was in school herself, studying at night after she put her kids— my mother and her brothers—to bed. I know she would want Kate to have it."

"That's very generous of you, Maggie. Are you sure?"

"Positive. You tell Kate I'll be there Saturday night to congratulate her and that I expect to see her wearing Gram's watch."

When Henry departed, Maggie dashed back into her daughter's old room and quickly dressed before anyone else stopped in. She returned to the kitchen to grab a bite to eat and clean up. While washing up the dishes in the dishpan, her hand lingered momentarily on the mug Duncan had used. She pressed the mug to her chest, heart thumped wildly. He loved her!

She felt giddy and young, like a teenage girl in love for the very first time. She hummed a little tune, one of the songs her mother used to sing. Before she knew it, Maggie was twirling around the kitchen, dish towel in hand, crooning Nat King Cole's *Orange- Colored Sky*:

> *I was walkin along, mindin my business,*
> *When out of an orange-colored sky,*
> *Flash! Bam! Alakazam!*
> *Wonderful you came by.*

Jennifer Wixson

I was humming a tune, drinking in sunshine,
When out of that orange-colored view
Flash! Bam! Alakazam!
I got a look at you.

Her mating pair of ravens had recently returned, showing off their second set of offspring. Maggie heard their raucous squawking from a tree outside and threw open the window over the sink. "I love him!" she called out, wanting someone or some Thing to hear her confession. The little family of Corvids cawed and dispersed in different directions. Romeo and Juliet, however, inured to her odd ways by now, remained nearby to watch her. "He loves me, too!" she informed the pair. In return, the birds garbled what to her prejudiced ears seemed like a note of approval.

Unable to contain herself, Maggie whirled around the kitchen, humming another tune. She loved him! Oh, how dearly she loved him!

When she and he were together she felt whole—and wholly at peace. It was though the two of them were a chemistry experiment, she was the acid and he was the base, and when they came together the burning agony of life was becalmed. Alone she was nothing; together they could face anything.

When she thought of him—or was with him—gravity didn't exist. Her spirit floated free from pain, free from suffering, free from guilt and shame. She recollected every line of his face, the sure movement of his hands, and the seductive curve of his smooth-shaven chin. Every detail of his being was impressed upon her memory and yet that memorization had occurred so naturally she had not even known she was taking inventory of him, keeping every precious piece of sacred information safe so that she could return to lovingly linger over it in her mind's eye again and again.

277

She recollected every word Duncan had ever spoken, every gesture he'd ever made: the way he had taken her arm the first day they'd met; how poignantly he'd hugged the gnarled maple tree; the light-hearted twirling of his Red Sox cap; and, most sacredly, the feel of his comforting arms around her. Why, she had loved him the moment she had laid eyes on him! From the very moment in which she had stepped out from behind the tree and noticed something was different about him.

Could that be possible?

Yes, she loved him! If such instantaneous love was impossible, then it must have been a miracle—meant to be. She loved Duncan out of a fullness of heart that made her feel more alive than she'd ever felt before. She longed to care for him, to be his helpmate and his best friend. She wanted to nurture him, to encourage him, and to watch over him, and she wanted him to be the one to do the same for her.

Suddenly, the awful reality of the situation hit Maggie in her gut so hard she felt as though she'd physically been kicked in the stomach. The blow took her breath away.

How could she break her engagement with one brother and immediately turn around and throw herself into the arms of his twin? How stupid had she been! She had engaged herself to marry the wrong brother! Was there ever such a dilemma?

Whether Duncan loved her or not—and Maggie was certain that he did—how could they take the chance of ruining his brother's happiness? The two of them must set aside their mutual love and desire and *carry on as though their love didn't exist*. They couldn't hurt David; it wasn't fair to him. Poor David had asked for nothing—and offered her everything. He had asked her to be his wife and she had accepted him!

278

A greedy, niggling voice inside Maggie's head whispered that she and Duncan need only wait a little while after breaking her engagement to David, a little while until everybody in town had forgotten all about their engagement, a little while until David himself had moved on. Then, when it was safe, she and Duncan could get together!

Maggie, remembering her dark night of the soul, however, resolutely set her jaw. She mentally berated herself for such small-mindedness and selfish thinking. She knew how proud David was. How precious—and precarious—his sense of self was to him. There would never be a 'safe' amount of time to pass that would make it alright to him that Maggie loved his twin—and not him. How well she remembered David's pride in her at the engagement dinner! She recollected the way he had possessively patted her thigh and joked about her "wild side." She also recollected David's disdainful words to his brother the night of the award dinner when Duncan innocently wondered what might have happened had he met Maggie first: "But when did you ever outrun me, Bub?" No, Duncan must never "outrun" David!

And Duncan was so large of heart, so generous of spirit! He would understand. She knew he would. Duncan was the most honorable man Maggie had ever met. She felt she knew him so well that she was sure he would never, ever reveal his love for her—to her—or to anyone else, especially not to his twin.

If only she had never agreed to marry David! She never loved him, she realized now. She had only accepted his proposal because she had been caught up in the thrill of the moment. She had been flattered by his attention and excited by the prospect of helping David with his work. Also, if the truth be told, she had wanted to hedge her bets by securing a partner for her later years. Why, oh, why had she taken such a wrong turn?

Was there no turning back? No one to whom she could go to for advice? Who would listen to her torrid tale without judging her?

Then Maggie remembered her mother, Rose Aberdeen Walker, resting peacefully in her grave in the Crosby Cemetery along the banks of the Sebasticook River. Her mother! She had wanted to visit Rose for weeks now, and here was her opportunity. She could share her dilemma with her mother!

She would go to Rose! She would return home— to Winslow.

Chapter 20
Along the Sebasticook

Maggie experienced a surge of nostalgic longing when contemplating returning home to Winslow. She recognized in the concept of 'home' the universal human desire to return to the safe and loving harbor of one's childhood, which in her case was not much more than twenty-five miles from the little red schoolhouse where she lived. Despite her proximity to her old stomping grounds along the banks of the Sebasticook River, she had not revisited the scenes of her youth for more than twenty years. Maggie hadn't visited the old family land because it was too painful for her. Two ungainly McMansions (McMansions by Sovereign standards, anyway) had sprung up during the past two decades in the pasture beside her family's former home.

But Maggie knew every stone wall, every tree and bush, every granite outcrop, and every curve of ridge on those hundred and fifty acres, for she and Peter had trod them all—hunting squirrels, chasing rainbows, fishing for pickerel, and running free as the wind. Despite the presence of the McMansions, she decided she would slip back home, as stealthily as an Indian. She and Peter had often pretended they were Native Americans, playing hide and seek in the fields and forest. They might as well have been Indians for they shared a philosophy similar to Native Americans, both believing they never owned the land so much as the land owned them.

Her heart raced with excitement as she motored through the sleepy little neighboring town of Benton Falls—going past the little white church and meeting hall—and coming onto the Garland Road in Winslow along the bend of the Sebasticook River by the outlet stream to Pattee's Pond, where Peter's great-grandparents had lived. She drove up the hill, past Peter's family's farm, idly wondering what her nephew Bruce or his wife Amber would think if they saw her drive by. Maggie slowed her car before reaching Sid Roberts' old place, knowing as she did that a legal right-of-way to the Crosby Cemetery lay beneath a stretch of lush, perfectly manicured lawn. She turned onto the right-of-way, grateful that the ditch crossing remained intact after all these years. The cemetery's access road, which ran along the stone wall separating Sid Roberts' house from the Crosby house where Maggie was born, was visible only to eyes of yesteryear. She drove halfway down to the cemetery and left her car in the woods, hiking the rest of the way downhill on foot.

When Maggie was five, her father and uncle had each taken up one side of the drop-heel buggy shaft of an abandoned buckboard they had found in the barn and had given her and her younger sister a wild ride down this very hill. The buckboard had run away from the two men and crashed into a copse of fledgling hardwoods. She paused beneath a stand of mature trees and pushed through the wild raspberry vines and sumac bushes growing underneath and sure enough, there it was—the buckboard! The wagon's soft gray wood and iron seat was intact and the rusty step was still attached. She heard her sister's laughter on the wind and her father's cries to: "Jump! Jump!" She and her sister had abandoned ship just before the crash, laughing hysterically, oblivious to danger at their young age.

She breeched the upper meadow, heart in her throat. The cemetery was still there, of course, keeping watch upon the ridge, surrounded by its iron fence, sagging and bent with the passing of time. Several hardwoods and two or three pine trees, which Maggie had not even noticed as a child, towered over the cemetery, offering shade and a sense of maturity to the somber but picturesque scene. Soft shards of light poked through their intermingled canopies, dappling the ground beneath the trees, creating an ever-changing kaleidoscope as the lazy breeze tousled the leaves and pine fronds. The grasses and wildflowers in and around the graveyard were tall, but not overgrown and Maggie realized that someone must have mown the graveyard once or twice this year, most likely around Memorial Day. A few faded American flags fluttered in the breeze, heralding the graves of Civil War and World War I and II veterans. No one had been buried in the cemetery since Rose in 1963, and no one had been buried there before that for nearly a decade. Peter was lying at rest with many generations of his family several miles away, in the large neighborhood cemetery, which was situated on the back side of the Hodges farm, accessed by the Eames Road.

Maggie pushed through the rusty gate, which squeaked when it swung open as though rarely used. A female bobolink flew up from the tall grass, startling her. The striped brown songbird issued a sharp trill and flew to the furthest fencepost, trying to draw Maggie away from its nest. Mindful of the bird's nest, she carefully made her way into the cemetery. Some of the two dozen headstones had toppled over since her last visit and now appeared to slumber peacefully on the ground. But the large Crosby monument stood tall and proud, valiantly keeping watch over this section of the Sebasticook River, waiting for scions of the family who Maggie suspected rarely returned to their original port of call. Rose's headstone, a gorgeous white piece of marble just as her mother had wanted, was still intact, holding down the southwest corner of the cemetery. Around the back of Rose's stone sprouted a family of tall, leggy lilacs, offspring of the original tree that she and her father and sister had planted.

Overcome by a rush of love, Maggie knelt before her mother's tombstone. She reverently touched the face of the cool, smooth marble. "I'm here, Mother," she said, tears in her eyes. "I've come home."

Was that a reply she heard murmuring on the breeze? An invitation to sit and talk? To tell her mother everything that was going on in her life?

She cleared away the dead leaves and bits of lilac debris and settled herself down into the soft grass in front of Rose's stone. A patch of daisies cropped up near her mother's grave and Maggie plucked one, idly pulling off the long white petals one by one until there was only one petal left: he loved her! "He loves me," she told her mother joyfully. "He loves me!" She broke apart the irresistible center disk and hundreds of the damp, tightly-packed yellow florets tumbled into her hand. "I hope these are grandchildren, though, not children," she joked.

Maggie tossed aside the defrocked daisy and proceeded to relate aloud—as though her mother was sitting across the table taking afternoon tea with her—her dilemma with the two brothers. The bobolink on the fencepost warbled. Other songbirds twittered from the safety of the treetops. The fragrant air in the meadow swam with the intoxicatingly-sweet scent of milkweeds, just beginning to open their beautiful mauve florets. The cheerful daisies bobbed their heads in the mid-summer breeze. A patch of cinnamon fern crowded up against the black iron fence from the outside as though eavesdropping on Maggie's romantic tale of woe. Several of the larger ferns poked frilly green fronds through the bars offering her an occasional consoling pat on the back.

How good it was to get everything off her chest! How foolish she had been to worry!

Maggie, being here in the company of those who had once walked the earth—but were now gone— realized that her perspective on life was beginning to shift. Her perception of reality telescoped to take in multiple generations of her family. She considered some of the challenges her ancestors had faced, those people who had blazed a trail for her and helped through their own lives to make her the person she was. She wasn't sure what would happen next or even how she would resolve her personal dilemma, but suddenly she had faith that everything would be alright. The future would be what it would be and she would accept it with grace, as her mother had accepted her own fate with grace and dignity. Rose had taught her daughter not only how to die with dignity, but also how to live—to live with love and joy!

The July sun beat down. The breeze quit; not even a poplar leaf quivered. The birds retired for their mid-day nap. The heavy perfume emanating from the milkweed and the ferns made Maggie feel drowsy. Before she knew it, she was asleep.

She awoke later, not knowing what time it was, although the shadows around the cemetery seemed to be longer. She rubbed the sleepy seeds from her eyes and stretched her cramped legs. She was in the process of getting up when she heard the telltale squeak of the cemetery's rusty gate behind her. She whirled around. Duncan!

"Darling," he cried, arms outstretched. He covered the distance between them in three strides and clasped her to his chest. "I've been so worried about you, my darling!"

Maggie leaned against him, her heart exploding with joy. He loved her. He loved her!

"Are you OK?"

Was she OK? How could she be better! "Oh, yes," she murmured.

"Say you love me!" he directed, raining kisses upon her face and neck.

"I do love you!"

"And will you be my wife?"

"Yes!" she replied, without thinking. "Wait—no!" She was still engaged to David! What about him? "Oh, Duncan! What are we going to do?" A little sob escaped her.

"Hush! There's no need to cry," Duncan assured her, stroking her hair, which somehow had come undone and tumbled down her back. "We're going to love each other like all good husbands and wives, that's what we're going to do."

Maggie gazed up into his honest, handsome face. Two hot tears rolled down her cheeks. "But what about your brother?" she beseeched him.

"Oh, no, you're not going to get away from me that easily, my darling! For once in my life I do believe I've outrun him." Duncan daubed her tears with the hem of his shirt. He glanced around the cemetery, took Maggie by the elbow, and steered her to an open area where no one was buried. He pulled her down to the ground. Duncan lay beside her in the soft grass, keeping a firm hand upon her, as though fearful she might disappear at any moment.

Maggie closed her eyes, overcome by relief. Love washed over her in warm waves. The earth spun beneath her and birds soared above. Time stood still.

He tickled her face with the fuzzy end of a stalk of timothy to get her attention. "Say you love me," he demanded again.

In response, she snuggled closer to him. "I do, Duncan, but ..."

"No 'buts', Maggie," he ordered, maneuvering himself so he could gaze deeply into her eyes. "Do you want to be my wife?"

Maggie's heart thumped. "Oh, yes!"

"Good! That's all I need to know. The rest can take care of itself." He rolled over on top of her and pinned her against the ground with his warm body. His mouth demanded complete submission. Maggie closed her eyes and surrendered.

Later, when they had sated themselves, she lay in the crook of his arm, watching the poufy white clouds drift by overhead. "You're pretty sexy, for a minister, you know," she said.

"Mmm, you're not so bad, yourself. Do you bring all your dates here?"

She giggled. "If I did, they didn't live to tell about it. Speaking of which," she continued, sitting up, "how on earth did you know where I was? And why did you come to my house this morning? You never said."

Duncan closed his eyes, ignoring her questions. Maggie gave him a slight poke in the ribs. "I'm serious. I want to know."

He groaned and rolled over onto his side, offering Maggie his back. "Go away, woman. Can't you take a guy's marriage proposal at face value and leave it at that?"

"No, I can't. Because, technically, I'm now engaged to two men—and the other guy is your twin brother."

"Oh, him."

"Yes, him! What about that little problem?"

Duncan sat up, his demeanor suddenly serious. He took Maggie's hands within his own, caressing them. "That's something you and I will deal with together, my darling. We'll tell David the truth, honestly and forthrightly. Do you think my brother would want to marry a woman who was in love with another man? Especially if that man was me? I'll answer that question for you. No, he would not."

"But that doesn't make what we're doing right!"

"Wait—I'm not done. Since I arrived in town, I've been watching the two of you. I came to the conclusion early on that David doesn't love you, not in the way you should be loved, the way a husband should love his wife."

"Nothing ever happened between us," Maggie whispered, anxious to reassure him on that point. "I never ..."

Duncan stopped her with a kiss. "I don't care," he said. He laid his cheek against hers and stroked her hair. "It doesn't matter. You love me."

"I do!"

"When I realized my brother didn't love you, I was determined to keep you both from making what I thought was a terrible mistake. Unfortunately, as time went by, I began to suspect my motive was no longer disinterested. You see, I'd fallen in love with you myself. I think I loved you from the first moment I saw you." Duncan reached over and plucked a daisy, placing the flower in her hair. "How could I not love you? You were so natural, singing and dancing down the Cross Road, shaking hands with the trees."

"What a strange sight I must have been!"

"A wonderfully strange sight! I've never met anyone quite like you. Heck, I think I was probably a little in love with you before we met, I'd heard so much about you from Nick." He threaded a second daisy into her hair, pulled away a little and surveyed his handiwork.

Nick! How would he react to the news? "Won't he be angry when he finds out about us?"

Duncan laughed and leaned back, elbow resting on the ground. "Nick? He's been singing your praises to me for the last year and a half. He had it all planned out, Maggie, how he'd introduce us, we'd fall in love, get married, and live here in Maine as one big happy family."

"How can that be? Nick's the one who introduced me to David!"

"Let me tell you, there's not a day goes by in which my son hasn't regretted that mistake. It never occurred to Nick that his confirmed bachelor uncle might want to seek the solace of a permanent companion in his later years. Poor David! And poor Nick, too. All my son's hopes were dashed the day we told him about your engagement. He had been worried about your relationship with my brother before that, which is why he was so anxious to get me to Sovereign, but until that day he supposed you were just another one of David's temporary playmates. He never believed his uncle would actually pop the question."

"No wonder Nick was upset! I thought he didn't want me as part of your family."

"Oh, he wanted you in the family, alright! Just not as his aunt."

"So that's why he never called me 'Aunt Maggie.' Of course, everything makes sense, now."

Wonders of wonder—when Maggie married Duncan, she would inherit a son! "What if I'm a terrible stepmother?" she worried. "I never was the world's best mother. Nellie will vouch for that."

"I ain't scairt, as my buddy Leland would say. I know how much you and Nick mean to each other. I was only half joking when I told you I was envious of your relationship. Probably I'll spend my declining days playing second fiddle to my son."

"Never!" Maggie cried, clasping and kissing one of his sensitive hands. "Although, if Nick gets married and has children, I can't make any promises," she immediately qualified, letting go of his hand. "I do want grandchildren and Nellie doesn't seem inclined to oblige me anytime soon."

"I knew it," he groaned. "No more daisies for you."

"But Duncan, you haven't told me yet why you came to my house this morning? And how did you know where I was? Nobody knew I was coming to the cemetery, not even Nellie."

He patted the ground beside him. "Lay back down, darling, and I'll tell you everything." Maggie willingly obliged and he tightened his arm around her. "I came to your house this morning," he continued, "to tell you I was leaving Sovereign for good."

"Oh, no!"

"But the moment I saw you in your bare feet and bathrobe, I knew I couldn't leave, at least not until I found out what was wrong. I knew David wasn't meeting your emotional needs—I saw how disappointed you were when you reached for him at the engagement dinner and he wasn't there. And obviously I was aware David couldn't meet your spiritual needs. Enter Duncan Faulkner, the white knight, to rescue you, although, in my defense," he added soberly, "I was only thinking of you this morning."

Maggie squeezed his hand, but said nothing.

"I was going to tell you I was leaving town just before I slipped out the back door, but you stopped me. Of course, I think at that moment I'd probably have confessed my love rather than my leaving," he admitted drily. "Not long after I arrived back at Nick's place, David called and wanted to know if Nick or I had any idea where you'd gone. He'd just returned from his camping trip ..."

"Right! I forgot about that camping trip. Sorry, go on," she urged.

"Anyway, you'd left him some sort of cryptic voice mail about needing to talk and he was angry and upset, guessing that you wanted to break off the engagement. When I heard that, I began to have hope for the first time—hope that you might love me, not him. That would further explain your dark night of the soul, too. But when David told me you weren't answering your phone ..."

"I left it in my car."

"... and you weren't at home, either, I began to worry about you. Somehow, it just came into my head that you had come here, to visit your mother. You told me on the outing to Sovereign Gore that you wanted to come here and I even remembered the name of the cemetery because my Kindergarten teacher was Mrs. Crosby. So when David pressed me again for where I thought you might be, I told him you were probably at the cemetery."

Surprised, Maggie sat up again, hugging her knees to her chest. "You did?" She glanced around the height of land, half expecting David to step out from behind a tree at any moment. "Then where ..."

"Don't worry, darling. He isn't here." Duncan sat up beside her. He brushed a stray strand of hair away from her eyes. "I expect he's at the other cemetery by now."

"What other cemetery?"

"The cemetery where your husband and his family are buried. I'm afraid I wasn't very honest about *which* cemetery and David naturally assumed you went to visit your late husband's grave. I didn't enlighten him, either," he concluded, with an impish grin.

She burst out laughing. "Oh, you! You're hopeless," she declared. "And you had the nerve to worry me this morning about the state of my soul if I lied?"

"I didn't lie," he pointed out. "I just didn't tell the whole truth. What is it they say? 'All's fair in love and war'," he quoted.

"What am I going to do with you!"

"Love me, I hope." He dropped a light kiss on the tip of Maggie's nose. "There's no going back now, darling."

"Nothing could ever make me go back! I love you too much for that. But I do have a little backtracking to do with my friends and neighbors. Nellie, I think, has suspected me for several weeks now. She probably knew before I did that I was in love with you and not David. Funny, sometimes you don't realize how far down the wrong path you've gone until it seems as though it's too late to turn back," she mused.

"It's never too late to turn back," he stated firmly. "Not when so many lives are at stake."

"How do you think will David take the news, when we tell him?"

"Not well, at first, I'm afraid. But then he'll find someone else, as he always does, and move on. Although I had hoped my brother might be ready to settle down. That might have been part of what attracted David to you in the first place—not that you're not attractive in your own right, darling, but you do belong to a very loving, caring community, which he does not."

"In that case, you'd better thank Leland the next time you see him."

"My ole buddy, Leland? And what am I thanking him for?"

"For making me aware what a treasure you are! One of you can't abide to be in the same room as Leland and the other is his new best friend. How can two brothers—fraternal twins, too!—be so different? How is that possible?"

"God only knows. I used to ask myself the same question when I was young. I even asked our mother once why David and I were so different."

"What did she say?"

"Mother told me not to worry about it. I remember her exact words, too. She said: 'Never mind what your brother does with his life; chart your own course.' And that's what I've done ever since."

"What a remarkable woman! We owe a big debt of gratitude to our mothers, don't we?" She glanced at her mother's grave. Suddenly, one remaining question popped into Maggie's head. "How did you ever find your way in here? I can count on one hand the people who know how to get to the Crosby Cemetery."

"Do I look like the kind of man who's afraid to ask for help?" Duncan replied, feigning hurt. "Let me assure you, I'm not. I followed my GPS to the Garland Road and stopped at the first house where there was a truck in the yard, rather, a tractor in the yard. A nice young man—your nephew, I believe ...?"

"Bruce! Of course, *he* would know."

"Exactly. Bruce took time out from changing the oil on his John Deere to carefully explain the best way to get here, through the back forty, naturally. He was even gracious enough to suggest I leave my car at the farm so you wouldn't hear me coming." Duncan winked at her, his hazel eyes twinkling with delight.

"You, men! You always stick together, don't you? Wretched beasts."

"But you love us anyway, confess?"

"Alas, I do."

"We might have some explaining to do, though, when we return to get my car. Amber came out of the barn while Bruce and I were chatting. Naturally, after we were introduced, I had to explain my mission."

"Naturally!"

"I promised her I'd bring you back to the house so you could tell her all about it." Duncan rose up as he finished speaking, pulling Maggie to her feet beside him. He brushed some dirt and grass from her clothes and then dropped a kiss on her forehead. "Well, darling? Shall we go take our medicine?"

Maggie nodded her acquiescence, her heart too full to speak. The gate squeaked a final time as Duncan led her out of the cemetery. He took her hand and they walked back to the farm, through the flower-strewn summer meadow, like children on their way home from school. Maggie never once glanced over her shoulder to get a final glimpse of the cemetery. She had a lot of living—and a lot of loving—left to do. It was time to look to the future.

Chapter 21
Conclusion

For the sake of brevity, allow me to bring our little tale to a swift—but happy—conclusion. After leaving Bruce and Amber's house, Maggie and Duncan went back to retrieve her car. During that short trip they agreed to break the news to David as gently and quickly as possible. On the drive home from Winslow Maggie phoned her soon-to-be ex-betrothed and arranged to meet with him that evening. Later at the old schoolhouse, while holding hands at the kitchen table, she and Duncan informed his twin honestly and compassionately that they were in love and intended to marry.

As Duncan had predicted, David was angry and upset. At first, David couldn't believe that his brother had stolen a march on him, unable to fathom that any woman could possibly prefer Duncan to him. When Maggie earnestly assured him this was so and pointed out all that she and Duncan had in common, David grudgingly admitted that his brother and his former fiancée were more suited to one another than he and Maggie had ever been. Eventually, he wished them well and departed abruptly for Cambridge, having previously committed, without ever conferring with Maggie on the subject, to return to Harvard to teach that fall.

By the time autumn arrived—as Duncan had also predicted—David had acquired a new playmate, one of his former students, whom he brought to Sovereign in late September and introduced around at the annual Harvest Supper. This year the Harvest Supper was being held as a fundraiser for Wendell and Rebecca. The concerned community hoped to replenish some of the nest egg stolen by the nefarious financial representative, Bill Gagnon, who was still on the lam.

"I can't believe I've been replaced by a teenager," Maggie whispered to her fledgling spouse as the two of them settled down to eat at one of the long banquet tables. She and Duncan had eloped in August and to the satisfaction of all their friends were now happily ensconced in the old schoolhouse.

Maggie munched on a crisp dill pickle, idly watching as her new brother-in-law squired his date through the hazards of the church's crowded buffet line. For some reason, the way David's hand lingered possessively in the small of the young woman's back irritated her. She was reminded of her former fiancée's attempt to flaunt his possession of her at their engagement dinner.

"Diane's thirty-four, that's hardly a teenager," Duncan pointed out. He used his fork to smash down a fluffy white mound of mashed potato. "Pass me the butter, will you, please?"

"Well, thirty-four is certainly a far cry from my age, which shall remain numberless," she retorted, handing Duncan the butter plate. She observed him load up his knife with butter. "Don't take so much. It isn't good for you, dear."

Unfazed, Duncan smothered his potato and squash with soft, sweet butter from Scotch Broom Acres. "You're not going to be one of those nagging wives, are you?"

"Certainly I am. I'd like to have you around for a while, especially after the all the drama I went through to marry you and not your brother."

"Yeah, Dad, go easy on the butter," interjected Nick. "I'm with Maggie on this one."

"You two always stick together," his father grumbled, but Duncan obediently returned some of the offending condiment to the butter plate.

"I'll take your side, Mr. Faulkner," Kate spoke up, spritely. She and Duncan had been an item since the outing to Sovereign Gore, much to Maggie's delight. "You should take as much butter as you want. We should all enjoy each day to the utmost, because we never know what tomorrow's going to bring."

"Amen to that!" agreed Duncan. Nevertheless he refrained from helping himself to more.

"Ain't thet the dem truth," said Leland, coming up and catching the tail end of the conversation. He dumped his full plate onto the table and unceremoniously joined them all. "I knew you was my kind o' gal the fust time I seed ya," he said to Kate.

Kate giggled and rewarded the old woodsman with a conspiratorial wink.

Wendell leaned forward, elbow on the table. "Pass the buttah down to this end, Duncan. Or ain't you done with it yet?"

"I'm not sure. I'm waiting for my wife to tell me what to do."

Maggie gave her husband a light jab in the ribs. "Don't be a goose! Pass the butter to Wendell."

"See? Now I know what to do." The plate of Scotch Broom Acres butter made its way down the table toward Wendell.

When the condiment reached Rebecca's hand, however, the blue plate came to an abrupt halt. "Can anyone get in on this discussion?" she inquired. "Because butter isn't good for you, either, dear," she continued, turning to her husband. "Your cholesterol is way too high and Tad and I would like to keep you around for many years to come."

Wendell shrugged good-naturedly. "Cain't argue with thet."

Duncan gazed longingly at the sweet Jersey butter. "I never had real cow's butter until I came to Sovereign. Now, the woman who introduced me to its delights tells me I can't have it!"

Leland leaned back in his aluminum folding chair and snatched one of the butter plates from a neighboring table, handing the cache to Duncan. "Don't say I nevah give you nuthin', son," he told Duncan.

The Episcopal minister's face visibly brightened. "Thank you, Leland. I owe you one. Actually, I owe you more than one."

"Eh?"

"Thank you for being yourself, my friend."

Leland scratched his head. "Don't think I kin help thet."

"My point exactly." Duncan sliced off a large portion of the purloined butter and proceeded to eat his dinner with great gusto, much to Maggie's dismay. She began to feel as though she was going to be annoyed with both Faulkner brothers that evening

After everyone had finished eating and drinking a congenial hush settled over the table. Nellie and Doctor Bart took the opportunity to announce to their friends that they were expecting a baby. They had already shared the news with Maggie and Duncan earlier in the week, Maggie naturally thrilled to discover she was finally going to become a grandmother. The announcement was received by the table with joy, congratulations, and some back-slapping.

"How exciting!" Rebecca gushed. "That means Tad will have another playmate. When is the baby due?"

"Late March," Doctor Bart replied. "Nellie and I wanted to wait until we knew everything was OK before we told you." His wife's hand was lying on the table and he covered it with his own. "She's going to keep working at the clinic until the baby comes, despite her doctor's objections."

"You're not my doctor," Nellie reminded him. "My OBGYN has given me the green light to work as long as I want."

"Still, I wish you wouldn't work so hard."

"Says the charcoal pot to the black kettle," Nellie teased. Nevertheless she rewarded her husband with quick kiss.

But the biggest surprise came at the very end of the evening when Ryan MacDonald got up to announce that the fundraiser for Wendell and Rebecca had raised more than $100,000. Most of the donations were small amounts given by their friends and neighbors; however, Maggie discovered later that Henry and Hannah had given $25,000 and Miss Crump, the watchful owner of a working gravel pit, had donated $50,000 to the fund.

There were audible gasps of surprise when Ryan made his announcement. Rebecca wept at the news. Wendell put his arm around his wife, attempting to console her; however, even his eyes were wet. Some of their friends and neighbors clamored around the couple, offering their congratulations and best wishes.

"Thank you so much, all of you dear, dear friends," cried Rebecca. "Now little Tad will be able to keep the old Russell place in the family for at least another generation! We're overwhelmed by your generosity. I don't know what to say, except that ... we love you all very much!" At the urging of Shirley Palmer and several others, she and Wendell began making the rounds of the banquet hall, much like a newly-married couple, stopping at each table to chat and offer their thanks to those present.

David Faulkner, who had been unusually quiet most of the evening, observed the popular couple socialize for a few minutes and then pushed his coffee cup aside. "Ready to go, babe? I am." Without waiting for his date's reply, he stood up. He re-buttoned his coat and adjusted his shirt sleeves.

Diane gazed up at him with adoring eyes. "Whatever you say, David."

But David wasn't listening. He had turned his back on his date in order to survey the quickest way out of the crowd. Seeing the hurt look on the young woman's face, Duncan wordlessly arose and assisted Diane out of her chair. "Thanks," she said, gratefully.

David turned around and caught Duncan in the act of helping Diane into her coat. A mocking smile flashed across his handsome face. "Always the perfect gentleman, aren't you, Bub?"

"I try to be," Duncan replied, unperturbed. "Will you be joining us for Thanksgiving, David? I understand Maggie cooks a mean turkey."

David frowned. "Probably not. I only get four days off at Thanksgiving."

"What about Christmas? We could have an old-fashioned holiday; hang stockings on the fireplace in the living room and everything."

"Christmas might be doable. But I can't commit at this point. I'm taking a group of underprivileged freshman to Baja next semester to study the migration of the gray whales and I'll have a lot of prep work to do."

"Sounds like a worthy endeavor. Is Harvard picking up the tab for that?"

"Actually, no. I won a grant from the Gates Foundation to help level the playing field for minorities pursuing a career in the sciences. Historically, minorities have faced many obstacles and this intensive semester will help the students catch up on some of the science they missed by attending grossly underfunded public high schools."

"Well, if you do decide to come for Christmas, I hope you'll stay with us," Duncan continued, returning to the issue at hand. "We have plenty of room, don't we, Maggie?" His wife stood up beside him and Duncan slipped an arm around her waist.

"Please do, David," Maggie added. "The invitation includes you, too, of course, Diane."

But David dismissed the offer out of hand. "Thanks, Bub. The B&B in Unity works just fine for us."

Hugs were given and David and Diane departed. Maggie, observing the couple pick their way through the laughing, jostling crowd, silently gave thanks to God for sending her the deserving Faulkner twin to love. Where would she be now had she married the wrong brother? For the thousandth time she wondered what she had ever seen in David Faulkner! Maggie wasn't sure how or even why she had started down the wrong path, veering away from her love of God toward a life of egocentric selfishness. During her dark night of the soul she had been horrified to see what a self-satisfied, small-minded person she had become. Fortuitously, however, Duncan had come along and reminded Maggie of her better self. Even before she was aware she loved him she had begun to reverse course. "It's never too late to turn around," Duncan had stated. "Not when so many lives are at stake." Thank God it *was* never too late!

Duncan held out her jacket. "Ready for bed? I know I am. And before you ask," he continued in a suggestive tone, head bent close to her ear, "I meant that as it sounded."

Maggie chuckled and slipped her arms into the coat. "Sounds good to me! But I do have one question for you before we go, dear."

"I knew it," he groaned. "What now, my curious darling?"

"Why on earth do you still allow your brother to call you 'Bub'? Frankly, it's damned annoying!"

"Oh, that? It's the least I can do," Duncan replied, cheerfully. "After all, I won the race, didn't I?"

The newlyweds returned to the little red schoolhouse, where they retired to the upstairs bedroom. Maggie had discovered that it didn't bother her in the least that Duncan shared the same bed in which she had once snuggled with Peter. Nor did she mind that Duncan hung up his shirt on the back of the bathroom door where Peter's shirts had once hung or stashed his shaving accoutrements on the little shelf Peter had built for his own use. She never compared the two men; she had plenty of room in her heart for both of them. Her love for her childhood playmate had softened like rain water, while her love for Duncan was fresh and new, like the air after a summer thunderstorm. Soberly, she realized now that the love she had shared with Peter had prepared her to recognize and appreciate Duncan's rare personal gifts, which a less mature Maggie might have overlooked. And so we will say 'goodbye' to Maggie, the minister of the Sovereign Union Church. We will consign her to the loving care of Duncan Faulkner, where for all intents and purposes she lives happily ever after.

The End

The Sovereign Series

Five novels by Jennifer Wixson

The Sovereign Series is a five-volume work of fiction by Maine farmer and author Jennifer Wixson. Set in the fictitious farming community of Sovereign, Maine (pop. 1,048) the town is populated by good-hearted and lovable residents, such as the old chicken farmer Wendell Russell and Sovereign's retired music teacher Miss Hastings. Memorable characters weave in and out of the five novels like good friends dropping in for a cup of tea.

Visitors to Sovereign partake in the felicity that abounds in this picturesque hamlet of rolling pastures and woodlots, whether while sharing a picnic with our little group of friends at the Millett Rock or wandering with lovers beside Black Brook. Readers, like the residents of Sovereign, become imbued with an uplifting sensation much like that described by Ralph Waldo Emerson as "a certain cordial exhilaration … the effect of the indulgence of this human affection." In Sovereign, love is truly— sovereign!

Book 1, _Hens & Chickens_ (White Wave, August 2012) – Two women downsized by corporate America, Lila Woodsum, 27, and Rebecca Johnson, 48, move to Maine to raise chickens and sell organic eggs and discover more than they bargained for—including love. _Hens & Chickens_ opens the book on Sovereign and introduces us to the local characters, including Wendell Russell, Miss Hastings, the handsome carpenter Mike Hobart, and the Gilpin family. A little tale of hens and chickens, pips and peeper, love and friendship, _Hens & Chickens_ lays the foundation for the next four titles in the series.

Book 2, _Peas, Beans & Corn_ (White Wave, June 2013) – The romance of a bygone era infuses Book 2 in The Sovereign Series, when Maine Army Guardsman Bruce Gilpin, 35, returns to Sovereign with the secret dream of restarting the town's old sweet corn canning factory. He's encouraged in his mission by the passionate young organic foodie Amber Johnson, 21, who reawakens his heavy heart.

The course of their true love becomes muddied by their well-meaning mothers, however, and by the arrival of Bruce's ex-wife Shelia and the handsome corporate attorney Ryan MacDonald, who hits town to rusticate. History pervades this little tale of hummingbird moths and morning mists, horse-drawn sleighs and corn desilkers, and the words of the poet Emily Dickinson, who could have been describing Sovereign when she once wrote: "I went to Heaven – 'Twas a small Town."

Book 3, *The Songbird of Sovereign* (White Wave, July 2014) – In Book 3 of *The Sovereign Series*, Miss Hastings reveals the secret of her youthful heart, a tragic lost love that has lasted a lifetime. While gracing the stages of New York as a teenage musical prodigy, Jana Hastings' career is cut short by consumption (tuberculosis), the wasting disease. Panicked, her parents seek treatment for their daughter at a sanatorium in central Maine, where she meets and falls in love with fellow TB sufferer Henry Graham, 27. Henry's gentle goodness transforms the young Miss Hastings, and his love reaches beyond the grave to positively touch the lives of hundreds of Sovereign schoolchildren over the course of the next seven decades.

Book 4, *The Minister's Daughter* (White Wave, August 2015) – Although she is tall, blonde and lovely, Nellie Walker, 22, daughter of Maggie Walker, minister of the Sovereign Union Church, is also selfish, supercilious and vain. When an unforeseen event leaves Nellie alone in the world, she returns to Sovereign and initiates a desperate search for the father whose identity her mother has never revealed.

Helping Nellie through this dark time is the compassionate country doctor, Metcalf Bartholomew Lawson, 31, known locally as "Doctor Bart." His love for Nellie has long been suspected (and encouraged) by her mother, although to date Nellie has exhibited little use for her pedantic suitor, a man more at home among herbs and rose bushes than cityscapes and boardwalks. Maggie's childhood friend Peter Hodges also provides Nellie with much needed comfort and support, when Nellie is forced to face – and overcome – some long-held prejudices.

Book 5, *Maggie's Dilemma* (White Wave, October 2017) – Nearly three years after the death of her husband and childhood friend Peter Hodges, Maggie becomes involved with the noted environmentalist David Faulkner, Walden's uncle, who has come to teach at Unity College for a year. Before she knows it she and David are engaged.

Maggie believes she's done the right thing—until Duncan Faulkner, David's brother (Walden's father), an Episcopal minister, shows up in Sovereign. Spending time with Duncan, Maggie comes to realize there is a world of difference between the two men. She quickly discovers-- too late!--that she's engaged to marry one brother, but is in love with the other.

Further complicating Maggie's life, an investment advisor from the city, with whom she has the slightest of acquaintances, has used her name to drum up business with her friends. Should she give them a heads-up that he could be nothing more than a Wall Street wolf in sheep's clothing? Or should she keep silent and let the chips fall where they may? Maggie chooses to say nothing, and as a result Wendell and Rebecca could lose the farm!

For more on *The Sovereign Series*, visit our website:
www.TheSovereignSeries.com

Other Writings by Jennifer Wixson

<u>Fiction</u>

Hens & Chickens (Book 1 in *The Sovereign Series*)
Peas, Beans & Corn (Book 2)
The Songbird of Sovereign (Book 3)
The Minister's Daughter (Book 4)

<u>Non-fiction</u>

Learning to SOAR!
Under the Apple Tree *(Coming Summer of 2018)*

<u>Regular column</u>

Letter from Troy, *Islandport Magazine*

Jennifer Wixson

Maine farmer, beekeeper, and author Jennifer Wixson writes from her home in Troy where she and her husband (fondly known as the Cranberry Man) raise Scottish Highland cattle and cranberries. A graduate of the School of Hard Knocks, Jen also admits to a Master's Degree in divinity from Bangor Theological Seminary.

You can follow Jen on Twitter @ChickenJen and find the latest on her various writing projects at:

www.facebook.com/Jennifer.Wixson.author